Dear Santa, Get Bent

One of nine reindeer that pulls Santa's sleigh, Dasher wants nothing more than to find a partner, a mate, someone to be with. With the restrictions in the workshop, she has only one choice—she goes to the human world and starts trying men on for size.

The down side to mating with a human is that they don't remember her the following day. The depressing point is that none of them have the stamina to keep up with her and there are no second chances. Every time is the first time with a human.

When she is assigned to a shop that needs an emergency audit, she enjoys the thrill of digging through the messy paperwork, and she has plans for the proprietor. One time might be enough if it was with him.

Argus has been sent to bring back a reindeer, but the woman with smouldering dark eyes is more than he was banking on. She seems nice, but he wants her naughty.

Malled by Christmas

Dancer joined the exodus from the workshop in a chance to experience life and possibly love.

She focuses on life and finds herself working in a mall as a security guard. Watching humans in their preparations for Christmas gives her a feeling of purpose and renews her energy for the holiday.

A new photographer at Santa's Grotto gains a crowd and Dancer's admiration. He handles children with skill and coaxes smiles out of the most recalcitrant little ones.

Dancer catches his eye, and she acknowledges the mutual attraction. A bit of light flirting and fending off attackers creates a bond that definitely embodies the spirit of giving.

Sleighing Her Elf

Prancer has no problem with her place on the team, but she wants to experience some of the wonderful new vehicles she has been seeing every Christmas Eve.

When she enters the human world, she assigns herself to drive a snow plow. It is everything she wants at a safe distance from any and all human interference. She wants to watch them, not be among them.

It worked out well for her until the night she hit the snowman on the side of the road, and it was occupied.

Merkoss thought he was on his way to intercepting one of the reindeer with a few weeks to go. He leaves the workshop and ends up encased in a snowman, moving through time as well as space. After being struck by the snow plow, he finds himself facing his target, but he only has twenty-four hours to convince her that she should return to the workshop. Time is of the essence.

Hung by the Fire

Vixen chooses life with astronomy, and she ends up as an educator and a researcher for a tiny observatory struggling to make ends meet.

When Vi arrives, she makes an impression and takes over most of the day-to-day operations, which is fine until an elf comes calling.

Xander has been sent to bring Vixen home, but he doesn't know how he will go about convincing her that it is a good idea, until he asks her out and she tells him what she wants.

Magic and wonder are the hallmarks of Christmas, and these two have it in spades.

Twisting the Pole

Comet is five hundred years old by human standards of linear time, but in her mind, she is the same young woman taken out of the Middle Ages by Santa.

Being pulled out of her time to become one of the Christmas reindeer had been harsh but better than being stoned or hung as a witch.

Her foray away from the workshop takes her to a modern past, a Ren Faire. The clothing and traditions are familiar, and she spends time grieving for a family lost many Christmases ago.

Salk is a coal elf of the naughty-or-nice department. His job has been to find those who are definitely naughty and punish them. He never imagined that he would find a reindeer who needs his nice side more than anything else.

Blizzard of Heat

Cupid launched herself into organizing a branch of Legal Aid only to meet a handsome lawyer who sends her senses into disarray.

Watching the families who needed help and those who were paid to help them was an education. No one stayed unless they had a feel for the job and all of those working with her want nothing more than relief of stress for their clients.

When Tyr arrives as holiday relief, he sweeps through their caseload like magic. His interest in late-night takeout and casual chatter are enough to catch and keep her attention, but when she realizes who and what he is, her holiday season goes from snowbound to hot.

Bells and Chains

Doni is having fun during the weeks before the holidays. She has never enjoyed herself more. After a variety of successful jobs, her boss sheepishly asks her to take on one more client before the holidays strike.

The private club caters to those with an adventurous bent and the money to ensure their privacy. Doni needs to bring a little joy and sparkle to their themed rooms, and she dives into the project with enthusiasm.

Bern has been watching for the reindeer to cross his path, but he never expected it to come in such an amazing form. Christmas has never looked more perfect.

Licking His Cane

Blitzen enjoys fixing things, and the machines that make Christmas sweeter need attention, too. As Belinda Litzen, she is a one-woman repair shop catering to all the overworked bakeries in town.

When a candy shop has a rolling machine down, she shows up to save the day and meets a candy maker who gives her a visual sugar rush.

Rex has been waiting for his reindeer to show up, but the repairwoman was not what he had imagined. Instead of brown, she was golden, and instead of shy, she met his gaze head-on.

She is his first reindeer, and he is her first wolf.

Nice and Naughty

Ru was born in a forest and soon recruited by Santa. He wanted her to help harness the remains of long-dead deities. Christmas is coming into fashion in the human world and that is a lot of energy to take advantage of. He moves her back in time, and together, they build the workshop.

Ru has one problem. Santa tricked her and locked the collar around her neck. Her other forms are no longer hers to command, and without them, she can't be whole.

It has taken her over a thousand years, but she finally has a way to claim her freedom, and if Santa cooperates, Christmas won't be hurt.

The characters and events in this book are fictitious. Any similarity to real persons, living or dead, is coincidental and not intended by the author.

Copyright © 2016 by Viola Grace
ISBN: 978-1-987969-13-9

©Cover art by Carmen Waters

All rights reserved. With the exception of review, the reproduction or utilization of this work in whole or in part in any form by electronic, mechanical or other means, now known or hereafter invented, is forbidden without the express permission of the publisher.

Published by Viola Grace

Look for me online at violagrace.com, amazon, kobo, B&N and other ebook sellers.

Operation Reindeer Retrieval

By

Viola Grace

Prologue to Dear Santa, Get Bent!

Ru calmly walked another stack of files to the cabinet and slowly sorted through it as she sought the alphabetical corollary. Her band and the bands of her siblings rattled on her arms under her sleeves. It made it hard to concentrate.

For the last two months, she had managed to keep management at bay while her sisters were out in the human world. It was her job to be the decoy, as she was the only one who was bound to Santa's sleigh.

With the way the bands were buzzing, it was likely that someone wanted to do a briefing regarding this year's path through the changing global weather patterns.

Ru promised herself that she would ignore them until it wasn't possible. Unfortunately, she knew that that particular moment was here. She could hear footsteps in the archive. There were never footsteps that didn't belong to a reindeer in the *nice and naughty list* archive.

There was only one reason for someone to make their way into the territory of the team—Santa wanted an audience.

"Hello? Where is everyone?"

Ru whistled sharply. The footfalls headed her way. She kept filing. It was what the reindeer did during the off-season. They were confined to the archive and did all the paperwork for the previous season. It was terminally boring and the reason for the visit today.

She could feel the presence of the elf behind her.

"Where are the others?"

Ru continued to file the verifications of the fulfillment of the nice or naughty requirements.

"Rudolph. Where are the others?" Administrator Rin wasn't shrill, but he wasn't completely calm.

She turned when she finished her batch and looked at him

with her hands folded in front of her. "What others?"

He lifted his monitor—the flat display that told him where the reindeer were at any given time. Rudolph's glow was red; the others were gold.

She shrugged.

"He is going to hear about this."

She shrugged again.

"Come with me."

That was surprising. "Leave the archive?"

"And the stables. Santa needs to know about this."

Ru walked with him to the upper level and through the crystalline gateway that normally blocked her progress. With Rin's hand on her shoulder, she slid through the gateway and into the main hall.

Santa was sitting with his mail and flipping through the letters that the elves had selected for special consideration.

Rin cleared his throat. "Boss, I have Rudolph for you."

Santa looked up, his pretty elven features glowing brightly in the reflected light of his crystal palace.

"Rudolph. Come and have a seat. I have been trying to contact you and the others from the team. Where have you been keeping yourself?" Santa patted the chair next to him and smiled.

Ru moved toward him and took the seat. "I have been where I always am. I am in the archive or the stable. Isn't that where I am supposed to be?"

She tried to hold in her frustration, but it lashed out.

Santa put the letter he was reading aside. He waved his hand and a pot of tea appeared between them. "Tell me what the problem is."

She sighed. "The reindeer have decided that since we have gone through five hundred seasons, it is time we strike out on our own. A woman can only take so much frustration."

Santa poured the tea. "Rin, where are the reindeer?"

Rin checked his tablet. "Boss, it says that they are all in here, with you."

"Ru, can you push up your sleeves, please?"

Ru pushed her sleeves back to the shoulder. On each arm were four tracking bands. Each engraved with the name of the reindeer who should have worn it. Ru's was still around her neck. She couldn't remove the ruby if she tried, and she had really tried.

Santa set the cup of tea down in front of her. "Where did they go, Rudolph?"

"In a nutshell? They have gone to get laid. For five hundred years, we have gone into heat, and for five hundred years, we were not allowed out to seek a mate to ease our need. We are not allowed to live like normal women, even for a while. We are tired of it. So, we worked out a strategy and implemented it. I would wear their bands and they would get some life experiences."

She picked up the cup and sipped at the minty tea.

Santa closed his eyes. "Christmas is in a week. What are we supposed to do about the missing reindeer?"

"Ask them to come back?" Ru smiled over her teacup.

Santa opened his eyes and narrowed them at her. "How?"

"Give us freedom to roam here and to seek sexual partners among the elves. You are all high elves; there isn't a size problem. We want to be able to find companionship. It is important. Do you know what five centuries without touching someone does? It isn't fun."

Santa nodded. "Fine. I will consider it, but how do we get them back *now?*"

Rudolph smiled. "You are going to need to send out some bait."

Santa turned to Rin. "Get the eight best-looking and most amenable guys from the naughty-or-nice department. If they are able to convince the reindeer they are after to come back, they can keep her. Or she can keep them. Whatever."

Ru smiled. It was working.

Rin scrambled away, and Ru sat sipping at her tea.

Santa sighed. "After all these years, they just snuck away?"

"They broke out, but no. They each wrote you a letter."

She patted the pockets of her gown and found them. With a flourish, she brought out a stack with Dasher's signature on top.

"Here you go."

Santa took the letters with bemusement. He opened Dasher's envelope and stared at the contents, reading the first sentence aloud. "Dear Santa, get bent!"

He glanced over at Ru through his crystal-blue eyes. "That

seems a little harsh."

Ru nodded. "It is years of frustration; keep reading."

He did, and his skin paled even further as the torture of a thwarted mating season was outlined to him. He shivered, and by the time he had recovered himself, Rin and a gathering of eight very strapping and attractive elves came through the portal.

"Rudolph, please remove the reindeer bands. They will be needed to find the ladies." Santa's voice was kind.

Ru removed the bands, one by one, and they were given to the elves as their mission was explained.

"You are on Operation Reindeer Retrieval. We need those ladies back, and we need them here in the next few days. Charm them, seduce them, but get them to agree to return. They have to be willing."

The elves looked down at the bands, at each other and a few exchanged the items they were holding. Ru smiled. It seemed that the reindeers' auras came through in their collars.

One of the men looked to Santa. "Boss, how are we supposed to find them?"

Santa scowled. "Can't you sense them?"

The men of the naughty-and-nice list shook their heads.

Ru snickered.

Santa turned to her. "You know where they are."

She shrugged. "I have no idea. We deliberately didn't share this kind of information, and I believe that this is why."

Santa sighed. "Rin, take her to my office."

Ru got to her feet, shook out her gown and left Santa with his representatives.

They had a lot to discuss.

Santa watched the elegant woman with the small rack of horns as she mounted the stairs to his office. The letter had been concise and something he couldn't ignore. It was a letter to Santa from Dasher, and she was mad.

"Gentlemen, it seems that my flight team has gotten a little frustrated with going through years of seasons without being able to find a mate. If you think of someone more suitable to take your place, by all means, hand off the band. I hadn't realized my team was so desperately unhappy, and if giving them a mate will keep them happy, I am willing to offer you up."

The men shifted, shrugged and nodded. Santa kept his smirk to himself. While the elves were allowed to leave during the off-season for personal recreation, they could not bring humans back to the workshop. Having a lover at home would be a great temptation, and as always, Rin had chosen the right men for the job.

"The reindeer are travelling using Christmas magic, so as you are all aware of what that entails, you can come up with the likeliest means of finding them yourselves."

He got to his feet and waved them off. "All of our resources are at your disposal. Good luck."

Santa gathered the letters from the reindeer and headed up the steps to his office. He had matters to attend to, and Rudolph could shed a light on certain aspects of it.

Dear Santa, Get Bent!

Dani Sherwood went through the sheaf of paperwork and occasionally looked up to examine the holiday decorations.

Metal tinsel, plastic arrangements of manically cheerful snowmen mixed with the sweetest angels she could imagine crafted of sugary treats.

"Do you have everything you need, Ms. Sherwood?" The office manager smiled loosely as the holiday party continued in the boardroom.

"I do. Thank you."

"Is there anything I can do for you?" His smile was hopeful.

Dani twisted her lips. She couldn't tell him that they had already had a date, dinner, sex and she had left their encounter with a lack of enthusiasm. None of her lovers remembered her after they parted. It was part of the Christmas magic she had brought with her.

"No, thank you. I have a date later, and I don't want to be late. I will just lock up the books and see you in the morning." She finished her data collection and closed her laptop.

"Oh, we won't be here in the morning. We are closing for the holidays. We won't be open again until the new year."

Dani blinked, "Of course. How foolish of me. Well, happy holidays."

She put the books back in the safe and gathered her laptop and notebooks. With her bag over her shoulder, she eased past the party and headed for the parkade. Working for a living among the humans had become her favourite part of this excursion.

Being the first reindeer to leave Santa's workshop out of season in five hundred years, she had immediately gone to a bar and sought out a suitable partner for sex. The end result had been less than satisfactory. Humans just didn't possess the stamina she needed to reach orgasm.

Dani wasn't a quitter, she tried over and over again with different males, but the result was always the same. A rush to their pleasure and she was left waiting until she could bring herself to orgasm. She didn't see what the elves saw in the humans. Maybe it was different with the women, but Dani wasn't that curious.

She got into her small car and drove the twenty minutes to the office of Accelerated Audits. The offices were manned twenty-four hours a day to serve a variety of clients. Dani worked the evening shift.

"Dani! Did you finish at Morgan Corp?" Ula Andrews smiled as she came in.

"I did. I just popped in to tidy up some details. I should be out of here in an hour."

"I don't know what we would have done without you this year." Ula grinned and returned to answering the phones.

Dani smiled and took up her position at her desk, thinking of co-workers past.

Ru had been stealing Christmas snowflakes for the last decade. When she had gathered enough, the team put their plan into action and escaped for the human world. Wearing holiday magic, Dani was accepted as a normal human because of the snowflake she had pressed into her skin.

Holiday magic was a funny thing, but Ru had been looking into it for decades before she started to snitch the magical snowflakes on the Christmas runs. Most of the falling stars turned into snowflakes on the way down, but Ru's position at the head of the team put her in the perfect location to grab them as they approached the workshop. It was only a few minutes during the homeward run that made the magic available, and Ru had grabbed every flake she could find, one at a time.

Now, with the exception of their mastermind, the team was out in the human world and enjoying what it felt like to be desired and to do a job that folks respected. It was truly a delightful vacation where each reindeer could pursue what she wanted to do in her off time.

Dani liked accounting. She enjoyed nothing more than working with the files and numbers, balancing, finding discrepancies and working through them to bring everything into the light.

She finished the Morgan Corp files and prepared the package

that her company would forward when the business was open after the holidays.

Dani sighed and packed up her bag. Ula was between calls. "Well, I am on my way out. Anything on the books for tomorrow?"

"Not yet. I will keep you posted. Are you on call tonight?"

"You bet." Dani winked. "Talk to you later."

"You had better." Ula winked and took the incoming call.

Nocturnal accounting was a new thing to Dani, and it was a new thing to this city. Having folk who were willing to head out in the dark of night and work on the books of any business that wanted to pay was definitely a niche market.

In the last six weeks, she had balanced the books of three corporations and two mobsters. The audits had been harrowing, but Dani had had a ton of fun. The different aspects of human life were fascinating to watch.

Whistling holiday music, she got in her car and headed for home. If she was on call, she wouldn't be able to drink, but she could still head out and enjoy watching the humans flirt, tangle and dance.

Dani sat in full party gear and watched as the bar patrons laughed, drank and clung to each other. It was more fun to watch than it was to participate in, and Dani wondered when that had happened.

She had been at The Frozen Cork for three hours when her phone buzzed. A slight leakage of magic let her answer it in a dome of quiet. "Hello?"

"Is this Ms. Sherwood of Accelerated Audits?" The deep voice was as intriguing as the opening line.

"It is. How may I help you?"

"I have just taken possession of a pop-up store at the mall, and I need an express audit before I begin business. Are you available to go over things this evening? I don't want to miss much shopping time."

"Understandable. What is your address?"

He rattled off a location near one of the malls.

"I can be there in twenty minutes."

"I will put some coffee on."

Heading to a business in the middle of the night for a mysterious audit put some of the excitement back in her time away from the workshop.

She hung up, stood up and worked her way out of the bar. She had her computer to collect and an assignment to get to.

While she was at her home, she made a quick call to Ula to confirm the job.

"Seriously, Dani. He called in and asked for you specifically."

"Really?"

"Well, he asked for a female auditor with dark hair who had started within the last three months. I figured it was a recommendation from one of those private gentlemen's clubs or something." Ula chuckled. "You seem to be popular with them."

Dani rolled her eyes and locked her door as she headed back to her car with her bag over her shoulder. "I am popular with all kinds of men. It doesn't mean I can work with them."

"Well, this is a straight-forward assessment of current business practices and stock levels. It shouldn't take you more than two days."

"Right. I have heard that one before."

Ula was notorious for downplaying the amount of work involved.

"Talk to you tomorrow, Ula."

"Have a nice consult, Dani."

Dani hung up and got into her car. Her reflection in the window had shown her that her horns were still very much a part of her, but when she was around humans, they disappeared.

Keeping her horns was a weird effect of the magic that she was pleased with. She would really miss her horns if they altered in any way. Humans saw what they expected to see, and they saw her as human.

The drive to the location was quick, and her lips quirked in a grin as she parked near the door. It was a lingerie shop.

Silken Mystique was proclaimed in elegant, tasteful letters above the door. Dani got her computer bag and headed to the door, knocking briskly.

The shadow that filled the doorway was not that of a petite shopkeeper. The door unlocked, and it was pushed outward. "Ms. Sherwood?"

"I am."

"Please, come in. My name is Argus Breathewaite, current

owner of this establishment." He cleared his throat. "I wasn't expecting you to show up in leather."

"I wasn't expecting to go to a client's business this evening. It is a compromise that I am here at all. Please call me Dani."

She smiled at the inventory. In the dim light, the silken jewel tones glowed in peignoirs, camisoles, gowns and more delicate garments that led back into the shop. She wanted to touch them all, rubbing them against her cheek, her skin.

He latched the door behind her and led her further in. "The woman who owned the shop before me was not the best bookkeeper. I need you to do an audit of the business in its entirety."

She sighed. "How long do I have?"

"I need to be up and selling or I will miss the entire season." Argus smiled.

She stared at him, his long brown hair brushed the back of his collar, his skin was a deep tan and he had far more the look of a farm worker than a lingerie shop owner. That said, if he was selling, the ladies would be buying. Something about him screamed sex.

She muttered, "I don't think sales will be a problem."

"Well, I need to get in my final order before the holidays. For that, I need an inventory check, and there isn't room in here for more than two people. Will you take me on?"

She blinked rapidly at the images that those words evoked.

Dani licked her lips and looked up at him. "I think we can get this in motion."

His lips tightened and his eyes brightened. "I see. Well, then, I will need to show you the office."

Dani braced herself, but was still a little stunned to see the piles of paperwork that were on every surface. She took a step forward, and one of the piles began a slow slide to the floor.

Acting on reflex, she moved to match her name and dashed in to grab the falling paper. "I believe you mentioned coffee?"

Argus chuckled. "How do you take it?"

"Double cream, double sugar. Extra strong." She snorted. "I will try and make heads and tails of this mess."

He chuckled. "Back in a minute."

She had a minute, so she used her reindeer magic to stop time and organize enough of the paper to free up two chairs and enough of the desk for her computer and a cup of coffee.

When he came back in, she was setting up her laptop and was sitting at the desk.

"Wow, you work quickly."

She grinned. "Accelerated Audits are done with speed and care. Working quickly is what we do."

She fired up a new file, and the basic spreadsheet was ready for her data input. The company name went on the header and Argus Breathewaite went in under proprietor.

She asked him about any assets, the finances and how the banking was arranged.

When she had the basics down and her coffee was empty, she went back to her bag and groped around for the clipboard.

"What kind of an inventory system do you have?"

"I don't know."

She wrinkled her nose. "Will you come with me?"

"Lead on."

The low rumble went through her bones. She sighed and headed for the storeroom.

The space was barely large enough for her to turn around. When Argus came in, it was positively intimate. His body heat warmed the entire space.

She grabbed at a box and hauled it toward her. The contents were wrapped in plastic, and she opened it carefully. "It seems that each item has a care tag, and you create inventory stickers at the main terminal."

He frowned. "How did they know what they had in stock if they didn't tag it before setting it in here?"

Dani rubbed her forehead. "She didn't."

She stood and lifted the gown up, examining it closely. It looked lovely, but there were stitching errors. "I need to examine the stock out front in good lighting."

"Why?"

"Under the terms of the purchase contract that I read, she promised that all the stock was of saleable quality. That is not the case for this particular gown. It is a factory second."

Argus sighed. "I feared as much. Let's go and take a look."

She wondered that if he had guessed it was crappy stock, why he had bought it at all.

An hour later, Argus was on the phone and placing a stock-replacement order to be shipped as quickly as possible. Dani was a little surprised that he had found someone to take on the order at such short notice, but he seemed completely confident in the timing of the order.

"We will have it in two days." He smiled. "I know folks who are excellent at emergency manufacturing."

Dani hid her smile. She knew some excellent makers as well, but she wasn't in a position to call on them. The workshop was off limits.

Dawn was creeping up, and she rubbed her eyes. "Well, I think I need to get some breakfast and some rest. I will be back this evening."

"Excellent. May I join you for breakfast? There is a wonderful restaurant just across the parking lot."

Dani blinked. "Oh, of course."

She had her bag and her laptop. She slid her leather jacket on and watched as he grabbed his own jacket and keys.

After locking up, he offered her his arm, and he nodded toward the building across the way, decorated with vehicles that were slowly filling up the lot near its doors.

Bemused at the courtly gesture, she took his arm and walked with him to Champion's Breakfast.

Once they were seated in a cozy booth, he asked her, "What made you become a nocturnal auditor?"

She wrinkled her nose. "I have always had a head for numbers and most of my working life has been after sundown. It seemed a natural choice."

He nodded. "It is just surprising that a woman of your beauty has brains as well."

She wrinkled her nose. "I put them in my letter to Santa when I was five. He delivered."

Argus blinked and slowly smiled.

"Argus is a strangely old-fashioned name, isn't it?"

He chuckled. "It is a family name going back a few generations."

"The giant with a hundred eyes." She sipped at the coffee between her palms while she looked at the menu.

"That is a strangely precise knowledge."

She wrinkled her nose. "My family and I are big readers. We do tons of reading during the off-season."

He inclined his head. "Brothers? Sisters?"

Dani nodded. "Sisters. Lots of sisters."

The server came up, and Dani ordered a stack of blueberry pancakes with a side of sausage.

Argus ordered bacon, eggs, toast and a side of pancakes.

As the light brightened, the buzzing of activity became a noise-dampening hum.

Argus leaned forward. "So, where were you when I called?"

"A local bar. I was people watching." She smiled.

"Just watching?"

"Of course. I am on call."

He chuckled. "Well, I am grateful that you are. I wouldn't have spotted the manufacturing details until it was too late."

She sighed. "I have to ask. Did you buy it sight unseen?"

"I did. I have an agent who acts on my behalf when I am interested in a new project. The urge just struck me, and so, here we are."

"Seriously? You just bought a stocked shop on an impulse?"

"It is a better use of my time and money than any of the other options." He shrugged.

"Well, I suppose that as long as I get paid, I don't really care why you do what you do." She snickered.

Their food arrived, and they each sat back as the large platters were placed in front of them. The stack of pancakes could have fed her in her reindeer form. It was huge.

She was halfway through when he asked a question that caught her by surprise.

"Are you seeing anyone?"

Dani blinked rapidly. "Um, no. I have had my fun and am waiting until after the holidays before I put myself out there again. Are you seeing someone?"

He smiled. "Not this year. I have been waiting for someone who sparks ideas."

"Sparks ideas?" She raised her brows.

"Yes. To find someone that makes you want to be adventurous, want to dazzle them and, at the same time, curl up in front of a fire with them. That is what I want."

She nodded and pushed her plate away. "Get a dog."

He paused and then laughed. "It does sound rather pretentious."

"It really does." She chuckled and yawned. "Well, this has been fun, but I have to get going before the rest of these pancakes become my pillow."

"Have a nice rest, Dani. It has been a productive first meeting."

She yawned and reached for her wallet.

He put his hand up. "I have it."

She winked. "Keep the receipt and declare it on your taxes. Consider it a business meeting."

Argus nodded. "See you this evening?"

"I will be here at six."

"See you then."

She got to her feet and left the diner, heading to her car as the parking lot filled in around it. She was glad it was a ten-minute drive. She wasn't up for much more time awake than that.

The trip was quick, and the moment she got in the door, she started stripping. Bed was calling, and she didn't even have time to contact Ru. She would call her later, after she rested.

Dreams should not be that hot. Dani woke and her body was still throbbing with the feel of Argus's mouth on her. It was funny, because she had no basis for the memory.

She scooted up her headboard and wrapped her arms around her legs, concentrating on calling Ru. To her surprise, there was no response.

Rudolph always responded. If she wasn't answering, then the moment had arrived. Santa knew his reindeer were missing.

"Damn. Well, there goes the vacation." Dani sighed and headed for the shower. She had always intended to go home. It was just that she wanted to experience the build-up to the holidays like the humans did. She wanted to see their excitement as the holiday got closer and be part of their approach in whatever way she could.

Her position as auditor made her particular participation a little odd, but she was giving folks peace of mind before they headed into the new year. It was part of the preparations, and she was happy to be able to help in her own small way.

She checked her email and caught up with the office, giving details of her participation in the organization of the business and an estimate of how long it would take. She had given Argus until Christmas Eve eve. She would help as much as she could, but she had to be back at the workshop before Christmas Eve.

If Argus didn't need her help that long, she would just find other things to do to welcome the season. It was her first time interacting with humans face to face, and she was loving the experience of seeing the lights and decorations for the season she usually lived in with no extra fanfare.

At the workshop, Christmas was just another day, only with more work, not less. Out in the human world, it was bright, filled with food, emotions—dark and light—and hope for what might happen next. It was wild.

Dani finished her shower and tried to contact with Ru again. This time, there was a spark of communication. It was enough to tell her what she needed to know. The elves were coming.

Dani made her breakfast, or brunch if she wanted to be fussy. Four hours of sleep had charged her up, and now, she had to pick an outfit to wear to work.

It took her an hour to pick out a sensible yet sexy dress. It dawned on her that she might be crawling around or helping pack up inventory, so she switched her choice to slacks and a clinging top with a cowl neck that showed cleavage when she bent over.

Her curls bounced as she bent, and she looked into her reflection. With a scowl, she went and changed her underwear into a bra that plunged and hiked her breasts up at the same time. It would be silly to ignore the attraction between her and Argus, and if she had gone to all the trouble to arrange to be with him, one night from him wasn't too much to ask. She was simply laying out the welcome mat to let him know that she would accept any move he made.

"How did you manage to get this much stock sent overnight?" Dani was opening boxes with a carefully wielded cutter.

Argus grinned. "I know a few people."

She pulled one of the chemises out of the box, and she nearly moaned at the feel and colour. Dark rainbow silk was spilling over her hands in a cool wave.

"This is wonderful." She held the silk up against herself and turned from side to side.

"Try it on." Argus was leaning against one of the display cabinets.

"That gets filed under highly inappropriate."

He shrugged and continued to verify the contents of the boxes against the packing slips. "Fine, but don't be surprised if the sizing isn't quite right. I have no way of checking, personally. You would be doing me a favour."

Her inner clotheshorse wanted to try the silk on, so she took it to the change room and followed her instinct.

The touch of the silk on bare skin was everything she thought it would be. The chemise fell to mid-thigh, and it clung to her curves and draped softly everywhere else.

She wanted to see it in the three-way mirror, but that was out in the hall between change rooms. Dani opened her door and snuck out, loving the look of the dark silk on her body when a change in the atmosphere got her attention.

Argus was standing next to the change room archway. "Well…" He cleared his throat. "The fit is perfect."

"I think so. The fabric is amazing. What is your profit margin on these? If it is less than two hundred percent, you are giving them away." She ran her hands down her belly, over her hips and to her thighs.

Sighing, she returned to the change room and got back into her black trousers and her draped shirt.

When she tugged back the curtain, Argus was waiting.

Dani couldn't help it. She yelped in surprise. "Don't do that."

He grinned. "What?"

She reluctantly slid the silk chemise into his hand. "Don't lurk outside the change room door. It will be bad for business or will keep you so busy you will not be able to attend to anyone else."

He chuckled and stepped back. "I have staff arriving to deal with clients."

She sighed with relief. "Oh, good."

She eased out of the change room. "I think I will make that chemise the first purchase of your shop. Let's get back to inventory."

He stroked the silk in his hand slowly. "I shall put it aside for you."

Dani smiled brightly. "Thank you. Now, that is enough of a

break. Back to work."

It took them two hours to register all of the new stock, and Dani sat with the laptop, pricing the glorious collection while Argus put up the displays. Her stomach rumbled and Argus looked at her.

"Would you care for some dinner?"

Without waiting for an answer, he pulled out his phone, and his thumb moved rapidly on the flat surface. He slipped the phone back in his pocket and smiled. "It will be here in ten minutes."

"What did you order?"

He grinned. "Pizza. I always order from them when I am in town."

She grinned. "Excellent. I have experimented with a few local places, but I always enjoy trying something new."

The prices she was inputting were reasonable. Wherever he had gotten the clothing, they had charged him an excellent price, including shipping.

Sitting on the floor, surrounded by boxes, she didn't realize how locked up her butt was until she set her laptop aside and tried to stand. "Oh, damn."

Argus was putting a bra and panty set on a padded hangar. "What is it?"

"My butt is numb. Hold on while I fight myself to my feet."

He chuckled and came over to help her up. "Take my hands."

She placed her hands in his, and he pulled her to her feet. She smacked up against him. He held her hands and pressed them to her lower back, pinning her to him.

She enjoyed the feeling of being pressed against him, but when he released her hands and started to massage the feeling back into her butt, she squirmed.

"While I appreciate the effort, we have a lot more work to do."

He sighed and kept kneading until tingling in her butt went from pain to pleasure. "There. Now that your muscles are relaxed, you can take a seat behind the counter and not the floor."

She wrinkled her nose. "Thank you."

His hands remained on the curves of her ass and her pelvis was pressed against a definitely interested cock. The knock at the front door broke up whatever was going between them.

Argus sighed, and she felt it rustle her hair. "Pizza is here."

The knock sounded again, and he let her go. Dani staggered a little and leaned against the counter. Perhaps she should just have sex with him tonight. He wouldn't remember it the next day. They would be back to business as usual.

The man who brought the pizza was shrouded in shadow, but he handed it over and disappeared into the night. Argus closed the door and latched it with a quick click. He approached the counter with the pizza box and the dangling soda cans.

She made room, and he set the box down. Argus went to the back, brought out some high stools and set one on either side of the counter. "Dig in."

Bemused, she pulled the lid of the box open while he popped the tops on the soda.

The smell was heavenly, the sight was absorbing and as she juggled the first slice out of the box, she was grinning with anticipation. Food at the workshop was anything you could imagine, but if you had never had exposure to the outside world, your imagination was limited.

This was a recipe she was taking home with her.

Dani groaned happily as she chewed. The flavours spread throughout her mouth, mixing hot, salty, sour, spicy, sweet, creamy, meaty and cheesy.

Argus watched her and grinned at the noises she was making. "If I had known you would be that enthusiastic, we would have had it for breakfast."

She wrinkled her nose and kept eating until the first slice was gone. When the first was history and the second was cradled in her hands, she smiled. "Pardon my enthusiasm. My family has a pretty limited food palate for the most part."

"Never apologize for enthusiasm. It is a genuine reaction that is appreciated." He lifted his own slice and bit into it with straight white teeth.

The pizza was devoured and only the darkened patches remained on the cardboard to show that anything had been there at all.

Argus packed up the box, and Dani headed off to wash her hands. She didn't want to chance a grease stain on the merchandise.

She sipped at the soda and looked at the pricing tags she had been generating on the printer. Each tag had a bar code and a physical description of the item along with the price. No tag swapping would be possible. The item had to match the description on the tag.

She took up the tagger and stood next to Argus as he unpacked another box. He stripped off the plastic, and she tagged it before setting it aside. They made quick work of the box and then hung the delicate garments up in companionable silence.

"Do you wear much of this sort of thing?" Argus held up a peignoir set.

She grinned. "Occasionally. I have a few items that I keep for myself. When I wear them for someone else, it kind of ruins the vibe for me."

He blinked. "Really?"

"Once you have worn something like this for a lover, you can't really wear it with another one. Well, I can't. Other women have different hang-ups. Not recycling lingerie with lovers is one of mine."

He cocked his head and leaned against the counter, his hands moving easily against the silk gown and robe on the satin hangar. "Interesting philosophy."

She shrugged. "I am making it up as I go along."

"When do you wear the lingerie you do keep for yourself?"

She grinned. "Movie nights, eating popcorn and takeout. Dancing in my apartment and sliding around in my socks."

He froze, and then, his lips curved in a delighted grin. "You have just given me an idea for an advertising campaign."

"If you want it before the holidays, you had better get on that magic phone of yours and make some calls."

Argus jerked. "Magic?"

She smirked and kept working. "It is just a reference to you getting whatever you need from it."

"Oh. I will be back. Just a minute."

He left her alone while he went to the back with his phone out and thumb dialling.

Humming Christmas tunes, Dani kept working until he returned.

Argus took the silky fabric out of her hands. "How would you like to help me with my advertising campaign?"

She narrowed her eyes at him. "How?"

"I need a model, and you are right; if I am to get this advertising up and running, we need to move fast. A friend of mine is a photographer, and he has access to Santa's Grotto at the mall."

"So, what?"

"Would you model some of this lingerie for the ads?"

She frowned. "You are kidding."

"I am not. He is gathering props from around the mall before they close. One of the guards will meet us at the door."

Surprised, Dani checked her phone. The mall closed in twenty minutes, their night shopping ended at midnight.

"I am guessing you need an answer now?"

"Preferably, yes." He smiled.

Dani wrinkled her nose and looked at him, his earnest expression in his rugged features. "Fine, but I am having Ula bill you for time and a half."

He bowed low, and there was something familiar in that gesture. "Please, select your clothing. Don't pick anything you wouldn't normally wear."

Dani frowned. "What did you want to put on display?"

"A little of everything, but only if it is your personal style."

She nodded. "Right. I guess I have to go shopping."

The rainbow cami was a given. She flicked through the bra and panty sets on hangars before digging through the boxes for what she wanted. As she found what she was looking for, she set it aside before scanning it into stock. No stock was going missing on her watch.

The pile of garments was intimidating, but if she was going to show off the store's contents, she needed a selection. The combination of colours would flatter her and the fabrics would feel wonderful. She even included a garter belt and stockings, just in case. She didn't wear them often, but she liked the reaction when she did.

She folded all of the clothing carefully into a bag, wrapped outfit by outfit. When she was done, she looked up and saw Argus smiling with her bag and jacket in his hand.

"Ready when you are. I thought your laptop could double as a prop, since that is what you were talking about."

She shrugged. "And depending how long we go, I can just head home afterward."

He walked toward her and tucked her jacket around her

shoulders. "I plan to go all night."

She blinked, blushed and fought her way into her jacket. "We will see how long the photographer can last."

He scowled and stiffened a little. "If he makes one move toward you, I will tear his arms off."

She chuckled. "If he takes pictures of children, he probably has his decorum down. From what I have read, parents take their children's safety seriously."

Argus nodded. "I know Nero well, but control has its limits."

"Nero? Another good and old name."

He looked like he wanted to say something else, but he settled for, "Well, let's get going."

The walk was short, but the silence between them suddenly got tense. Dani wasn't sure what she was doing, and Argus seemed to be conflicted about what he was asking for.

Dani's tension melted when the security guard met them at the door.

The woman had long golden hair and a name badge that read *D. Certic*.

The teammates had promised not to keep in touch during their time in the human world, but it seemed to be fate that Dani had ended up next door.

"Come on in. Management has signed off on it. They wouldn't refuse Nero anything." The guard smiled.

When they were inside the mall, the door was locked up after them. It looked like Officer Certic ran a tight ship.

Nero was waiting in Santa's Grotto with a huge pile of bags. His long black braid swung against his spine as he moved the tripod to get the best angle for both throne and tree.

"My name is Dana and you can call on me if you need anything. Nero has my number. I am going on my rounds." The guard nodded and wandered off into the maze of the mall.

Dani wanted to hug her, but it wouldn't have been appropriate. There was no way for their alter egos to know one another, and getting too close to their true names would blow their covers. Dani was surprised that Dana's wasn't blown already. She was moving with superhuman grace.

"Hello, I am guessing you are Danielle? My name is Nero, and I will be doing Argus this huge favour tonight." Nero smiled, but it was obvious that he was tired.

"Call me Dani. I will be happy to make this as painless as possible."

"Good, because the collection of props that Argus had me gather are leaving me a little confused."

Dani chuckled and looked for a place to set her jacket down.

"I have set up a change room for you behind the throne. Get into whatever you like and grab the props you want. When you are ready, I will start shooting."

Argus smiled. "I will bring some of the props over and you can pick the ones you like."

Dani sucked in a nervous breath and went to strip and come out in underwear.

She was ready to emerge wearing a camisole and matching robe when a soft hiss got her attention.

Smiling, Dani headed to the rear of the privacy screens, and when she pushed the edge apart, Dana was standing there with a makeup kit.

Dani mouthed a thank you, but Dana was already working with eyeshadow, lipstick and mascara. The powder gave her a soft iridescence and set her teammate's efforts. "Knock 'em dead."

As quietly as she had arrived, Dana disappeared. She was the quietest reindeer, known for her footfalls, or lack thereof. Every movement was a dance.

Wearing the makeup as a subtle mask, Dani felt a bit better about sliding into the throne wearing slouchy socks and a cheeky grin. She draped her legs over one arm and leaned against the other with her laptop in her lap and the boot screen glowing brightly.

Nero called out for her to adjust her posture, and she tilted her head and arched her back. The camera clicked, and soon, she was getting changed again.

In peignoir hanging ornaments on the tree, reading her tablet while lying on her belly in bra, panties, garter and stockings with her legs crossed at the ankles.

Outfit after outfit, pose after pose, until she had even used her leather jacket and a length of chain for a bra shoot.

When she emerged for the final shot, Argus was sitting on Santa's throne wearing a tuxedo, and he patted his lap. She was wearing the thigh-length dark rainbow chemise, and she settled across his thighs.

Argus's arm came around her and pulled her against him.

Nero spoke softly, "Tell him what you want for Christmas."

Argus leaned down, and Dani put her arm around him to pull herself closer.

"I want to take you back to my place for a night I can remember."

Her lips were next to his ear, and she could feel his breath on her cheek.

The clicking of the camera coincided with the tightening of his body under her. Argus turned his head toward hers, and she brought her lips a millimetre from his. "This could get awkward."

"Why?"

"Because I really want privacy right now, and he is clicking away."

Nero chuckled. "I am done. Great shoot. I will take a look at the images and send you the proofs. For a non-professional model, you did well, Dani."

"Thank you." She could feel Argus's erection under her thigh. There didn't seem to be a safe way to dismount. He solved the problem by standing up with her in his arms.

With careful strides, he walked her to her changing area and set her on her feet. "See you when you have gotten dressed."

Her hands shook as she got into her street clothes and shoes. The chemise was folded and carefully put into the bag with the others. This job was going to cost her. She loved the feel of silky things.

She emerged, and Nero was already breaking down her change room. The props, including the socks, were already packed up and ready to go back to the shops in the morning.

Argus had the tuxedo back on the hanger in record time. She didn't know where he had changed, but she really didn't want to think about it. Wherever it was, it was on camera somewhere.

She grabbed her bag and slung it over her shoulder, picking up the shopping bag full of lingerie at the same time.

It was three in the morning, and they had plenty of time before dawn.

Dani thanked Nero and kissed his cheek. "It was weirdly fun."

The imprint of her glossy lipstick was clear on his pale skin. Dana was going to go ballistic. Dani had a feeling that she had put her foot down on Nero to mark him as her own. The lipstick would just make things a little interesting for the day.

Argus took her hand and led her out of the mall, intersecting with Dana on their way. She let them out and locked up behind them. "It was nice seeing you, Dani."

"See you in a few days, Dana."

Dana winked and turned to resume her rounds.

"What is in a few days?"

"The pre-Christmas sale. I am a fan of Christmas Eve shopping."

"How do you know she is working Christmas Eve?"

"We had rapid-fire girl-talk while I was changing."

They walked through the silent lot and across the small lane that separated the mall from the line of shops.

She flexed her shoulders. "I think that I should make the first purchase at the shop and then head back to my place."

She paused. "Would you care to join me?"

"Are you sure?"

Dani looked at his solemn features. "We won't be working together much longer, so this is your one chance. I won't ask again."

In the middle of the near-empty lot, next to her car, he pulled her to him and kissed her. "Then, my answer is yes."

She was shocked at the contact, recovered and went on her toes to deepen the kiss. Kissing was her favourite part of foreplay.

When they parted for a moment, she whispered her address. "Apartment twenty-four."

"I will see you there."

She got into her car and tried to focus. It was a straight drive, and she realized when she pulled into her parking spot that she still had the bag of clothing with her. She sighed and carried it inside.

A sleek red car pulled into the visitor parking, and she waited while Argus joined her. He took the bag from her while she managed the keys and they walked through the lobby and up the wide and winding flight of stairs to the second floor.

She opened her door and led the way into her personal

space.

"Somehow, I expected something more...frilly, less functional." Argus followed her in. He closed and latched the door behind him.

"I am the only frilly thing in here. I grew up sharing space, so keeping my personal space tidy is important to me."

She hung her jacket up on the hook, kicked her shoes off on the mat and gave him the nickel tour. "This is my living room, that's the dining room, there is my kitchen and the bedroom is down the hall."

Her Christmas tree was decorated, and there were eight presents underneath it.

"Who are those for?"

She cleared her throat. "I mentioned I had a lot of sisters."

"So you did."

He took her hand and pulled her down the hall to the bedroom.

She stifled her grin at his eagerness. Her smile faded when he entered her bedroom, flicked on the light and pulled her into his arms.

"Don't you want the lights out?" Every human she had had so far had wanted dim lighting.

"No, I want to see every inch of you, and I want to remember it."

She tried not to feel sad at the likelihood that this would fade with the morning light. She wanted him now, and she was going to give in to her urges. Tomorrow would take care of itself.

Dani threaded her fingers through his hair and kissed him, holding on as her tongue duelled with his in a slow, wet rhythm.

His hands pressed against her back and cupped her butt, holding her against him. She stroked his neck and caressed her way down his chest as her blood rushed in her ears and her heartbeat took over.

He pulled her shirt upward and unsnapped her bra on the way. When his thumbs skimmed the fabric up, they took everything with them. They parted for a moment while her clothing was pulled over her head, and she shivered as she pressed her breasts to his chest, the points of her nipples scraping the soft fabric.

"Aw, I wanted to look." He chuckled and stroked the side of

one breast.

"You can look when I am a little warmer."

"I feel a challenge in the air." His hands roamed over her spine and down to where her back curved into her butt.

"You can feel whatever you like as long as I get to warm up." Her fingers toyed with the top button on his shirt, and she started to open them, one by one.

She pressed her lips to the skin of his chest as it slowly came into view. He shivered, and when she had finally pulled the tails of his shirt free of his trousers, he groaned.

The fine line of hair that snaked down his chest and disappeared into his pants was tempting. So, she gave into temptation.

She slipped out of his grasp and to her knees. With careful fingers, she unbuttoned his trousers and slowly unzipped them. She slid her hand in and found silk. The sensation of silk and heat had its own reaction inside her, but she eased the thick rod of his cock out so that she could taste him.

He groaned, and she smiled around the head of him as she sucked the tip into her mouth. Salty sweet greeted her as she licked the hole in the tip and leaned to take more of him into her.

Dani tugged at his trousers, pulling them lower on his hips so she could grip naked skin. Her personal warmth was ratcheting up in marked degrees. Her pussy was slick, her channel ached and she wanted her trousers off.

He groaned again, and she pulled back, looking up at him, and used her grip on his hips to pull her upright. She found his hands already on the fastening of her jeans and when she was loose, she pried her clothing off, kicking it free.

Gloriously naked, they faced each other, and it was a long and endless moment before one of them made a move.

Argus stroked her cheek and smiled. "You look glorious in the light."

"You are rather stunning yourself. I thought half your musculature was due to your clothing. Nope, you really have muscles on muscles."

"But am I your type?" He kept stroking her face and neck.

"You are definitely my type. How about me? Do you go for the brainy brunettes?"

He smiled. "From here on in, they are on every wish list I make, but I already have the one I want right in front of me."

"Nice answer."

Argus bent until his lips were brushing against hers. "Can I fuck you now?"

"Since you asked so politely, yes."

His lips returned to hers as he gripped her waist, carrying her the few steps to the bed. He sat down and settled her across his lap in a parody of the photo shoot.

"Now, little lady, have you been naughty or nice?"

She squirmed as he moved his hand over her hip and between her thighs.

"Define naughty." She kissed him and coaxed him into a ravenous duel of lips.

"When you lure others into doing what they wouldn't have done under their normal circumstances. That is naughty."

She whispered against his lips. "I am definitely nice then."

"Oh good. I have always had a soft spot in my heart for nice girls."

"And a hard spot anywhere else?"

He chuckled and lifted her to straddle his lap. He delved two fingers into her and moved hard and fast until she was whimpering and moving with each thrust. When she was panting and clinging to his shoulders, he replaced his fingers with his cock, and he pulled her onto him.

She groaned as she worked him into her with slow circles of her hips. When he was finally inside her, she started to rock. He leaned back flat on the bed and cupped her breasts while she rode him.

He reached between them as she rocked and plunged, stroking her clit. Her downward thrusts now elicited a yelp from her as her clit's sensitivity was finally catered to.

Sweat gleamed on her, and he rubbed at her nipples, squeezing the mounds of her breasts until the pleasure-pain pulled another string inside her and yanked her over the edge. She screeched in surprise when her orgasm hit and held tight to his chest, her nails leaving furrows of red in his skin.

He waited until the inner clasp of her muscles slowed, and then, he gripped her hips, pulling her up and down, working her on his cock with his own beat.

Argus bounced her, her breasts jolted and she was forced to cup them to keep them from moving around. His beat could be felt in her back teeth. The jolting was tremendous.

He grunted, lifted her off and turned her so that she was kneeling on the bed on all fours.

Her inner beast liked this idea. When he slid into her wet heat, she groaned, and when he started rapid thrusts that pushed his cock against the front wall of her channel, she was all for it.

Her breasts swayed, but he reached under her and gripped them tight while he pounded into her. She could feel his tension growing, and the urgency fuelled her own. A second orgasm was on the way, and she prepared to miss out on what seemed to be a phenomenal release.

He released one of her breasts and rubbed her clit from the front in time with his thrusts. She rocked back against him and hope began to blossom as the release got closer.

A sharp flick on her clit sent her over, and she heard his shout of release in time with her inhalation. She breathed in, and her chest locked as her body dealt with the energy spilling out through her.

Her channel clenched around him and held him tight as his cock spasmed inside her. He held still, and his body trembled for a few minutes before his cock softened and he slid out of her. With a low groan, he dropped to her side and she followed suit.

Argus pulled her against him and rubbed his face in her curls. "I would very much like to try that again."

She yawned. "We are going to have to wait. I defy stereotypes. Right now, I just want to rest and enjoy the moment."

"I fully agree with that statement."

She wrinkled her nose. "Get up."

"What?"

"I want to get under the covers."

He chuckled, got out of bed and folded back the sheets on his side. When his side was ready, he rolled her over and repeated the preparation, tucking her into her bed without her having to do more than grunt.

Light tickled the edge of her curtains, and she rolled over to look for Argus. Tears pricked her eyes when she discovered the sheets behind her were cool. He was gone.

She wiped her eyes and headed for the shower. If the mist was in her face, her tears would be undetectable, even to herself.

She had to get herself together. She would be working with him at six, and he wouldn't know why she was upset.

She left the bathroom wrapped in a towel with another working at her curls.

Argus was sitting on her bed, and he had two square boxes with him, as well as some coffee cups.

"Since I didn't think either of us would be up to cook, I brought breakfast to you."

Dani blinked in surprise. She had already grieved him, and here he was.

He patted the bed. "Come on. Let's have a picnic and then change the sheets."

She moved toward him with the slow jerky patterns of a marionette. "The sheets are fine."

She settled next to him and took the box he handed to her.

He leaned in and kissed her. "They are fine for now. Who knows what will happen next?"

He waggled his eyebrows, and she giggled. He had liberated some utensils from her kitchen, and she opened the box to find blueberry pancakes drowned in syrup with a side of sausages.

"There is a lot of syrup here." She gave him a wry look.

"I have plans for it."

It was more of a promise than a threat, but she was careful to save as much as she could. When she set the box aside, he handed her her coffee, and she slurped happily.

"You looked surprised to see me." He leaned against her headboard and smiled.

"I was. I thought you had crept out and forgotten all about me."

"I don't think I will be forgetting anything. It isn't every day that I get to make love to a reindeer."

Her coffee wavered in her hand. She cleared her throat. "I beg your pardon?"

"Well, I wasn't sure that first moment, but now that I have seen those delicate horns coming out of your head, I am fairly certain. Dasher?"

She scooted back, but he grabbed her ankle. "How do you..."

He sighed and slight shifts in his appearance took over. His face grew leaner, his body more graceful and his ears pointed through the thick waves of his hair. "Argus Breathewaite, at your service."

"You are an elf."

"I am."

"From the workshop." Her mind was scrambling to make sense of it.

"Yes. Did you think that no one would come for you?"

"Well, I did write Santa a pretty nasty letter. He probably wasn't impressed."

"He was very impressed. He was just surprised that no one had mentioned anything earlier."

"How could we? We never have any contact with anyone until the week before Christmas."

"Will you come back?" His thumb was massaging her instep.

She blinked. Of course they were coming back. How did he not know that? They just wanted their time to live, to become real beings in the eyes of others in a different capacity than hauling a representation of the holiday around in the cold, dark night.

"What is Santa offering?" She smiled slightly and arched her foot in his grip.

"No more segregation. You can mix with the other occupants of the workshop and even have time in the human world if you want it."

He set the box to the side table and pulled both of her feet into his lap. He massaged and she wriggled happily.

"Anything else?"

"Private quarters and you can socialize with any of the occupants of the workshop, in any way, at any time."

"What do you think of that?" she groaned as he struck a spot that seemed to be connected to nerves on her inner thigh.

"I think that you are a woman I would like to spend more time with, outside working hours."

She blinked and cocked her head while her body rioted. "What do you do at the workshop?"

He grinned. "I am one of the investigators for the naughty-or-nice list. You definitely qualify as both."

"The Nice..." She groaned again, and she felt herself get wet for him.

"Yes, Santa sends out investigators for situations that are a little murky. I track my target, make an assessment and report back. I am sure that you would be welcome to come with me on those assignments." His hands reached up to stroke the back of her knees.

She gasped and her coffee wavered. He took the cup from her hand and set it on the side table.

"Why this sudden change of policy?" She bit her lip as he flicked off her towel and pulled her up to straddle him.

"I don't know, but when we left, Santa had Rudolph in his office, and they were in negotiations."

She met his gaze as he reached for the box of syrup and flicked it open. With his eyes locked to hers, he painted her neck and breasts with the faintly blue syrup.

Her voice wobbled. "What are you doing?"

"Negotiating. Christmas needs you." He ran his tongue across the sweet trail. "I need you."

She shivered as his tongue lapped at her nipple. When he drew it into his mouth and suckled hard, she shook in his arms.

He slid three fingers against her mound, spreading the slick invitation until his digits moved effortlessly. He slipped one into her and teased her as he continued to suck at her breasts, one after the other and back again.

She rocked against him and moaned as her senses all came online.

"What do you need?" He lifted her with an arm around her hips so he could reach the trail of sweetness that had cascaded down her belly.

"I need you. Anything else I can deal with, but right now, I need you."

He grinned and turned, placing her on her back and drizzled the remaining syrup over her. "Good, I am in the mood for dessert."

She wanted to laugh, but when he pressed his mouth against her, she moaned. His hand moved between her thighs, fingers shifting in and out in a steady beat as he sucked on her skin and nibbled at her breasts, slowly working his way down her torso.

When her navel had been cleared of all blueberry syrup, he

moved lower.

It wasn't blueberry he was after now; it was her.

His shoulders held her thighs apart as he used his tongue on her, lapping at her clit and stabbing into her with hot, wet thrusts.

The heat was amazing, but she wanted more.

Her hips moved against his mouth, and she reached down, grabbing his pointed ears with care. He lifted his head and moved up her body. His jeans were still keeping them apart, but she undulated against him.

"I want you now, please."

"That was both naughty and nice. I like it."

His clothing disappeared in a flash of Christmas magic. He thrust against her, and it took a few blind slides before he found her opening. She groaned as he moved into her, shaking when they were finally coupled.

Argus thrust, she lifted and soon, they were pounding against each other, both seeking the other's release.

The light outside grew brighter, and they rolled from side to side, each position stroking different portions of her inner anatomy.

Dani held tight to him as he rocked inside her, and when she was on top, she stroked his chest as her hips moved to impale her ever deeper.

It could have been minutes, hours or even days. When he reached between them and stroked her clit, she yelped in surprise and fell forward as she shook uncontrollably.

He gripped her hips and pumped upward, once, twice, and then, he groaned as his cock jerked inside her.

She lay across his chest and panted, a smile forming on her lips. "What do you want for Christmas, Argus?"

He stroked her back. "I want that, with cranberry syrup. So that you know we are in the holiday spirit."

She laughed and drew circles on his chest with her fingertip. "I think that can be arranged if I don't have to head back to the stable after the night shift."

"Santa is willing to give you whatever you want to keep you on the team." His hands moved over her spine.

What the reindeer wanted was time during mating season to find a mate, but if they were being offered one all year round, that was fine with her.

"Could you be content with me and not an endless string of humans?" The soft question hung in the air.

He stroked her back and the curve of her hip. "I could indeed. You are not the only ones who are looking for more than just a physical release. We want companions for our lifetime, but that isn't possible with humans. When Santa offered us the chance to convince you to come home, by any means, we jumped at it. A chance at a reindeer? It is a dream come true."

"You dream about reindeer?" She chuckled. "For one month a year, I dream about sex."

"I think I can help you with that." He stroked her spine again.

"You know, I think you can." She sighed. "Where is the collar?" She leaned up and looked at him, blowing curls away from her face.

"Collar?" He blushed slightly.

"Yes. The band that I wear that tells Santa where I am." She grimaced and shifted until he was no longer inside her.

"It is at my place. I did not think it appropriate to bring along."

"Well, I had hoped to stay here until the twenty-third, but if I have to make a choice, I will go home with you."

He sat up and dumped her to the bed. "You were planning to go back to the workshop?"

She leaned up on one elbow. "Of course. We are a team. I would never leave Ru to pull the sleigh on her own. That many hopes and dreams are heavy."

"The others?"

"We will all be back at the workshop before Christmas Eve. It is our duty to our own family."

He chuckled and grabbed her in a hug. "That is the best news I have heard all week. You are definitely firmly on the nice list."

She stroked her hand down his ridged abdomen and wrapped her fingers around his surging erection. "I think I want to shoot for naughty."

He pried her hand away, chuckled and rolled her to her stomach, pressing kisses along her spine. "I think naughty might be within your grasp."

His tongue trailed patterns along her back. Naughty was certainly something he was familiar with.

Dani stood in the shop and looked around. It was ready for business.

"So, you really own a bunch of boutiques around the country?"

Argus grinned. "This is the first lingerie shop, but yes. It is how I keep track of those who have gotten what they asked Santa for. Assessing the grown-up gives Santa a better idea on the result if he gives a child precisely what it asks for. All year round, I travel to the boutiques and stores, checking in on who has made a career of being naughty and why."

Dani finished checking the terminal, and she put through the first sale.

Argus blinked. "What are you doing?"

"I am not going to take the items that I used for the shoot. This is the first sale for the shop."

He walked up behind her and wrapped his arms around her. "I could have written those off as samples."

"Nope. If I am going to wear them and enjoy them, they will be mine, not yours. I wear the silk because I like it. If you like it, that is a benefit to you that you can deal with."

She glanced over her shoulder and placed a tiny kiss on his jaw.

She asked him, "So, have you contacted Santa?"

He grinned. "Yes. I have told him that I would have you home on the twenty-third. Until then, we are free to remain here and get this shop up and running. Are you willing to stay and help?"

"I am. On the twenty-third, my collar goes back on and I will get you home in record time." Dani winked.

"The snowflakes are pretty fast."

"No one moves faster than Dasher."

Argus faced his mate in her business form. "Somehow, I expected you to be smaller."

She bent her foreleg and gestured with the huge rack of antlers. Her eight-foot-high shoulder was within reach if he used the boost.

Argus grinned and followed directions, getting on her back and holding the nearest of her antlers. It was before dawn on the twenty-third and the shop was booming. He had appointed a manager and clerks. They should be able to manage in his absence. If not, he and his auditor would be back in the new year.

Dasher took three steps and launched into the air, her hooves carrying them upward until a portal opened in the sky. In a flash, they were home.

Argus looked around and hoped that the others had made it back in time.

Christmas magic was strong, but it needed the reindeer to spread it around the globe.

Prologue to Malled by Christmas

Ru handed her the Christmas snowflake with the utmost care. Dancer returned the favour with the sealed letter to Santa.

"So, I just put this on my skin and stick to my alias?"

Ru nodded. "Yup. Just like Dasher. Press it against your skin and think of your alias and what you want to do. It will bind to you and let you remain with the humans as one of them. They won't think anything of you simply turning up for work."

"And I have to stick to the alias?"

"You do. Christmas magic needs honesty to power it. Splitting your name to incorporate your actual name is part of that honesty."

"What happens if the alias slips?"

Ru smiled. "Then, you are going to flare high and wide on Santa's radar. Your time out from under their gaze will be over."

Dancer held the snowflake between her finger and her thumb. She eased her tunic away from her shoulder and pressed the snowflake into her skin. "Dana Certic."

Her collar popped off, and Ru caught it, wrapping it around her wrist. "Two down, six to go. Now focus on what you want."

Dana Certic closed her eyes and imagined where she wanted to be. She wanted to be around people, wanted to be able to watch to her heart's content and able to gain access to male companionship when it was available. She wanted a small home and a modest vehicle, just like any other human woman.

The blizzard of magic surrounded her, and when she opened her eyes, she was standing in a hallway where she could see humans walking around inside a huge space and there was a weight around her hips. The magic filled in the blanks. Dana Certic was a mall security guard.

Malled by Christmas

Dana wandered on her rounds, keeping a close eye on the crowds that were milling toward Santa's Grotto.

She had spent weeks working with the other security officers in finding children and catching petty thieves before they could make it out of the mall.

She had located nineteen *lost* vehicles and lost track of the number of hands that had patted her backside.

The mall Santa was one of the butt-patting offenders. Children were perfectly safe with him, but any woman with curves had to be on guard. That was one lap she wouldn't be sitting on again.

A wailing screech came from the grotto, and Dana moved to help with the fuss. She stifled a laugh and moved toward the child who was gnawing at the leg of the photographer.

The mother was trying to negotiate with the toddler, and the photographer was trying to pull the camera off the tripod to bludgeon his attacker.

Dana knelt next to the child. "Hey, sweetie. I think Santa has a candy cane for you if you let go of that man. The flavour has to be nasty."

She stopped the photographer from hitting the child, and she stroked the chubby cheek, giving the little girl a tiny bit of Christmas magic. The girl released the photographer, and he jerked away, cursing and clutching his leg.

In the lineup, mothers put their hands over their child's ears. The mother snatched up the child and rushed away.

Rolling her eyes, Dana headed over to the photographer and looked at the bite. "You are going to need stitches. That little girl had more than two teeth."

"This job isn't worth it. They won't smile. They bite and claw. I hate the little bastards."

Dana smirked. "They can be trying."

"I fucking quit!"

Dana blinked. "Hang on. I will get Toby to bring a first aid kit."

"Fuck that. I am getting my stuff and going. They can find another sucker for this freak parade."

He got up and stalked past her, packing his gear into his bag and walking out.

The hapless Christmas elf came over as Dana got to her feet. "Is he gone?"

"He is. Contact management and tell folks that they can't get their picture with Santa tonight." She brushed off her knees and wrote the notes down in her book before she resumed her rounds.

Several parents took their children out of the line when they learned that no photography was available, but there were many others who stayed and waited to see Santa. Dana resumed her rounds with a spring in her step. The Spirit of Christmas was alive and well.

The next day, Dana was getting ready to make her rounds when she ran into Toby.

"Dana, you will not believe the amazing photographer that management brought in. He is great with kids. The line is circling the grotto. I think half the moms are just wanting to pose in front of him."

Dana grinned. "This I have got to see."

She left the security office and made her way through the mall. The crowd around the grotto was tempting for pickpockets and petty thieves. Mothers left bags unattended while wrangling their children, and it was part of Dana's job to make sure that their bags didn't go walking.

It was late in the afternoon, and since the kids were out of school, it was just the parents getting off work that flooded the mall when Dana was on her evening shift.

Toby was right. There were a ton of women in unseasonably short skirts with their children in tow. It was nearly laughable, but it provided a gathering that might cause an issue.

Dana walked around the edge of the crowd and kept an eye out for opportunists. The women in elf costumes were moving things along, and Santa was working with grim determination, his Ho-Ho-Ho's were resounding in the grotto.

The new photographer was getting kids to smile and their mothers to swoon. Dana circled to get a good look at him while still doing her job. When she realized it was impossible, she just went about her rounds.

She located two lost toddlers and called the police on three detained shoplifters before the mall closed. Getting everyone out while remaining polite and cheerful was her speciality.

The elves and Santa groaned and stretched as they were finally free to be themselves again. The photographer was cleaning his lenses, and Dana walked over to introduce herself.

She could see his dark hair as she crossed the glittering grotto. "So, you are the man who rode to the rescue?"

He looked up at her and smiled. His eyes were brilliant emerald, and his hair was midnight silk held back in a neat ponytail. "The timing lined up."

She took on the persona she was used to by now. She extended her hand. "Hi. I am Dana."

"Nero." He inclined his head and shook her hand with a warm, dry grip.

"I will be on duty most evenings while you are here. If your ardent admirers get to be too much, just call." She released his hand and turned to leave.

"Is that all?"

She glanced over to the elves in bells and pointy shoes. "Ask Tasha and Lena. I introduce myself to everyone who is here after hours. It makes it easier to remember who is who after hours."

Santa cleared his throat.

"Oh, and Timothy. Sorry, Timothy."

Nero grinned. "Fair enough. I am pleased to meet you. You have a keen eye."

She blinked. "How so?"

"You moved between four petty thieves and their targets before they could grab the unattended bags. It was well done."

She cocked her head. "You saw that?"

"I have a keen eye as well." He winked.

He was really handsome. Bizarrely handsome. Dana bobbed her head and said, "I am sure I will see you tomorrow."

His slow smile burned in her mind as she finished her search of the mall and went out to the parking lot to identify all vehicles left in the space overnight. Employees were supposed to park in a specific zone near the rear entryways; any other cars were suitable for towing.

She tried not to tow any vehicles unless they were abandoned for more than twenty-four hours, but there were two candidates out tonight in the same spaces as the night before.

Dana called in the towing company and turned a blind eye to the vehicle with the couple giggling and rocking the springs. If they were still there in an hour, she would tell them to move along, but her human brain knew that privacy was sometimes hard to find.

If the laughter had not been mutual, she would have interrupted. That had only happened once so far, but she was a firm believer in mutual consent.

Dana returned to the inside of the mall, checked in with Jonathon in the security office and checked the grotto for any children sleeping under the tree.

The last two hours flew by, and she changed clothes before leaving the mall. There was an open ice rink on her way home, and she loved to skate when everyone was asleep.

She put on her skates and queued up her music before slipping in her headphones and taking to the ice.

Dancing on the ice was almost as much fun as spinning around her apartment, but here, she could go faster. She spun, twirled and swayed from skate to skate around the rink where only two other people were enjoying the solitude.

She skated until her nose was cold and her hands were pale. It was time to go home. She had her thermos of hot chocolate standing by and a puffy duvet and warm bed at her house. It was time to get going.

Dana made a face as she got behind the wheel. She was beginning to hate time. It ruled the human existence and made every day into a chore instead of a joy.

After the ten-minute drive from the rink to home, she grabbed her favourite fairy tales and headed for bed with another cup of hot cocoa.

Nero's face was in her mind when she closed her eyes. She looked forward to seeing him the next day.

"Dana, we have a security call in Rikcmon's Toys. Requesting that you handle it."

Dana answered her walkie-talkie. "On my way, coward."

"Damn straight."

She smiled and headed for the toy store.

The clerk pointed frantically to the back of the store, and when Dana arrived, it was obvious that the woman with the stroller was locating high-dollar-value items and tucking them under the blanket.

Dana melted back behind one of the aisles, and she slipped up and out into the mall, just outside the door. It wasn't stealing until the woman crossed the threshold of the store, so the moment she did, Dana appeared at her shoulder. "Please, come with me, miss."

The woman jerked and tried to run, but Dana reached out and pulled her to a quick halt with one hand on the back of her coat.

With her strength and height, she walked the crying woman to the security office with ease.

She called the police, made the report and itemized the stolen items. The woman sobbed, but Dana didn't hear it. If the items hadn't all been of high price, she might have believed that the woman just wanted the child to have a toy to open at Christmas. The adult warnings on the video games were also a giveaway to the true motivation.

"If you could also remove the vest you have on under your coat? You have at least seven pounds of goods there, based on your posture."

The woman scowled. "How do you know that?"

Dana shook her head. "Based on your neck and wrists, you are not that heavy."

The woman started crying again, and it was just in time for the police to arrive. The hostility that turned on was amazing, but Dana simply ignored it, handed over the report and mentioned that the woman had additional items on her. The police patted the woman down and had her open her outer layer. The vest within was indeed loaded with expensive items.

Dana wrote them all down so that the toy store would know what was stolen, the police signed her report and the shoplifter was escorted out to the police car. Dana finished the last of the details, filed the incident report and got back into the mall.

She picked up her walkie and muttered, "Thanks for that."

"No problem. Take a swing by the grotto. Things are clogging up again."

"Slave driver."

She put the communicator back on her belt and headed for the grotto.

The women were all making eyes at Nero, and it made for a lot of loose and missing children. Dana gathered them up and returned them to their inattentive parents.

It was a challenging duty, but she managed to stop all the tears and get the children matched with their moms.

The rest of the night went by in a blur, and by the time they had ushered out the last shopper, she was more than ready for a break.

Nero was packing up his cameras, and he smiled at her. "Hello, Dana. How are you this evening?"

She grinned. "Exhausted."

"Aw, too bad. I would love to give you a foot rub, but I get the feeling you are still on duty."

"I am, but that does sound nice." She looked at him as he zipped up his leather jacket. "Do you need an escort out?"

He shook his head. "I shouldn't think so."

"We got a warning about mall lots being hit after hours. They seem to be preying on mall staff. I think I will have to insist."

Nero gave her a considering look. "Fine, but you have to wear a coat."

She shrugged. "I don't need one. Cold isn't a problem for me."

He chuckled. "Right. Of course. Well, I am ready. Protect me."

She rolled her eyes and walked to the doors, locking the inner door behind her after he had passed. He led the way to his vehicle, and the low red car was definitely flashy enough for some attention.

When he was inside his car, he looked at her. "Thank you for the escort."

"You are welcome. You have quite the way with the ladies, so I thought it would be wiser to make sure none of your fans stalk you."

He grinned. "It is my burden. Good night, Dana."

"Good night, Nero."

He waited until she was back in the mall before he drove off, and Dana went on to the glamourous job of making sure that all the bathrooms had been emptied of occupants.

She was counting the hours until she could skate. Suddenly, she had a ton of energy and really wanted to spend some of it before she tried to sleep.

She was halfway through her shift when she saw Nero waving at her. She came over and looked at him. "You flapped?"

He scowled. "Yes. I have a favour to ask of you."

"Shoot."

"I have already checked with management, but I have a friend who wishes to use the grotto for a fashion shoot. Would you mind keeping the lights on for a few hours?"

"Management said yes?"

"They did." Nero waited patiently.

Dana looked around at the huge lineup. "Okay, sure."

He beamed, and her heart thudded in her chest. "Thank you."

She nodded and returned to her rounds.

When everyone was out at the end of the night, she tried not to look shocked when she saw a familiar face outside the door. Dasher was looking at her with what she was sure was the same surprise on her own face.

She brought Dasher and her male companion inside and directed them to the grotto.

It seemed that Dasher, or Dani as she preferred to be called, was going to change and pose in a variety of lingerie.

Dana supposed that everyone had their own thing, but she knew that Dani was going to have a problem when it came to makeup.

Dana went to her locker to grab her makeup kit and then headed out on her rounds. When she came back to the rear of the improvised changing area that had been assembled, she scratched at the wall.

Dani pried the wall open and smiled brightly. Dana opened her makeup kit and went to work to paint her workmate with the natural-but-sexy look.

When she was finished bringing out all of Dani's striking features, she slid the kit under the tree and returned to her work, making the rounds over and over, noting the parked cars in the lot that were not supposed to be there.

She returned to the mall and watched the last of the photo shoot from a discrete distance. It was obvious to her that Dani was interested in the man whose lap she was in. Dana smiled. Dani had wanted sex over everything. Based on the look in her friend's eyes, she was going to get it.

When they left, she waved farewell to her teammate and locked up behind her. Nero was setting aside all of the items that he had borrowed from the different shops to use as props.

"I don't suppose you can lock these up for me?"

She sighed. "Of course."

He smiled. "Thank you."

"Just a moment."

She slipped to the tree and grabbed her makeup case. "Ready?"

He grinned. "I thought that she had done a great job with her makeup."

"I can tell, she left lipstick on your cheek." Dana smirked and shrugged. "She looked like she needed a hand."

"You are very good at assessment."

"You have mentioned that before."

They walked through the halls until she got to the security office. She left a note for the morning staff regarding the different shops involved in the samples. She included a note in the computer and another on Jeffrey's locker.

She put the makeup case back in her own locker and turned toward Nero. "Are you ready to go?"

He nodded. "Just let me get my cameras and I will be happy to head home for the night."

She followed him to the grotto and led him to the doors near where he parked.

They were nearly to his vehicle when lights flared a few rows away and one of the silent cars roared toward them.

Three young men charged out, demanding Nero's cameras.

He swiftly prepared to defend himself, but Dana was in charge of his security, so she moved forward.

Martial arts were a form of dance and so was bar brawling. She used both techniques to get them to the ground. The three men groaned.

Nero was near her. "I called the police."

Apparently, that was the magic phrase to get two of the young men up and moving. They staggered to their vehicle and left. The third man couldn't move. Dana was sitting on him.

She looked up and nodded toward the security camera. The entire event had been caught on the camera.

Nero asked, "Are you all right?"

Dana grinned and then noted that she had a bloody nose. It was either that or she had bitten one of the buggers.

"I am fine. I heal quickly."

The lights and sirens marked the arrival of the police, and what followed was a set of interviews that took her to the end of her shift. She had called Jeffrey in early and explained the situation. He arrived while she was explaining that she had the make and plate number of the car for the third time.

Nero's calm voice confirmed everything she said, and finally, she shrugged. "Well, my shift is over. I am going home."

The police appeared nonplussed. "We aren't done."

"I am standing outside, and I don't have a coat on. We have been here for an hour and even the butthead who tried to attack me is in a nice warm police car." She faked a shiver.

Nero snorted.

"I have the recording of the event in the office. If one of you will follow me, I will have Jeffrey make you a copy and then I can go home." She smiled brightly, and the officer seemed dazed. It was enough for her, and she headed inside, telling Jeffrey which camera and what footage.

She really just wanted to go home and get some rest.

Nero followed her in, trailing after her like an elegant puppy.

She stopped in the centre of the hallway. "What is it?"

"I realize that the timing is not ideal, but I would like to invite you to a formal ball this weekend. I have asked Toby, and he said that you have the night off."

Dana was more stunned by that than the attack. "A ball?"

"The Snowflake Ball. It is a charity event that I have photographed in the past. This time, I am one of the paying masses."

She was trying to figure out what to say, but what came out was, "I don't have a dress."

"You work at a mall. I am sure that something will appear

that suits you." He smiled and took one of her hands, kissing the inside of her wrist.

"Well, then. Yes."

The police officer was behind Nero and rapidly getting closer.

Nero inclined his head. "I will see you home."

She paused, looked around and nodded. "Give me ten minutes."

She took the officer to the security office, showed Jeffrey how to find the file and set it to copy to disk. When that was running, she changed out of her uniform and into her normal clothing. Her skates were in her car.

"Okay, I am out of here. Officer, I hope you have a charming evening."

She swanned away and met Nero in the hall. "I am not going home yet."

"Where can I follow you?"

"I get my own stalker? Nice." She chuckled. "I am going to the all-night skating arena."

"They have one of those?"

"Follow me and find out."

She had to stop and give all her contact information to the officer who was actually writing things down, but when she was behind the wheel with Nero behind her in his own vehicle, she had to admit that her day was looking up.

After a short drive with her red shadow, she pulled into the arena lot and smiled as his car pulled up next to her.

When he got out, she chirped, "You have seen me here safely. Job well done. Go home, you look exhausted."

He shook his head. "I can stay awake long enough to see you home. Do you do this every night?"

She shrugged and grabbed her skates from her trunk. "Yes. I find it relaxing."

He followed her into the arena, and she showed her pass to the clerk on duty while jerking a thumb toward Nero. "He is here to supervise."

He nodded and returned to his computer.

She led Nero to the seats and got her skates on. When she got to her feet, he chuckled. "So, you are taller now."

She made a face. "Still not taller than you are."

"Genetics in action."

Dana nodded and made her way carefully to the ice. When she was firmly on the frozen surface, she took off with all the energy that she had been holding in.

Time blurred with the joy of motion as she shifted, twisted and felt the icy caress of wind on her cheeks.

Her hair fluttered as her speed caused it to flick and flip.

She listened to the pitch of her skates on the ice, jumped, turned and, after close to an hour, she pulled herself to a halt.

She was sweaty but relaxed when she left the ice.

Nero was standing next to the entryway, and he offered his hand. "You are amazing on ice."

Dana winked. "You should see me on silk sheets."

He paused, and a slow smile crossed his lips as he steadied her toward her shoes.

She unlaced her skates and slipped her feet into the sneakers that she favoured. Her skates were dried off and tucked carefully back in her bag, and then, she got to her feet.

"Okay, now, I am on the way home, and then, you will head to your own place, right?"

Nero smiled. "Unless you take pity and offer me your couch."

"I have a queen-sized pull-out couch. That should do." She put the skate bag over her shoulder and led the way back to the parking lot.

He rushed up next to her as they made it into the pre-dawn light. "You are serious?"

"I know where you work and can take care of myself. Follow me and you can spend what is left of the night on my couch."

Nero nodded and headed for his car.

Dana called herself nine kinds of fool as she drove home.

When he parked behind her and followed her to her door, she had definite second thoughts. As she stepped inside her home and invited him inside, she felt like she had just invited the devil. Her soul was definitely at stake.

Dana cleared her throat. "The couch is a fold-out. You should fit if you lie on it diagonally."

She walked to the linen closet, opened it and grabbed extra blankets and puffy pillows. She heard the squeak and thud as the couch opened, and she returned to the living room. The bed was folded out and Nero was removing his shirt.

She blinked in surprise as he peeled off the fabric, but her surprise turned to shock when she saw the distinct snowflake mark on the right side of his chest. The silvery sheen was visible, even from across the room.

"Is that a tattoo?" Her voice was high, even to her own ears.

He paused with his shirt over his forearms. "More or less. I am guessing that you have one somewhere on you."

Dana stepped back. "Why are you here?"

"I am here to retrieve one of the reindeer. We have some time, but I have to convince you to come back before Christmas."

She tried an obvious defense. "You are insane, is that it?"

"No, just your average, run-of-the-mill elf. You are a reindeer inhabiting the human world for the first time. No sense denying it, your horns showed themselves for a second while you were fighting those thugs tonight."

Her hand went to the crown of her head. "They did?"

"Just for a second. I wasn't positive until then, but that locked it in."

Dana blushed. "Damn. I didn't think about that."

She put the pillows and blankets down on the edge of the bed. "So, how are you going to do it?"

He raised his brows, and she watched his abs bunch as he opened the button on his jeans. "Do what?"

"Convince me to go back with you?"

He unzipped his jeans, and she turned her back. He chuckled. "I will think of something, but I thought asking you out on a date was a good start."

She suddenly remembered. "Right. Formal evening in two days."

She heard the springs of the bed squeak as he slid under the sheets and he reached for the blankets.

"Yes. You have to dance with me." He settled, and she heard him give a deep sigh.

A small peep behind her showed that he had tucked the bedding and sheets to his hips and the rest of him was gleaming and naked.

She bit her lip and closed the drapes. "Set your alarm if you need one. The drapes keep most of the daylight out."

He grunted, and she saw him illuminated in the light of his

phone. "Thanks for the tip. Argus mentioned that his reindeer was nocturnal, and it never struck me until now that it is probably when you are most comfortable working."

She shrugged and locked the door, turning off the hall lights as she headed to her bedroom. "It is all that we know, after all."

Nero listened to the footfalls and Dana's movements in her bedroom.

The loneliness of her last statement speared through him. At the mall, humans, who had accepted and welcomed her as one of their own, surrounded her. To go back to being locked up at the workshop wasn't a fate that he wanted for her. She needed light and life.

If she let him, he would like to offer it to her. To hell with Santa's protocols. He hadn't left the research department of the naughty-or-nice list in order to enslave one of the loveliest, most graceful creatures that he had ever seen.

She would be free after Christmas whether Santa liked it or not. She deserved freedom.

Nero settled back on the surprisingly comfortable bed and let sleep overtake him. He had his plan.

Dana slept her four hours and got up, moving as quietly as she could. She took a shower and wrapped herself in a thick and plushy robe before sneaking out into the kitchen to make some coffee.

Being stealthy in her own space was a little awkward, but she did the best she could.

The low rumble from the couch made her freeze in her tracks. "Can I get a cup of coffee out of your preparations?"

Dana cleared her throat. "Sure. Can I offer you some cinnamon raisin toast? I can't get enough of the stuff."

"Please. What time is it?"

"Around eleven in the morning. We got in kinda late, so I stayed in bed as long as I could."

"Four hours of sleep?"

"The team has a lot of stamina. We rest when we are given unlimited time to do so."

"So, you rest on Christmas day."

"Pretty much. After that, we do all the filing for the naughty-or-nice list and spend our time wondering what we would do with unlimited freedom every other day of the year."

He gathered the sheet around his hips and got to his feet. His braid had come partially undone, and the loose hair was swaying as he walked. He opened the blackout curtains and smiled at her.

"Somehow, when I imagine you in bed, I don't think of that robe."

She held her arms out while the coffee machine chugged away. "Don't you like these cartoons? I find that just looking at the robe makes me smile. You should see the onesie that I managed to find in my size. I am all about comfort."

When he looked down, he let out a blast of laughter.

She wiggled her reindeer slippers, and the noses lit up with a red glow.

"And amusement. You would not believe the kind of things you can find at the mall."

He grinned. "I would believe just about anything. I found you there, after all."

She cocked her head. "How did you find me?"

"Christmas magic and one very important fact, you are female and carry the Spirit of Christmas with you wherever you go. You glow with it."

Dana paused for a moment, and then, she cleared her throat. "Right. The coffee is ready. Put your pants on."

He obeyed immediately, dropping the sheet.

She whirled and turned her back to him while he broadcast a feeling of smugness through her home.

The toast ejected, and she jumped, slathering butter on the hot surface of fruit and bread before pouring a cup of coffee and moving around to her eat-in counter.

She returned to the kitchen, poured him a cup of coffee and popped the raisin toast into the toaster.

Without looking into the living room where Nero was getting dressed, she managed to hop onto her stool and faced the counter as she ate her normal breakfast.

When the toast popped, he took up her field of vision as he buttered his toast and picked up his coffee, walking around to sit next to her. He was completely dressed, and she glanced at him. "When do you start work?"

"David is there until three. I will start just before you do."

"Well, you are an excellent and patient photographer. Do you really enjoy the kids as much as you seem to?"

He nodded. "Of course. This is the job that I do all year round. I seek out the naughty and the nice, taking in how they react to those around them."

She paused, "You get to travel away from the workshop?"

"I do. The entire naughty-or-nice-list department has something to seek out specifically. I specialize in kindness toward siblings."

Dana finished her coffee while that sank in. He got to see the children that Santa was bringing gifts to.

"Well, this explains the reports that we spend the rest of the year scanning and filing." Dana grimaced.

"The reindeer do that?"

"Yup. It is our make-work job for the rest of the year." She set her coffee cup on her plate and went around the corner to wash them and put them away.

"What are you doing for the rest of the day before work?" He seemed hopeful.

Dana gave him a stern look. "I am shopping for a dress."

He gave her a shy smile. "Ah, right. So, you are still coming with me?"

She rolled her eyes. "I said yes. I meant yes."

Desperate for a distraction, she turned on the television and flipped to the news channel. The images of the mall raiders from the night before were identified next to their mug shots and clips of her kicking them down kept scrolling on repeat.

"Oh, geez. I had better check my phone." She headed to her phone, and sure enough, there were dozens of messages that she hadn't heard. She turned the sound on, but kept it low because the notices kept coming.

She checked her email and the mall was giving her a few days off until the furor died down. They were geared toward families, and they didn't want to draw any of the news crews.

She returned to her spot next to Nero.

The messages were requests for interviews. Dana made a face at her phone.

"Well, I am guessing that you are going to have to shop elsewhere for your dress." Nero chuckled. He went through his phone and asked her, "What is your number? There is a shop that will definitely offer you an excellent selection just across the city."

She pouted, but gave him her number. A moment later, a ping from her phone told her that she had a message. "Thanks."

Nero smiled and patted her hand. "I promise to speak only good things about you if anyone wants to meet and greet the intended victim."

She gave him a narrow-eyed look. "Make sure that you do."

He nodded. "Well, I am going to head home and change before I have to go and face your adoring public."

He leaned in and gave her a quick kiss. She tasted coffee and cinnamon, barely registering the kiss before he was gone.

The cool air from the door opening and closing brushed against her face and snapped her out of her bemused stupor. "Right. Dress. Need clothing to shop." She muttered to herself as she returned to her bedroom to get dressed for shopping. The lights on her slippers lit with every step. Ru would get a kick out of them.

The gilded lettering over the shop was so elaborate that Dana couldn't figure out what it said. Regardless, she headed into the shop with a determined stride.

The woman behind the counter paused and smiled as Dana came inside.

The gowns on display took Dana's breath away. She had the feeling that the bank account and earnings of her time in the human world were about to be passed into one of those dresses.

Dana walked up to the woman and was direct. "I am looking for a dress for the Snowflake Ball."

The woman winced. "Last minute."

"I was just asked yesterday. We only met this week." Dana wanted to smack herself for making excuses for the last-minute nature of the gown shopping.

"Well, in that case, we had better get started." The brunette with the dancing blue eyes gave her a considering look. "May I make some recommendations?"

"Please. I have no idea where to start."

The experience began with the attendant getting her shoe size so that appropriate footwear could be matched to the gown.

Dana was tucked into a changing area while the attendant brought dress after dress. Two hours after she had entered the shop, Dana had a long, flat box in her possession and a smaller box with the matching shoes.

The bill was less than she expected. "Excuse me, you undercharged me."

The woman smiled. "I saw your picture on the news this morning. You did an excellent job of defending that mall worker, and kicking those guys to the curb was a moment that I definitely enjoyed watching. I gave you the shop worker's discount. Nobody needs to worry about leaving the mall during this season because thugs have decided to go after easy prey."

"I can't accept the discount."

"Too late. I have rung it through." She smiled brightly. "Merry Christmas."

Dana wanted to argue, but the woman's features were politely shuttered. There would be no arguing with her.

"Thank you. Merry Christmas." She nodded her head and left the shop.

She returned to her car, put the dress and shoes in the back seat and then headed for the nearest drive-thru. She wasn't fussy about food; she just needed to eat when she got hungry. Her toast had just worn off.

Well, with no work for the rest of the day and a dress to get home, she headed back to her place to hang up her purchase and try to figure out what she should do with the unexpected time.

With some dark glasses and her hair loose, she snuck into the mall just after eight in the evening to check on her domain.

Nero was wielding his camera with precision, and Dana had a sudden thought. What was the harm in sitting in Santa's lap for a photo?

She waited in line with the rest of the crowd, slowly shuffling forward step by step. When she was a few folks away from Santa, one of the elves stopped, stared and went running to Nero.

Dang. Ah, well. She stood straight, brushed lint from her jeans and the vest that she wore over her buttoned-down shirt. Her heels clicked softly as she shifted her weight on the tiled floor.

She was wearing her favourite outfit for her off days, and it included above-the-knee boots. Since her work was done barefoot and the rest of the year was spent in flat leather slippers, she enjoyed the heels and the feel of leather against her calves.

When she got up to the front of the line, there were only a handful of people behind her. It was nearly close of business, so she gave up her spot and went to the back of the line. She waited patiently, and when it was her turn, Santa beckoned her forward.

Dana had taken two steps when Santa got up and bolted. "Hey!"

Nero came forward and sat in the throne. "Come on, I am not letting you get on that lap. You have no idea what has landed on it before you get there."

Dana had caught the mall Santa with his girlfriend behind the trash bins, so she could see Nero's point.

"So, why are you taking his place?"

"I thought you could tell me what you want for Christmas. I promise to pass it along to Santa." He winked.

She mentally debated for a moment and then took a seat across Nero's thighs. "I don't really need to ask him for anything. I left him a letter."

He touched her jaw to get her to look up at him, and the camera snapped. "A letter?"

"Yes. We all wrote one. When we left, we gave them to Ru, and she was going to pass them on when it was figured out that we had scooted."

Nero leaned toward her, his lips brushing against her cheek, "What did you ask for?"

"A life. Friends. And something for my teammates."

She heard the camera click again. "Why are you taking photos?"

"Because everybody needs a picture in Santa's Grotto." His lips were so near hers, she could feel his breath whisper across her mouth.

She leaned toward him. "I know one thing I want to do."

"Yes?"

"I want to dance." She kissed him and heard the click of the camera. She didn't mind. She wanted to remember this moment any way that she could.

When he lifted his head, he smiled, "Then, dance you shall."

Dana didn't know why she had always been compelled to fuss with makeup and hair, but she was glad for the practice. She had grabbed her kit from her locker the night before and put the finishing touches on her face before she slipped her lipstick into her small clutch purse.

She hadn't bought the clutch; it had been slipped into her shoebox with a little note. *May the happiness of the holiday season keep you filled with joy. Leara.*

That little note had connected the dots for her. She had been fitted for a dress by one of the vast network of elves throughout the human world. No wonder Nero had sent her to that shop. There was a connection and that connection was magic.

Dana sighed and checked her reflection one more time. She looked like a normal human ready for a formal evening. She felt like a nervous wreck.

When the knock sounded at her door, she nearly jumped out of the golden beaded gown.

"Keep yourself together, Dana."

She walked to the door and opened it. Her escort for the night was resplendent in his tuxedo. "You look wonderful."

He blinked and gave her a small smile. "I was going to say the same, but you beat me to it. Dana, you look stunning."

She blushed and took a step outside.

"Don't you need a wrap?" He frowned.

She paused then shrugged. "Nope. I don't get cold. None of us do. We wouldn't be able to do our job if we did."

"Well, in that case..." He offered her his arm, and she turned to pull the door closed.

With her home secure, she took his arm and walked to his vehicle. He opened the door of the low, flashy red car and tucked her skirt in carefully. He had obviously done this more than once before.

She buckled up, and they were on their way to the ball.

He kept glancing over at her, and she turned her head toward him. "Why are you staring?"

"You just look so terrified. I promise, there isn't anything unusual about this night. We are just a man and a woman attending a fundraiser for the local children's hospital."

Dana nodded and tried to relax.

The lineup of expensive vehicles caused her to tense up again. When they arrived at the entryway, the valet ran around while Nero got out of the car and came around to her side, opening the door for her and taking her hand to help her out.

She got to her feet and snugged in close to his side as they entered the building. It appeared to be a museum and an old manor house together in one.

There was a checkpoint inside, and Nero produced two elaborately engraved invitations from the interior of his jacket.

They passed the checkpoint with a polite nod from the man at the door and headed up a set of carved stairs. Two young women with dangerous cleavage emerging from their gowns presented them with masks. Dana had a gold mask, Nero a black one.

He helped her tie her mask on and gave her a quick kiss. She didn't have time either to get outraged or to enjoy it. He tucked her hand around his arm and escorted her into the ball.

A waltz was already playing, and despite the modern gowns on some of the women, Dana was transported back to when she had watched a ball through a window on one snowy Christmas night.

"Would you care to dance?" Nero's voice was a low whisper in her ear.

She nodded, and he led her to the dance floor. He pulled her against him, and they were off.

Her skin was tingling two hours later as she paused to get a glass of lemon water while Nero spoke to some friends of his.

"You two have matching tattoos; how cute." The snide voice sounded from behind Dana, and she turned to see an elegant woman in a bottle blue gown.

Dana smirked. "They don't match. His is on the right side, mine is on the left and the designs are different."

The woman blinked. "I was his escort last year."

Dana sipped at her water. "Well, it is a charity ball."

The woman gasped, and Dana merely put her water down and left her to try and come up with a comeback.

She eased up to Nero's side, and he put his arm around her waist. Their dancing had definitely broken the ice when it came to physical contact. She didn't want to tell him, but dancing with him worked on her hormones ten times faster than seeing him only wearing a sheet. Guys were funny about stuff like that.

She smiled as the couple he was speaking to expressed their admiration for his latest photographic exhibition.

The woman smiled happily and asked Dana, "Have you seen his latest work?"

Dana grinned. "I have seen him working, but I haven't gotten to see the end result."

The squeeze to her ribs told her to behave.

The woman told her that she was missing out. Apparently, Nero had fans.

"Would you care to return to the dance floor?" Nero was already in motion when he asked.

"Why would I ever refuse that?" She laughed and swung into his arms as the music pulsed around them.

She swung the mask from her fingers and hummed happily as he drove her home in the small hours of the morning.

"Did you have a good night?" Nero looked over at her.

"It was wonderful. I can't thank you enough." Dana turned her head just in time to see another car surge toward them through the rear windshield.

She just had enough of a view of that her mind was nearly sure she recognized the distinctive grill when they were struck and Nero fought to keep the car from spinning end over end.

She didn't shout; she waited. She had been in crashes before while tied to eight of her closest friends. Nothing was solved by panicking.

They skidded to a halt and the engine shut down. Nose first in a ditch would make it easy for them to get out.

"Dana, are you all right?"

She looked into his worried gaze and blinked as he lost his human seeming for a moment. He was all elf, and she got the feeling that toy making was not in his repertoire.

"I am fine, but I am very angry." She looked in the side-view mirror and watched the approach of one of the idiots that she had thumped two days earlier.

She noted their posture and sighed. "They have guns."

"Lovely. You stay in the car."

She ignored him. "I fly over Texas. I am not afraid of guns."

She opened the car door and kicked her feet out, standing up with only a little effort. Her shoes were not made for grass and gravel.

She looked around with her senses, and when she knew that they would be unobserved, she sprouted her horns.

The other car door opened, and Nero came out, but he wasn't alone. He was carrying a blade half as tall as he was. She had seen that blade before.

"How did you get that?"

"Not the time, Dana."

She shrugged and turned toward the young men who were busy yelling epithets and threatening the bitch who disrespected them.

She waited for them to get closer, and then, she grabbed the first one and hauled him down to the ground, dislocating his arm. He screamed, and she heard a shot and then a shout.

Dana left her target and turned to watch Nero pulling three feet of the Spirit of Christmas out of the young man's chest. The thug dropped to his knees and a beatific expression took him over.

Dana grinned. "Stab this one, too. He keeps going for his gun."

Nero came forward and ran him through, leaving the touch of the spirit where the rage had been.

"You know what this is?" He raised his brows.

"All we have to read is the list and history books. Yes, I know the Spirit of Christmas when I see it. So, obviously, you are one of the ten who can wield it."

He nodded and looked at his car. "I don't suppose you can help me get that out of the ditch."

"First, call the police. We have located the guys from the other night. Then, I will push your vehicle back onto the road, though you may still need a tow."

He grimaced. "This is not the end to the evening that I had

intended. Did they shoot you?"

She looked down and cursed a blue streak. "I haven't even finished paying for this dress yet. Damn it."

Nero looked at her and chuckled, releasing the sword back into the ether where it lived and removing his jacket in one easy move. He tucked it around her. "This should hide the mark that isn't bleeding."

He made the calls, and she pushed his car back onto the edge of the road. The tow truck hitched his vehicle up while the police took care of the other two. Nero pointed out that one of them had a dislocated shoulder, and the police nodded.

A quick statement, a tow truck and a cab later and they were on their way to her home.

Nero was depressed.

"What is it, Nero?"

"This is not what I wanted for the evening."

She patted his thigh. "As I know all too well, what I want doesn't usually matter. You have to enjoy the moments that appear, not the ones you hope for."

"Can I borrow your couch again tonight?"

Dana smiled. "You can. I will even make a proper breakfast tomorrow."

"Unless I beat you to it."

She grinned. "That's the spirit."

He laughed and pulled her in close as the cab brought them to her home.

Once inside, she kept hold of his hand and hauled him to her bedroom. She had a plan, and she didn't care how it turned out as long as she tried.

Nero took the hint and slid his jacket off her shoulders. "I had no idea that you were impervious to bullets."

She chuckled. "Since humanity started looking for us on Christmas Eve, there were others who took aim to bring down the pagan symbol using weapons. We worked on the enchantments until we could manage to take anything short of a ballistic missile."

He set his jacket aside on the chair she kept for reading, and he stroked his hands down her shoulders, pressing kisses along the skin that he had just caressed.

Dana sighed and leaned back into his embrace while Nero

unfastened her gown, and it slid to the floor with a hiss and a rustle.

The starch of his shirt rubbed against her back as he pressed against her, wrapping his arms around her while he moved his hands over the front of her torso, learning her curves.

Dana surrendered herself to him and turned in his arms when he shifted her toward him.

She eased the studs of his shirt free and tugged at his tie until it slithered free. She was wearing her shoes and panties, nothing else.

"I think you are over dressed, Nero."

He chuckled and released his cuffs before wrenching the snow-white shirt off. She backed away as he unbuckled his belt and kicked off his shoes. She wished she had thought of that. Little straps bucked her shoes around her ankles.

He stepped back and peeled off his trousers, tossing them on top of his jacket.

Nero flicked off his socks and grinned as he stood. "Now, who is overdressed?"

She stepped out of the circle of her dress and walked over to the bed. "I am wishing that I had anticipated this when I picked out the shoes, but I was thinking of the dancing."

When she sat to remove her shoes, he followed her and knelt, taking her foot, setting the shoe on his thigh, and he unbuckled it with a few economical motions. "Why are you so crazy for dancing?"

Dana shrugged. "We all pick our different obsessions. It has helped to keep us sane over the centuries. We have tried everything from arts and crafts to solitude and a ton of things in between. I found that I like the freedom of movement."

As she said freedom, he released her second shoe and she wiggled her toes. "Thanks."

He grinned and leaned forward so that they were face to face. "You are still wearing more than I am."

She grinned. "True. You might want to remedy that."

"I intend to...in good time."

He kissed her, and she stopped the fleeting wonder of what he was waiting for when their tongues slid against each other and he lifted her to bear her back onto the bed.

Dana smiled as he moved over her and she could press her

breasts against his chest.

He woke her body with long strokes of his limbs against hers.

She felt her panties get damp when he kissed her belly, and she gasped when he used his teeth on the underside of her breasts.

Dana was shocked at the jolt she experienced when he sucked her index finger between his lips, swirling his tongue around it.

She shook with surprise and gasped. Her finger came free of his mouth with a pop, and he finally slid his hand between her and the golden silk and lace that were her only covering.

He leaned back to get them off her legs and flicked aside. To her embarrassment, they ended up on his jacket and trousers.

She only had a moment to focus on her errant underwear, because he moved over her and parted her thighs.

Dana looked him in the eye as he fitted himself to her and his cock slid inside.

She winced when he had a bit of a struggle to work himself inside, but he retreated and moved forward again. This time, the inward thrust worked just fine, and she gasped, arching her neck as the first course of pleasure spun outward.

When she caught on to his rhythm, she started moving in counterpoint. Nero's hair was still caught up in a braid, but he lost his human seeming while he was thrusting into her.

The beautiful features sharpened into a visage that was nearly cruel, but his focus on her took the danger out of her mind. There was no pain with the pleasure, so she simply enjoyed their dance.

She alternately clasped and clawed his shoulders and ribs as she approached her orgasm. When it finally snapped free, she was sure that she drew blood in addition to her howl.

He slammed into her hard and fast throughout her climax until his own arrived. Nero grunted and held his hips into hers with nearly bruising force.

He remained pressed against her until he slowly loosened his stance and dropped against her, pressing his lips to her shoulder.

She stroked his hair and traced the texture of his braid. "Definitely a good night."

He raised his head and kissed her. "I think so."

He withdrew from her and turned her on her side, spooning

her from behind. The sweat was still cooling on their bodies.

His lips were next to her ear when he spoke. "I know this is a strange comment, but I have your collar at my apartment."

She chuckled. "You were supposed to trick me into it?"

"Convince you to come back willingly. You are needed."

She smiled into the dimness of her room. "I know. We all know. We are coming back."

Nero paused for a moment. "What?"

"You heard me. The reindeer were always coming back. We just needed some time to have a life. To be with humans as one of them. To feel what it means to anticipate Christmas. You know. To be normal. We will all be home on the twenty-third. We wanted to stop being taken for granted and confined to the workshop."

He stroked her arm and moved his hand so that it rested on her belly. "Understandable. I didn't even know that the reindeer were shapeshifters until two weeks ago."

Dana chuckled. "Yeah, we were the original Mrs. Claus's little secret. She found us to provide him with a team that would keep him safe and enable him to do what he needed to. I miss her."

"How long has she been gone?" He nuzzled her hair.

She turned. "Don't you know?"

"I have only been at the workshop for two hundred years. He has been single the entire time that he has employed me."

"She died three hundred years ago. He had let his physical appearance age as she did, but she was human, and even his magic could only extend her life for so long. It was terribly sad, but he buried her, and we went into the sky on schedule that year."

"Which is why he looks that way during the flight." Nero spoke with dawning comprehension.

"It is a memorial to her."

"Interesting, so the modern world has created an entire industry around a memorial."

"For birth and death. It fits in with the pagan system rather nicely."

He chuckled. "Don't say that at the mall. I am pretty sure that Toby would skin you."

"He is a little touchy. I can't speak for the rest of the reindeer, but I like the feeling of Christmas. I had never realized that there was so much anticipation as it got closer. It is wonderful to feel."

"Would you leave the workshop again?"

She turned her head. "Of course, but the next time, I wouldn't want to sneak out. I would want to be given one of the snowflakes by Santa and leave with my head high."

"How did you manage to get them?"

She twisted until she was facing him. "Some things are my secret. You are going to have to deal with that."

His smile was delighted. "Are you planning on keeping me?"

"Do you honestly think you can get away from me? I can track you across the world and back again. All I need is the right incentive." She stroked her hand down the cobbled muscle of his abdomen and to the column of his waking erection.

His eyes sparkled and he dumped his human seeming again. "I think I can give you enough incentive to keep me on your radar."

"How generous. I await your offering." She squeaked as he grabbed her and rolled until he fell off the bed.

Nero lay on his back and positioned her over him. "Lady, I am yours for the taking."

She straddled him and took him until they were both exhausted and shaking.

It was a really good night.

Two days after the ball, she was back at work and Nero was snapping photos of children on their last attempts to get in good with Santa.

She had seen her collar, and it was sitting at home, next to her bag and fuzzy slippers. She was taking those home for Ru.

Work was still challenging, but knowing that Nero was going to hang around until the end of her shift gave her added incentive to make sure that everything was taken care of. The word incentive had never sounded so dirty to her own mind.

Every now and then, she caught his gaze and he smiled. They were on the final countdown for Christmas, and it was going to be a wild ride home.

Dancer was grinning at Nero. He looked distinctly uncomfortable. "Are you sure you can carry me?"

She laughed. "I am guessing that you have never been close to the team before it launches."

"No. As I said, you were kept very separate."

"Okay. You have my bag?"

He lifted it. "I have it."

She pried off the snowflake and pressed it to her collar for safekeeping. "Ready?"

He nodded. "Yes."

She shifted into her reindeer form and lifted her head as she towered above Nero.

"You are really large."

She snorted and shook her head. She knelt so that he could climb on, and when he had a firm hold on her horns, she got up and took the few steps she needed before running across the sky.

It was time to return to the workshop. She had to work in the morning.

Prologue to Sleighing Her Elf

Prancer opened the small box and took out the snowflake. "So, what do I do with it?"

Ru smiled. "It is how the elves meld with the human world. I am pretty sure you can manage it, Prancer."

"Penny. Call me Penny."

Ru nodded. "Righto. Penny it is."

"How much time do I have?"

"Well, it is eight weeks until Christmas, so keep track of the day, and on the twenty-third, head home."

Penny nodded. "I can hardly wait to feel what it is like to be alone in the human world."

Ru grinned. "Then, stop talking and get going. The sooner you are on your way, the sooner you can begin your new experiences."

Penny nodded and pressed the concentrated magical snowflake between her breasts.

In a moment, she went from the workshop to the human world, and she was standing in front of a huge machine. Her eyes went wide and someone called out, "Rancer! Get your ass in that machine. The highways aren't going to clear themselves."

With a grin, she climbed the ladder and situated herself in the cab, the magic of the snowflake told her what she needed to do and her spirit of adventure started up the monster under her.

When it warmed up, she checked her maps and rumbled forward, out of the yard and into the sea of white. Between her map, her compass and her GPS, she got on the highway, put the blade down and started plowing.

Sleighing Her Elf

Penny winced as she covered another car in the ditch. There were no signs of occupation, so all she could hope was that the owners of the vehicle remembered where they parked.

After nearly eight weeks of working as Penelope Rancer, snow plow driver, she knew her route and the dangers of it, like the back of her hand.

Driving along a snowed-in highway was not something she would wish on anyone. In the mountains, it could turn deadly if folks weren't careful, and if they were on the road, careful wasn't one of their strong suits.

She played her favourite tunes as she drove along, but the whiteout beyond the glass of her cab was a little distracting. With the blade down, she had to calculate every move, and a check in her mirrors told her that she was leading a parade of folks who wanted to get where they were going. They were depending on her to run them to another cleared road, and she was going to do it.

Her time in the human world had been surprisingly educational. She loved time alone. Two times, she had dated co-workers, but since each of the men had forgotten their night together a day later, it had made her want to concentrate on her work.

Each day that the sun was bright and her services weren't needed, she spent in her small cabin in comfy clothing watching a crackling fire and reading books. Fairy tales were her favourite.

She continued her shift, burying car after car and wincing every time.

At four in the morning of the twenty-second, she headed for home. She was plowing the right lane clear, and to her astonishment, she saw a snowman up ahead. She tried to turn to avoid it, but the flying edge of the arc of snow she was creating caught him. She heard herself scream as human limbs became visible as the snowman shattered.

She stopped her plow and got out, ignoring the small bites of snow against her skin. She skidded through the knee-deep drifts and fought her way to the man on the side of the road.

Man may have been an incorrect statement. She was looking at an elf. "Son of a bitch."

He was lying in the snow, all golden and pretty, but she could see bruises surfacing. "Come on."

She grabbed him by the arm and hauled him upright, walking him to her plow and pulling him bodily into the cab. There wasn't really room for him, but she put him in the seat and climbed in his lap. With a grunt and some focus, she got them moving again, and ten minutes later, she turned into her driveway, parking next to her cabin.

Her unfortunate victim was still dazed when she pulled him down and out of the plow. Elves were sturdy and there was plenty of snow for him to land on.

When he was down, she pulled him onto her shoulders in a fireman's carry and got him into her cabin. Penny eased him onto her bed and stripped him before wrapping him in clean, dry blankets. Her fireplace cooperated, and soon, a crackling blaze was cheerily flaring and heating the room.

Penny had noted the chill in his skin, and there was only one thing for it. She stripped, pried his cocoon away and crept under the blankets with him to use some of her body heat to wake him.

His skin was icy cold, and she wrapped her leg over him, rubbing his back with her free arm.

She watched his face until her eyes crossed. She needed him awake before she took the next step.

When his eyes flickered open, it was enough. She kissed him, parting his lips and exhaling a teeny bit of her magic into his body.

He started to warm up immediately.

She broke off the kiss and looked him over. His snowflake was just below his collarbone, and it glittered in the light.

He was a workshop elf, in relatively good shape, and now that he was warming up, she needed to check for damage.

Penny sat up and ran her hands over him, working across each limb with concentration until she had reassured herself that nothing was broken.

His erection seemed to be working fine. At least he hadn't frozen his cock.

She looked at his face, and his golden eyes were opened.

He licked his lips. "Why did you stop?"

She grinned. "Because you weren't broken and your body now seems to be on the way to heating itself. I will just run your clothes through the washer and dryer, and you can be on your way."

He sat up, and she got up, tossing the sheet over him to the waist. She gathered his clothing up and wandered out to her small laundry corner, shoving his clothing into the washer after she had gone through his pockets out of reflex.

A small, heavy object was inside his jeans' pocket. She picked it up and recognized her collar.

Her company had shuffled out behind her, and he stared at the small object in her hand. "I can explain."

"Start with your name, elf. It will speed things along."

"Merkoss. I am one of the elves assigned to the naughty-or-nice list." He inclined his head and bowed gracefully.

"You may call me Penny. My true name will be resumed soon enough." She finished loading the washing machine and grabbed clothing from her pile of folded clothing. Sweater, long shorts and high socks all went on in moments.

"Well, Merkoss. What kind of soup do you want to help warm you up? I have quite a selection."

"You aren't angry that I was sent to seduce you into returning?"

She shuffled in her socks across the floor toward the kitchen. "You can try. I am just wondering why you left it so late."

"What do you mean?"

She looked back at him.

"Today is the twenty-second; if I am to fly, I need to head home tomorrow at the latest."

He looked shocked once again. "That is impossible. I set out weeks ago."

"You do know that you were standing in the road with a casing of snowman around you. The bright scarf managed to catch my attention, and I missed hitting you with the plow."

He winced. "It felt like something hit me."

"Don't be a wuss. It was only three hundred pounds of ice and snow travelling at fifty miles an hour."

"You rescued me."

She selected two cans of chicken noodle and started to open them. "I wouldn't leave a human, and I didn't leave you."

He winced. "You rate elves lower than humans?"

"Elves can usually take care of themselves."

"Wait, what do you mean today is the twenty-second? I left the workshop weeks ago."

"It seems that the magic directed you into a snowman just now. It wasn't there two days ago when I last cleared that route."

Merkoss rubbed his head. "I am still a little cold."

She sighed and went back to her bedroom, grabbing a quilt and draping it over his shoulders. "Have a seat and tuck in. It will be a few minutes before the soup is ready."

Merkoss shuffled over to the armchair, and he tucked himself in. "This is very strange."

"What? My house or that you were a snowman?"

"That you are not startled or afraid of my being here."

"Why would I be afraid? All you could do was try to get me there a day earlier. I am already packed for tomorrow."

"You were already coming back?"

"Of course. That was the plan all along. We just wanted freedom to work off our heat and live in the human world for a time. I have enjoyed it." Penny smiled and added the water to the condensed soup and set it on the element while she made sandwiches and got crackers ready.

She set a kettle of water on, anticipating that Merkoss would need a little more heated liquid to get himself comfortable.

She settled on her couch and noted that she hadn't lit the main fireplace. With a grunt, she got up and created flame with the competency that came with practice.

As the flames began to crackle, she pulled the screen over and returned to the couch.

"You do that easily."

She chuckled. "It was always my job at the workshop. I mean, Vixen had her own skills with fire, but mine have been more direct."

He looked forlorn, tucked into the quilt and sheet. "Thank you for saving me."

"You are welcome, and you were lucky. If it hadn't been me, you might not have survived."

He licked his lips. "I tasted magic when I woke."

"Reindeer don't get cold, so I shared a bit of that with you. I will need to reclaim it before I go home, but you should be fine by then."

"So, you are really going back, with or without me?" He scowled.

She chuckled. "It isn't something to prick your ego. I would never let down the children of the world or Santa. The team needs all of us to fly, so we will all be there."

Merkoss huddled in his blanket. "So, what was this exercise for?"

She got up when the kettle shrieked. "I am fairly sure that the elves sent to get us are a form of sacrifice from Santa, to us. You are mine to toy with, my friend."

He looked startled at her levity. "You aren't surprised that we were sent out?"

"I would have been more surprised if you hadn't. Christmas reindeer can't properly mate with humans and have them remember us. There is no forever home for us away from the workshop. Elves are really our only choice." She shrugged and prepped a pot of tea. She leaned against the counter until the tea was done, sweetened two cups and brought them to her unexpected guest.

His hand appeared from the cocoon and accepted the mug with the reindeer on it.

She wandered back to her seat on the couch and listened to the pitch of the soup as it heated.

The tea's scent was bright with citrus and cinnamon. She inhaled deeply and sipped.

The soup started to bubble, so she put her tea down and went to stir it. With a smile, she got a huge mug down, put some crackers in a small dish and put a serving of soup in the mug.

She heard a splashing of liquid on the wood floor and turned to him. "Damn."

Penny pushed his blanket aside and lifted his head. He was shivering and out cold. She grimaced, climbed into his lap, and kissed him again, breathing heat into him from her unending supply.

His body jerked, warmed, and he put his hands on her hips. He returned her kiss with interest, and she slowly pulled back.

Her voice was husky as she murmured, "Your soup is ready, and I will get you some more tea."

"What did you just do?"

She climbed off him and backed away, "I am pretty sure you know what a kiss is."

"Not that. The magic."

"Oh. Didn't we go over that already?" She scowled.

He looked at her with glazed eyes. "Did we?"

She hissed and got the soup, looked around and strained it into a watering pot. First, she was going to warm his core, then she would have to put him in her bed again.

When she approached him, he looked at her with wary eyes. "What is that?"

"Chicken broth. You need warming up, and apparently, you are resistant to my magic."

"From a watering can?"

"Your hands are shaking too hard to hold a spoon. Now, open up."

She spent twenty minutes getting warm liquids into him and then carefully manoeuvered him out of the chair and back into bed.

He was awake enough to wrap her in his arms and hold her close. She didn't even have a chance to get her clothing off.

Merkoss settled against her and breathed deeply and slowly.

Penny gave up on her planned evening and let the even rhythm take her into sleep.

She woke several times when he was shaking in her arms, but a quick check on him and another blanket, he settled. When dawn finally approached, she settled her back against him, and he wrapped her in his arms.

He was aroused again, but his shivering had stopped. The arm around her glowed with warmth, and she was able to finally rest properly, knowing that she didn't need to be on alert for his having a seizure due to cold was enough for her to actually get some proper rest.

Penny sighed and grabbed her favourite pillow, pulling it to her face and snuggling in. She might only get an hour of solid sleep, but that was all she needed.

Penny woke when she smelled bacon. She sat up and looked around. The other side of the bed was empty.

Merkoss came into the bedroom wearing only his jeans and carrying a tray.

She looked and winced. "Damn, I forgot to put your stuff in the dryer."

"I figured it out." He grinned. "I have made you breakfast."

"Thank you, but you didn't have to."

"It is the least I can do considering that I stole a night's sleep from you."

"I should have realized that you were nearly frozen through." She scooted up in bed, and he put the tray across her knees. It was a lovely gesture, but she had to pee.

She sighed and looked down at the bacon and egg smiley face. It was impossible not to grin back.

"Thank you for breakfast."

"Thank you for my life. I don't know why the magic sent me there, or how long I was in that casing, but I am glad you got me loose."

She pierced the eyes of the happy face and dipped the bacon in the yolks. "I am glad I didn't hit you square on."

"I am glad of the same." He winked and sat near her feet. "So, what did you have planned for today?"

She swallowed and frowned. "I just wanted to go for a walk and enjoy the daylight and snow. I am soon going to be back on the night shift, and I will miss the feel of the cold of the snow mixing with the heat of the sun."

"We should do that then."

Penny chuckled. "You are barely warmed up. I don't think you really want to head back into the cold."

"For you, I would gladly do it."

She shook her head. "I can easily rearrange my schedule for a final day of watching movies and eating popcorn. I can't do those things back at the workshop either."

"You would do that?"

"Of course. You are here and that was not in my plans, so the plans will change." She crunched through the bacon and eradicated the rest of the eggs.

Merkoss took her tray away, which left Penny free to get up and take a shower.

She enjoyed the feeling of heat on her skin before drying off and wrapping herself in a soft cotton robe.

Her last day in the human world was going to be spent comfy.

She wandered into the living room, and her DVD collection had been arranged in front of the television.

Merkoss smiled and sat back. "I have not seen most of these."

She chuckled. "Is the popcorn on standby?"

"Of course."

She reached in and arranged a stack of her favourites. "Then, let's begin."

He had made tea and set it on the coffee table, and as she put the first movie into the machine, she glanced back and he was sitting in the chair.

Penny sighed. "You are never going to seduce me from over there."

Merkoss blinked. "I did not want to infringe on your personal space."

She grinned. "I have as much personal space as I want at the workshop. I need companionship today. It is the biggest thing that is missing for all of us."

He got up and moved to the couch. "And yet, you have chosen a solitary occupation."

She got up and grabbed the remote control, settling next to him on the couch and leaning against his shoulder. She started the action comedy and relaxed with another being in her personal space.

By the end of the first movie, his arm was around her and she was tucked against his chest. She sighed and moved away from him, putting the DVD away before tucking the next one into the machine.

"This time, it is a comedy."

She scooted around the coffee table, and she settled against him again. He put his arm around her, and he rested his chin on her head.

"So, Merkoss, what do you do at the workshop?"

He sighed. "I am an auditor. I take a look at the reports that the others bring in, and I make recommendations to determine whether the children are naughty or nice. I take those recommendations to Santa, and he approves them or not."

"Do you get out a lot?" She turned her head to look at him.

"Only when necessary. Two months out of the year are spent clarifying the decisions of the watchers."

"That is still more than me." She smiled.

Over the next half hour, she focused on him, on his body, the smells, the heat coming from his skin. She finally whispered, "So, when are you going to get around to seducing me?"

He blinked. "I was waiting for the romantic comedy."

She smiled, "Okay. That's up next. No pressure."

"I will be ready for it." He lifted one of her hands to his mouth, and he pressed his lips to her wrist.

She smiled and shifted closer to him as the movie continued to play out.

With her blatant permission expressed, he slid his hand into her robe, and cupped her breast as they continued to watch the movie.

She settled into his embrace, and when the movie was done, she felt cold. Every place that his hands had touched now wanted him back. She wanted to steal his heat and that in itself was a little odd. She normally put out more heat than she could use.

Her hands shook as she flipped the DVDs, and when the romantic comedy started up, she walked back to the couch and untied the robe.

Merkoss smiled, and she settled against him, but he pulled her across his lap. She looked at him, and he took the remote, setting it down on the coffee table.

The first kiss was sweet, and it rapidly changed to a roiling heat.

She twisted in his arms and wrapped her hands around his neck.

He moved his hands into her robe, and he stroked her skin with long, even pressure of his fingers, waking her nerves and sending his own particular energy into her.

She had no idea what he was doing until he found a spot just over her hip, and he ran his finger over the small patch.

Her nipples tightened, she felt a surge of liquid between her thighs and her breath caught.

"What the hell was that?"

He chuckled and pressed his lips to her neck. "I find the truth of things and make decisions."

She wasn't quite sure what that meant until he pressed his fingers along her spine and she arched toward him with a thud. He made a slight exhalation as she relaxed a bit, and he smirked at her. "Like that."

Penny cleared her throat. "That is an interesting skill. How did you come by it?"

He grinned. "Years of practice."

She leaned against his chest. "Hooray for practice."

On the screen, the heroine had just met the hero in a ridiculous way. Penny didn't really care.

She pressed her breasts against him and shifted slightly, dragging her skin across his.

He sighed and stroked his fingers down her back to tease the spot he had just applied pressure to.

His kiss was sweet, and she moaned into his mouth as that spot sparked a cascade of sensation that made her shake.

He took his time waking her, moving her in his lap until her robe was on the floor and she was straddling him. He bit at her lips, and she responded in kind.

Writhing on him took her past the heroine realizing that the man of her dreams might be the guy in front of her. Penny had to smile at her split attention, but she was a girl after all. She could multitask.

Finally, she sat up and started to work on his jeans. The button fought her for a moment, but she calmed and eased it free. The zipper went down with deliberate care. Males tended to get fussy if the zipper was too quick.

She slid her hand into the fabric, and the thick column of his cock sprang free. Penny didn't think she would ever get used to that. It was always sudden, like a perverse jack-in-the-box.

When his cock was free, she pressed a soft kiss to the head, lapping at the creamy salt emerging from the tip. She had always been a fan of the salt lick.

He groaned and arched his hips to coax her to take him deeper. She obliged with a few long sucks and then moved up his body, licking a trail from his groin up his chest.

When she got to his neck, she bit him gently and then not so gently. His grunt and the firm grip of his hands on her hips made her smile as she released him.

He murmured, "Do it again."

She switched sides and bit down again with careful control.

He reached between her thighs and pressed two fingers into her. His digits went in easily, and he quickly replaced his hand with his cock. The wide head pressed against her, and he gripped her hips to pull her onto him in short, controlled presses that brought him into her completely.

She closed her eyes and focused on the feeling of him inside her. Humans were heat, but it faded quickly. Merkoss felt like coal. He was lighting slowly, but he would burn a long time.

She smiled, then she began to ride him. Her hips moved in slow and steady beats to the sound of her own heart. His heart was faster, but she chose her own as counterpoint. He could pick when he was on top.

Penny no sooner thought of her smug position than he flipped her and pinned her to her own couch.

She draped one leg over the back of the couch and wrapped the other around him as he used his own heartbeat for the rhythm. Her body soon caught up.

She bucked against him, looking for more contact, more pressure, just more.

She clawed at his shoulders, and he pinned her hands above her head. He paused and lifted her legs until they were draped over his shoulders and pinned her hands again. The new position drove him deep, and she grunted with the impact of each inward thrust.

She felt a glow take over her skin, and her horns sprouted into short protrusions. She whined and gripped his hands with hers, bucking to bring her to release.

She could barely move in the pinned position, but finally, she moved just enough to send her over. The noise she made wasn't human, but neither was her lover.

He released her hands and reached under her to press that spot on her spine.

The pulses of release burst into flame, and she heard herself shout again. She clawed at his shoulders and smelled blood. He jerked forward, and his hips slammed into her with harsh repetition before he groaned and collapsed on her.

She was exceedingly glad that whoever had furnished her home had a comfortable and wide couch.

Merkoss had his head in the crook of her neck, and it was when she felt his lips curling in a smile that she knew she hadn't killed him. The heat she had given him had been paid back, with interest.

"Can you let my legs go now? This is getting less than comfortable."

He chuckled and slowly lowered her legs. He also moved out of her, which made getting the feeling back in her legs a lot easier.

She smiled as he grunted and squirmed with her until they were spooned together and watching the comical end of the film.

"That is going to be a nice memory until I get the nerve up to escape again." Penny smiled.

He held onto her with his arm around her belly. "This is where I have news for you. I would like permission to court you when we return to the workshop."

She twisted until she could see his expression. "Are you kidding?"

"No. Despite what you may think of us elves, we choose our lovers carefully. Well, I do at any rate. I have seen you returning from your annual rounds and been awestruck at the grace and strength that you have exhibited as you were led to the stables. You must have been exhausted, but you held your head high."

She chuckled. "Reindeer have stamina. Under normal circumstances, we can go all night."

"Well, with your big day looming, we should leave that for another night."

Penny sighed. The credits were rolling on the film. She should get up and change the disks, but she was content where she was.

Merkoss pressed a kiss to her shoulder, and the DVDs moved. The machine ejected the romance and the case floated up to catch it.

Penny was startled. "You can move things with your mind?"

"Sometimes it is necessary. I can only shift inanimate objects, but it does help with the filing."

The next movie was more action, and her DVDs settled themselves neatly as he continued to hold her.

She lifted her hand to her head, and to her relief, the horns were gone.

"Are your horns out at the workshop?"

She nodded. "Usually. We don't bother with human seeming when we don't have to, just like you guys."

"I like them. Until today, I have never seen you as you normally are."

"I think Santa wanted it that way. At first, it was to protect us from the aggression of males, but then, we took on the seeming of nuns. Unfortunately, we were nuns who went into heat, and being unable to satisfy that particular urge caused what can only be described as job in-satisfaction."

"So, you have been going into heat with no outlet for hundreds of years?" His astonishment was obvious.

"Yep. Researching the options that the humans had just made things more frustrating, and masturbation can only get you so far before you start looking at the vegetables at dinner with a lustful eye. That gets old quickly as well."

He shivered and held her tighter. "I can't imagine life without the touch of a lover."

"Well, we all charged out and tried our hand at sex with humans."

"How do you know how to do that?"

She winced. "I am not supposed to say."

"Do you know where your teammates are?"

"Of course." She shrugged. "It comes with being part of a group. Any of us can locate the others, and Ru has known how to find us this entire time."

"Why didn't she leave?"

"That ruby around her neck is her birthright, but it is also very easy to track. An alarm would have sounded the moment she left. She didn't want to risk our experiences for hers."

"You left her behind anyway?"

"She was in charge. She is our leader. She told us we could go, and we went with the promise to return." Penny chuckled.

"She even taught us to get around detection for the most part or at least delay it."

"Well, as none of the other elves managed to locate you, or even knew you were missing, I am guessing that she gave good advice."

"She did, but she always does. She might be the youngest of us, but she is definitely the most intelligent." Penny sighed.

Something was exploding on her television, but the light outside was fading.

"Penny, if you wish to go for a walk in the sunset, I would be happy to come with you."

She smiled. "Excellent. Give me five minutes to get dressed."

She rolled off the couch and landed on all fours. In a moment, she was up on her feet and in her bedroom.

When she was dressed and ready, she returned to the living room, she looked around for him. Merkoss was standing near the door wearing his jacket, jeans and boots. He was holding her parka and smiling.

"Are you sure you want to come with me? I am pretty sure that you aren't as weatherproof as I am."

"We all have our strengths. I am sure that you will help to warm me up if bits of me get frozen." He winked. "Again."

She slid into her parka and closed the front, stepping into her boots and bending quickly to finish the lacing. Merkoss gripped her hips.

"What are you doing, Merkoss?"

"Helping you keep your balance in the most entertaining way possible."

She snorted and straightened. "You can let go now."

He laughed. "Spoilsport."

When she was ready, they exited her cabin and walked into the brisk winter air. The sunset had painted the white snow in pinks and oranges.

Penny walked with Merkoss following, and she headed for the rise near her home. The view of the sunset over the hill and the snow-covered meadow. She crouched and looked out over the silence, the human world with the planes in the sky beyond and the lights blinking in through the trees from houses and other structures. It seemed so alone here, but there was always another human habitation just a few miles away.

The workshop was a different dimension from this place, both literally and figuratively. Here, there was peace and this moment that she could enjoy.

She turned and beckoned to Merkoss. He joined her on the hilltop, and she pulled his arms around her. "Can you see it?"

"The beauty? The sunset? Or the joy in your face?"

"Any of it. This is what I wanted, and I didn't even know it." She felt tears welling in her eyes. "They have all this beauty, and they still huddle in cities and towns. They stay inside when winter touches the world and ignore the amazing landscape that they are right in the middle of. They are blind."

He hugged her. "They are not blind, they just can't see through your eyes. I like what you see. It is a blaze of light that the world needs."

"The world needs Prancer, not the views of Penny Rancer." She chuckled ruefully as the stars crept out to light the sky.

"The world needs you both. I need you both, but that is something that you will have to decide as time passes."

"What? Whether I want my snowman all year round?"

He coughed uncomfortably. "I can't promise to freeze myself again, but I am willing to roll around in the snow to re-enact our first night together anytime you ask."

She felt the urge to return to the workshop pounding in her veins. "Well, we had better get back inside. I need to grab the rest of my presents for the girls."

He turned her in his arms. "Just one more thing."

He kissed her under the gathering stars, with the air they exhaled misting around them. Penny kissed him back and held him until the last traces of the sunset were gone. Eventually, they walked back to the cabin in the starlight with the glow from the sky on the snow lighting the way.

Inside her temporary home, she grabbed the bag of presents, and when she had everything ready, she grabbed her collar.

"You have it?" Merkoss seemed surprised. "I didn't think you would wear it."

"It is the uniform of my position, the mark of my particular magic." She unfurled it and looked at it with a heavy sigh.

"I can put it on you."

"No."

He quieted, and she pointed to the bag. "Grab that sack,

please. I will need you to hold it during the flight."

"You want me to..."

"Ride me. Yes. I want you to be on my back, holding onto my horns and keeping my stuff from crushing a small bungalow on the way home."

"As my lady wishes."

Penny had to admit that it sounded nice. She nodded and walked to the door. "Well, I suppose that there is only one thing left to do."

He followed her outside with his outdoor clothing all nicely fastened. "What is the last step?"

"I was only able to come here because of this snowflake, so I am guessing it had something to do with my home and means of transport." She chuckled and took off her parka, dropping it in the snow. She opened her shirt and held the small case in her hand, peeling the snowflake off with her right hand. She pressed it into the case, not wanting to waste it.

"Here. Put this in the bag or zip it into your pocket. I don't want it getting lost." She smiled brightly.

When the snowflake was secure, she kissed him one last time, and then, she buckled on her collar.

Prancer took over, and she became the reindeer. She turned her head and was unsurprised to see her home and the snow plow disappear in a swirl of magic.

She stamped her feet and looked down at Merkoss. He smiled and ran his hand over her side. "You are bigger than I remembered."

She stamped her hoof and jerked her head. He followed orders, and she stood as the bag was thrown over her shoulders. He mounted her next and got a good grip on her horns and cleared his throat.

"I am ready when you are, Prancer."

It was all she needed to hear. Half a dozen steps in the snow were all she needed to take off and rise above the treeline, her hooves churning the air and running on a current only she could see.

Her instinct guided her, and she headed home. The workshop awaited, and her one day of duty a year was just another day away.

Prologue to Hung by the Fire

Ru sat with Vixen in the main living area. "You don't have to go."

"I want to go, need to go. I have dreamed of seeing the stars and feeling warmth on my skin. Those two things are in short supply around here."

"Are you interested in a chance at love?"

Vixen chuckled. "If it happens, it happens. I am not going to make it my entire focus. I want to learn all I can and feel what it's like to be able to teach those around me about what I love."

"You are going to try and spill the secrets of the cosmos?"

"As much as I am able." She smiled slightly.

Ru gave her the small box with the concentrated magic in it. "Well, put this somewhere it won't melt."

"So, I just put it on and think about what I want and I will disappear?"

"Not disappear, be transported. You will be whisked through time and space to your destination and your life as Violette Xenic will begin, or rather, resume from a point in the timeline that you will remember."

"So, Violette Xenic is a real person?"

"She will be, once Christmas magic kicks in, which it can't do until you put the snowflake on."

Vixen nodded and handed Rudolph her letter to Santa. "I don't know what good that will do."

Ru smiled. "You will be surprised. Now, go, have fun and meet someone who makes you glad you don't have to wear twelve layers of clothing to fit in."

Vixen nodded, hugged her teammate and got to her feet. She focused on Violette Xenic and what she would mean. She focused on the stars, and she hoped for a good time. With her mind made up, she pried the snowflake from the box, lifted her shirt and pressed it at the base of her spine. It was a Christmas magic tramp stamp.

The world swirled and faded, and she was on her way to somewhere warm.

Hung by the Fire

Violette smiled and addressed the assembled donors in the observatory. "We are very lucky to have gained this position, and it is your donations that keep us discovering new phenomenon."

The crowd of donors clapped politely, and Dr. Violette Xenic inclined her head with a smile.

A deep voice boomed out from the rear of those assembled. "Dr. Xenic, what is the newest discovery from the Arbin Observatory?"

Violette smiled and grabbed her remote, dimming the lights and triggering the projectors. The auditorium lit up with a map of the stars. Just a tiny slice of the heavens and it was a view that Vi never got tired of looking at.

"The Cor-Tin-Xen meteor was discovered here, and it will be skidding close enough to fill the skies with bright sparks as we approach the holiday season. On December twenty-second, we will be in the full glory of the shower, and it was this observatory that found the incoming wonder."

The same man moved forward and raised one very elegant brow. "Wonder? Glory? You are not speaking like a scientist, Doctor."

"When you stop looking to the skies and feeling wonder, you may as well be in a coma. If this can't touch you, nothing can." She felt her cheeks heat.

The crowd chuckled at her, and the servers began to circulate through the star-speckled gala.

Violette set the projector and lights for a more comfortable level and started circulating with the donors. When she had decided that she wanted astronomy as her occupation, fundraising had not been part of her plan.

Unfortunately, she rapidly discovered that raising money

was definitely part of being a researcher.

Violette took a glass of white wine and circulated with the guests examining the equipment they had paid for. She answered questions, identified constellations and generally toned down her knowledge to what could be described in two-minute sound bites.

"It seems that our funds are going to good use, Doctor. You certainly put me in my place." The man who had spoken earlier appeared at her elbow.

Vi's mind spun as she tried to place him, but it took an embarrassingly long time before his name came to mind. Colin Zeller.

"Well, Mr. Zeller, it was never my intention. I simply wished to share my wonder with the cosmos around us." She inclined her head with a smile.

"That is abundantly clear. Do you put this much passion into everything you do?"

She focused on flirting and smiled. "Well, I do yoga so quickly that I did nine moves while I was talking to you without breaking a sweat."

He chuckled. "Talented and quick witted. Add in the intellect and you are a surprise in that amazingly charming package."

Colin shifted forward to slide his hand up her arm. Vi was about to back away when a strong, warm arm slid around her waist.

Whomever it was pressed a kiss to her cheek and whispered, "Sorry I missed your speech, sweetie."

Vi glanced up at him but could only see golden skin and dark-bronze hair. Her senses were spinning, and she pasted a bright smile on her face. "You have heard it all before."

He gave her a squeeze, and Zeller's hand fell away from her. "The wonder again?"

She chuckled and leaned against him. "All the time, every time."

Colin looked at them suspiciously. "I didn't know you were seeing anyone."

Her companion smiled a blinding smile. "Xander Ekwin. Pleased to meet you. We haven't been together long, but Vi makes a great first impression."

Vi looked at the men shaking hands and nearly applauded.

Xander had provided Colin with an easy out.

Colin nodded. "She surely does. Excuse me."

She waited until they were relatively alone and asked her companion, "Is this a service you offer to every lady getting hit on by a guy who thinks he can leverage a check for sexual favours?"

Xander smiled, "Only when the woman looks like she is about to get violent. I work in security so that is a concern I moved to address."

She chuckled. "Nice. Are you here working with a client?"

"I have just been hired by the observatory, actually. I am doing a sweep while you have unauthorized folks pawing at your exceptionally expensive equipment."

She took in his impeccable tuxedo, the snowy white shirt, jet buttons, gleaming black jacket and polished shoes. His clothing was expensive, so he was blending right in.

She looked at the golden cascade of her party dress and nodded. "The donors like to be able to see what they have purchased for the observatory. Don't worry, we get all the fingerprints and semen stains off the equipment before we use it again."

He winced. "That's graphic."

She chuckled. "When it comes to the stars, some folks go a little crazy. I am a bit of a lunatic myself."

"I would never have guessed."

She grinned. "I succumb to the charms of the full moon."

One of her assistants brought over another donor, and she excused herself. Her back felt cool, and to her surprise, she realized that he had had his arm around her the entire time and she hadn't noticed. It felt so natural.

She pasted an interested smile on her face and continued doing the rounds. It was part of the job that she hadn't anticipated, but at least she got to do it at night. Changing her schedule for the pleasure of wearing agonizing shoes and a gown that made noise whenever she moved was not her idea of a good time.

Three hours of weak white wine and explaining until her throat was hoarse and she was happy to see the donors begin to leave, depositing cheques with the director on their way out.

She bundled her skirt in one hand and climbed the ladder to the outer observation level. The night was firmly in charge, and there was no light pollution to interfere with the sky.

Green jungle and lava fields were shades of black on the ground, but it was the swirl of light that kept Vi's attention.

"It is an amazing view. I can understand why you have made them your life's pursuit."

She looked around, and Xander stepped out of the shadows.

She chuckled. "I have to pursue them. They can't come to me."

His laugh echoed off the metal walkway that they stood on. "I suppose that is true."

The wind tugged at the skirt of her gown, and the crystalline fabric swirled up before settling against her again.

"What are you doing up here, Xander?"

"I am just making sure that none of the guests crept out here for a cigarette. We don't want to lock anyone up here."

She looked at his expression as he tilted his head toward the skies. He was just as enthralled with the celestial dance as she was.

"Well, I am heading downstairs to shake the hands of the last of the donors. I am sure you will have no problem clearing the deck." Having a witness to her stargazing wasn't part of her evening's agenda. She turned and headed to the hatch she had climbed out of.

She settled on the first step and made her way down to the lower level. Vi knew every inch of the new observatory, and she didn't like strangers in her territory. She joined the stragglers on the interior deck and spent the next hour coaxing them into leaving while providing the observatory with a hefty donation.

Two of the men gave her a drunken hug goodbye and grabbed her ass, but there was so much fabric covering her that she simply patted them on the cheek with extra force and tucked them into their cars with their drivers rolling their eyes.

When they were gone, the director smiled brightly at her and took off with the cheques to record the details of each donation. Fred Anderson was a man with the heart of a calculator, but that is what a research facility needed. Until large grants started running in, donations kept the observatory moving forward.

Violette went through the facility and made sure that all cups, plates and wine glasses had been collected.

Xander interrupted her while she was juggling an armload of glassware. "Shouldn't the caterers be doing that?"

She sighed. "You would not believe the places that folks jam these. The caterer will give me a count so that I can continue the hunt for the missing tomorrow, but this gives me a head start."

"Somehow, I did not think that housekeeping in the observatory was in your job description."

"We do what we have to do to make our lives easier." She tried to move past him and eventually had to clear her throat. "Could you step aside?"

"Of course. You are the last person in the building. Where are you going?"

"The caterers promised to leave plastic tubs by the front entryway. I am going to put these there."

"Won't you ruin your dress?"

She chuckled. "Everything I have is wash and wear. I will just soak the gown when I get home. It will be good as new if I need it again."

He raised his brows. "That is silk."

She shrugged. "I am pretty sure that caterpillars get wet. It will be fine."

She didn't mention that Christmas magic was giving her the clothing she needed at any given time. It was a little odd, even by her standards.

Xander smiled. "Can I give you a hand?"

"Sure. Find some stray glassware and herd it to the tubs."

He inclined his head and disappeared into the shadows of the observatory.

She collected everything she could find and set it into the bins. When she was done, she checked out with the security guard at the door for the event and then headed home.

The small cottage that she lived in was surrounded by cooled lava. She parked her motorcycle and fluffed out her skirt as she headed into the house. Locking up was never an issue. Anyone who ventured across the field of rock was welcome to whatever they wanted.

She made a cup of tea while unzipping her dress, and she let it drop to the floor in a rush before she gathered it up and took it to hang on her bedroom door.

When she returned to the kitchen for her tea, she was wearing comfy sweatpants and a loose tee. She enjoyed the feeling of the smooth and warm bamboo floors under her feet.

She sipped at the tea while she opened her laptop and checked on the latest scans from the observatory. The meteor was on approach, and it would streak across the skies on the twenty-second. She wished that she could stay to help with the analysis of all the information, but she was going to be on her way back to the workshop the day after the shower, so that particular delight was going to be lost to her.

Violette grinned. She had plenty of memories of the stars already stored up. They would keep her happy while she was stuck in her home for the rest of the year.

She would miss looking upward and trying to guess what would happen next, but it had been delightful while it lasted.

She checked on the speed and trajectory of the incoming meteor and its entourage. If she was really lucky, the shower would strike nearby and she would be able to see what happened when pieces of the stars fell to earth.

Currently, the pieces were destined to land in the ocean, but her luck might be with her, and a small chunk might make landfall near the observatory. She would love to see a rock from space land and cool.

She climbed into bed with her laptop and looked at image after image of the approaching meteor.

She snuggled into the sheets with the images in her mind and the laptop closed next to her. Sleeping with technology took on a whole new meaning in her bedroom. Vi loved having the entire world within easy reach. Feeling connected had never been so easy.

The next afternoon, Vi was back in her normal uniform of a sundress and sandals. The skirt fluttered around her thighs as she drove up to the observatory, but the bike shorts she wore for just that reason kept her nice and decent.

She parked her bike and hiked up the stairs, entering her temporary domain.

The researchers and students were all at the terminals and discussing the incoming event with excited tones. The harvest of images from the previous night was giving them plenty of things to do.

Hung by the Fire

Excitement was going around. The director ran up to her and skidded to a halt.

"Six years, Xenic. We have enough funding for six years if no major overhauls of our equipment are necessary."

Vi chuckled. "Excellent. Of course, you will need to replace all the computers before then, so there is a few fifty thousands of dollars. Custom builds don't come cheap."

Director Wells scowled. "Don't harsh my happy with practical information."

Violette smirked. "Apologies."

"Not a problem. I have been thinking of selling tickets for the night of the meteor shower."

"The twenty-second? Who would pay to come to an observatory for that kind of thing?"

It was Wells' turn to smirk. "The same folks who came here last night to listen to you talk and explain the universe in terms they could understand. You made quite an impression, Xenic. The donations we got were definitely more than expected."

"I am delighted that the researchers will be able to continue their work for the foreseeable future."

"That includes you as well."

Vi blinked and shook her head. "Right. Of course. By the way, why didn't you let me know about the added security?"

"Oh, he was the request of one of the patrons. With all the money they have put into the telescope and the satellite, he was concerned that there was insufficient security here to keep his investment safe. It was fairly last minute, and I forgot to mention it."

Vi wrinkled her nose. "It's fine. Have you seen anymore glassware?"

"There was some found in the ladies room, but that was it. The caterers picked it up this morning when the cleaning crew was in."

"Good. I want to get to work, so if there isn't anything that needs my immediate attention, I am going to jump into the cosmos."

"Go nuts, Xenic. Do what you do best."

With that endorsement, Vi headed up to her station and started to go over the data that had been gathered the night before.

Hours passed as she checked with her team. The data was new and exciting, but then, for Violette, everything was new and exciting.

Weeks had passed here in the human world with the observatory as her focus. She had enjoyed every moment, but at home, on her calendar, the twenty-third was highlighted and covered with glitter.

The human world was fun, but the workshop was home.

"I think you need to take a break."

Violette came out of the data and looked around. Xander was leaning against her desk, and he looked pretty good, though the tux had been breathtaking.

She blinked and rubbed her eyes. "Don't you have some securing to do?"

"I have been doing it for hours. I am ready to head out for dinner."

She looked around and saw the telltale signs of her coworkers' meals. Her stomach rumbled and reinforced the need to get something.

"That is an excellent idea." She got to her feet and stretched.

"I would enjoy it if you joined me for a meal."

She paused and blinked. "Oh. Um, I suppose so. I was just going to hit the food truck down the highway."

He grinned. "I can do better, and it won't be much further."

She checked her watch and nodded. "Fine, but I only have an hour."

"We will be there in five minutes."

"Then, I guess we had better get going."

She leaned forward and locked her computer. She was outside in the heat of the afternoon before he made it through the door.

"You move very quickly when you want to."

She grinned and winked. "I need incentive. Unfortunately, that usually means food."

Xander chuckled. "Well, let's not keep you waiting."

Vi followed him to his vehicle, and she smiled slightly as he tucked her into the passenger seat and eased the door closed behind her.

When he settled into the driver's seat, she had to comment.

"Old-fashioned manners. Very nice."

He chuckled. "It is easier to treat all women as ladies. It makes for a much more pleasant life."

He put the vehicle in gear, and it glided down the drive of the observatory before he accelerated on the highway.

"Is a pleasant life one of your goals?"

"Everyone deserves to be happy. I just aim to pursue that happiness with someone else." His tone was matter-of-fact and had none of the pervasive leer that she had been on the lookout for the previous evening.

"So, do you pursue it constantly?"

"When the stars align." He grinned and pulled into a small drive that led up against a hill and to a small villa in the jungle.

"What is this place?"

"It is a tiny, private restaurant that only opens on request. I called them a few hours ago, and they had an opening."

She blinked. "How did you know I would come with you?"

"I was counting on the stars to align." He winked and parked on the gravel drive.

Xander was out of the vehicle and around to her side a moment later, opening her door and helping her out of his car.

If she had put any of the Christmas magic into the knowledge, she was sure that she would learn the car that she had just been a passenger in was worth more than two years of her salary. As it was, she just knew it smelled really great. Part of that was probably Xander.

He took her hand and led her up a stairway that approached the crest of the hill. When they got to the top, she gasped as the valley below was exposed in all its lush glory. He chuckled and kept leading her out onto a wide platform where a table was set for two. He held her chair for her, and she settled in before he took his own spot.

The server came from inside a building that was hidden in the green shadows. It was so well disguised that she was no longer confused at her not knowing that this place existed. It was designed to hide.

Xander said, "Hello, Timothy. How is business?"

Timothy grinned. "Slow and controlled. Just the way we like it, Mr. Ekwin. The chef's special for you and your companion?"

Vi quirked her lips. "Unless you have tacos."

Timothy chuckled. "No, but I promise that dinner will not disappoint. Enjoy the view. I will be back shortly."

She propped her chin on her fist and stared out over the valley and the small pockets of mist that gave rise to the memory of lava pools past.

The molten earth was never too far away, but the clear and light-pollution-free sky was considered worth the risk. Even Vi's home had the marks of the last lava flow around it. The field of stone that she drove across made the view of her home surrounded by green in the middle of the rippling rock all the more wondrous. The solar panels that she used powered everything she needed and gave her another thing to thank the stars for.

When she turned back to look at her dinner companion, he was staring at her with an indulgent smile on his lips.

"What?"

He chuckled. "You have the same look on your face now as you did looking through the captured images from last night. You are analyzing the valley."

"This is new to me. I hadn't realized it was here. I tend to get a little analytical when presented with new information."

Xander smiled, and Tim brought out cool, sweating glasses of water with lemon floating inside them.

"You seem to be master of the observatory. Does the director mind?"

Vi grinned. "As long as I can keep the discoveries coming in, I can do what I like."

"Do you ever worry about being beaten to the punch?"

She laughed. "No. The stars belong to everyone. The more that new items are discovered and studied, the more interest will grow. The more folks who get interested, the more funds will be directed into studying the stars. Perhaps, one day, we will be able to confirm that we are not alone."

Xander rubbed his chin as their food arrived. "I would not have guessed that you were a UFO fanatic."

She snorted. "I am not, but I do believe that there is more than simply science in the world and in the universe. To believe in possibilities is to believe in magic, and the magic in the stars is there for everyone to see."

The ravioli that was set down in front of her was drizzled

with an aromatic salsa. When she bit into the first of the plump pastas, she smiled in delight. "Tacos!"

Timothy winked and left them.

Xander took a bite and blinked. "Wow. Now that is a taste combination I was not expecting."

She smirked and started working her way through the plate.

"It is odd to see a woman of science glow so brightly when she speaks of magic."

She shrugged. "Magic exists throughout the world. It is a hidden power, but it is still felt in everyday life."

"You speak like you have firsthand knowledge."

"You probably have as well; you just didn't know it for what is was."

He finished his plate and leaned back. "So, you believe in magic, are a master of science, look for magic in the stars, wear an evening gown with style and ride a motorcycle in a sundress. You are a mass of conflicting situations. If I didn't know better, I would say that you are too much woman to be real."

She was sure that her pause was minuscule, but she had the feeling that he had caught it. "Many women have a variety of interests."

"You are not many women. I get the feeling that you are quite unique."

Vi shrugged and dabbed her lips with a napkin. "I am just like other ladies."

"If you insist, but I stand by my opinion. Women like you don't come along every day."

She decided to change the subject. "What drove you to security at the observatory?"

"The new equipment that was just installed has caused the investor a little bit of agitation. He wants it protected at all times."

She grinned. "So, who is protecting it while we are out to dinner?"

"Other members of my company. They are watching from a distance, but your equipment is under my serious protection." He winked.

"Good to know."

Another course arrived, and the salad was bright and filled with seeds and berries.

She was scooping up the last of the pumpkin seeds when he asked her, "So, you really do believe in magic?"

She finished her mouthful and took a sip of water. When she was done, she placed her hands in her lap. "I do."

"Why?"

"Because it has been a part of my life since the first moment I could walk. It isn't something to be dismissed, and it can be found anywhere you are looking for it." She waved her hand over the view. "If you don't think that is magic, you have a dent in your soul."

The dessert arrived in the form of a pineapple ice.

Xander nodded and ate his serving in silence.

She lifted her head and asked him, "So, what do you do in your off time?"

"I surf and help a friend with a small shop on the beach. His security is always an issue."

"Why?"

"He trusts everyone. He has no sense of self-preservation. Every sob story gets his attention, and his money flows like water." Xander shook his head in disgust.

"Does he have what he needs? I mean, does he have enough money to pay his own bills before he gives the money away?"

Xander scowled. "He does."

"Then, let him have his charity. It enriches the soul while you lighten your pocket." She smiled and finished her ice.

"That is an interesting way of looking at things."

"'Tis the season." Her expression was definitely smug; she could feel it.

He chuckled and checked his elegant watch. "Well, it is time to get you back to your workstation. Thank you for joining me."

He rose to his feet, and Timothy materialized behind her, pulling her chair out to help her to her feet. Xander held his hand out, and she took it to get herself to her feet.

With only a nod to Timothy, he led her back to his vehicle.

"Aren't you going to pay?"

"They will send the bill to my office, and it will be paid at the end of the month. One of the reasons they like a select clientele is so that they don't have to run a cash business."

"Well, the food was definitely worth the trip. I have never eaten mystery food before, but I enjoyed it."

He grinned and tucked her into his car before closing the door and walking around. "Excellent. If you are up to it, we can hit the food truck tomorrow."

She grinned. "Excellent. They do this thing with fries, pickled jalapenos, cheese and hot sauce that will melt your face."

"That sounds intriguing."

"Oh, you will see stars in full daylight." She chortled and rubbed her hands together.

"It's a date."

To her shock, she realized that she had just done that exact thing. She had just made a date.

She digested that on the short drive back to the observatory.

"Why are the observatories out in these remote areas?"

Vi wrinkled her nose. "In two words, light pollution."

"What?"

"The lights that let you navigate around cities and towns keep the telescopes from being able to do their work efficiently. In a bright sky, you can only see the brightest stars. In the darkness, the weaker, more distant lights can be seen."

"So, you do your best work in absolute night."

Violette thought about her normal job and taking off in the darkness, racing to beat the dawn around the world. "You could say that."

He pulled into the observatory lot and shut his vehicle down. "Well, thank you for coming with me."

"You are most welcome. It was fun."

He got out of the car and came around to open her door again. He took her hand and led her back to the observatory.

Vi looked at him and wanted nothing more than to instigate a kiss, but he worked for the observatory and she wasn't going to be around long. It wouldn't be fair to him.

She sighed, squeezed his hand and headed inside. At least she would have tomorrow.

"How in the name of all that is holy do you eat that?" Xander's eyes were watering, and he was on his third bottle of water.

Vi grinned. "Practice."

She watched him, and for a moment, he blurred. He became more elegant and his ears formed points.

Her amusement cooled, and she finished her lava fries. She didn't want to go home. Not yet. She wanted to see a meteor shower and be able to watch it until it finished its dramatic cascade.

"Violette, what is wrong?"

Should she blow her cover? He could be a regular elf, just out in the human world for fun.

"How long have you been on the island?"

He blinked. "This time? I have been here for three months. I spend my summers elsewhere."

She twisted her lips. "I saw your ears, elf."

He looked as if he wanted to argue with her, but her expression must have been no-nonsense.

He glanced around, and when he realized they were on their own, he leaned forward. "I didn't mean for you to see them, reindeer."

She narrowed her eyes. "I don't know what you are talking about."

"Oh, really? I have a collar in my car with the name *Vixen* engraved on the tag. It led me straight to you." His affable expression was gone; he was intent.

"So, what is your intention?"

"I am going to convince you to return."

Vi blinked. It seemed that Ru hadn't told Santa about their plan to come back when they had seen what they wanted of the world. Well, this could be fun.

"That is going to take a lot of convincing."

He smiled. "I am up for the challenge."

She shook her head. "I don't know. You were just defeated by French fries and some hot peppers."

"I was assaulted by them, not defeated." He gave her a narrow-eyed look.

She grinned. "Can I have them?"

He shoved the fries over and stared as she consumed them. "I cannot believe you are eating those."

"I will pay later, but for now, I am enjoying the heat. Do you have any idea how difficult it is to fly Santa in his holiday mode all over the planet? It is fricking freezing every time we stop."

"I have heard that the team doesn't feel the cold."

She wrinkled her nose. "Not physically, but since I have had no memories of being hot, truly and wonderfully hot from the inside out, my mind paints an image of the cold and holds it tight."

He shivered. "I can only imagine. Have you gone to the beach since you have been here?"

She shook her head. "No. I spend the days either asleep or at home. The light that caresses my deck is plenty."

"Where do you live?"

She wrinkled her nose. "You know the lava field across the highway from the observatory?"

He was wary. "Yes?"

"I live on an oasis in the middle of it. I think it is called a puhka?" She sighed. "It is close to where I want to be, and I can get back and forth with ease."

"As long as you ride the bike."

"Correct. Your lovely and elegant car has no chance to get in there."

"I suppose that I will have to adapt and find a way to get to you."

Vi grinned. "If you are serious about convincing me, you had better. Have you ever sat in the middle of a lava field? There is a silence that wraps around your soul. I love it."

"You don't worry—oh, wait. You can fly."

She chuckled. "I can indeed. Not in this form, but I can get up and running pretty damned quick."

"Is it a little weird when I say that I really want to see that?"

Vi shook her head. "No, most folks want to see one of us up close. It surprises folks when they see how big we really are."

"How big are you?"

"Close to nine feet tall with the rack. Humans lose the memory, but they keep the impression of the magic."

"So, that is why you are so fascinated with magic?"

"I am not fascinated; I just know that the world needs it. Even with the modern sensibility of commerce pulling away from the importance of the season, you still can't stop the magic. That is what Santa and the team is for. We bring the magic, and we keep it in their hearts and minds until the next year."

Xander leaned back, and he shook his head. "I can't imagine what it feels like to do what you do."

"As an elf, what is your speciality?"

He sighed. "I work with the naughty-or-nice list. My focus is on keeping folks who drain themselves and build up resentment toward those that they help. I try to tell them that they have to make sure that they are taken care of first, and then, they can care for others."

She chuckled. "So, what we were talking about yesterday..."

"I help him to choose the most deserving of those who come to him. I can see to their hearts."

"That is handy. What do you see when you look at me?"

"Generosity, joy and magic. It radiates out of everything that you say and do."

She raised her hand and made a few signals. He scowled at her. "What was that?"

A minute later, a new order of fries was in front of him. Fries, cheese curds and beef gravy. "There. That should sooth you."

He took a bite and then another. A moment later, there was a feeding frenzy taking over the elf.

When his gravy-stained lips lifted, he asked, "What is that?"

"Canadian thing. Poutine. From what I have heard, it is everywhere. Even *McDonald's* has a version."

"How do you know that?"

"We fly across Canada and even hit a few drive thrus. I can read no matter what form I wear."

He cleared his throat. "Do you mind if I get another?"

"No problem. We still have twenty minutes."

He got to his feet and headed back to the truck.

Vi smirked as she watched him walk, his change from handsome human to accessible elf had definitely increased his attractiveness.

She finished his discarded fries and sat there with a soda while he made his way back to her with his precious poutine.

His delight in the new discovery was obvious, and she was able to see some of the energy that she associated with elves. The only ones she had ever met helped to lash them to the sleigh every year. Those elves were jovial, but they spoke to each other and Santa, and seemed to forget that there were sentient beings inside the beast bodies.

When Xander pushed his paper tray aside, he smiled blissfully. "I can see the attraction for that food truck."

"I am sure that they are delighted." She chuckled, gathering up their discarded trays and getting to her feet to drop them into the recycling bin. She wiped her hands clean and tossed the napkins into the trash.

Xander came up behind her and fired his own napkins into the trash along with their empty soda cups.

"Ready to get back to work?" He smiled.

"I am. Tomorrow is my day away from the observatory, so I will see you on Friday."

He seemed a little surprised. "You are taking a day off so close to the shower?"

"I am working from home, as per my contract. If you can find my place, you are welcome to come over for coffee."

"You aren't going to give me any additional clues as to your location?"

"It is across the highway from the observatory. I can't be more precise than that." She wrinkled her nose. "I can always find my way home."

He sighed. "I will have to do my best."

They returned to the observatory, and as he helped her from the car, she smirked. "Bring food if you come out tomorrow. I haven't gotten the hang of cooking yet."

Xander's grin stayed on his face all the way to the doors of the observatory.

He lifted her hand to his lips and kissed her skin. "Have a good night of calculations, Violette."

"Have fun stalking in the shadows, Xander."

She waved at him and headed inside where her team was waiting with updates.

There was work to be done and darkness was coming. Time to look to the stars.

Vi sat out on her porch in a long jersey tank dress and a kimono-style robe with her laptop on her thighs. The sound of an approaching vehicle made her smile.

It appeared that Xander had found a way after all.

He pulled up on a dirt bike, and the box strapped to his back made her mouth water. He had brought takeout.

She set her computer down and walked over to the edge of the railing. "Congratulations. You found me."

He looked around. "I have to say that this is the most unusual home locale I have yet to observe."

He parked the bike, putting it on its kickstand, and he walked over to her.

She was still leaning on the railing when he kissed her. Her eyes widened in shock, and she debated what to do next. Reaching up and holding his head to hers seemed like the right thing to do.

He tasted like cinnamon. It was the strangest thing, but he tasted like heat. Unwilling to fight her instincts, she pressed closer and held on.

Xander pulled back and looked down at her. "I did not intend for things to escalate this quickly."

She looked down, and she had wrapped one leg around his and was holding him against her. "Well, there is something to be said for instinct."

"Would you like to continue this inside?"

Vi grinned. "After dinner. I am assuming that you brought food in that pack."

He nodded. "I believed that was the wisest course."

"Excellent. Dinner first, but I have a special spot to have it. We are going upstairs."

She had an evil smirk on her lips as she got plates and cutlery together on a tray with a pitcher of lemonade.

She led the way through her home, up the stairs, through her bedroom and out onto the deck that overlooked the surrounding lava fields beyond the small clump of trees gleaming and rippling in the sunlight.

"This is... incredible." Xander set the box on the table she gestured to. He looked around in wonder. "You can see for miles."

"Yup. I can even see the observatory if I want to." She walked to the edge of the railing and looked out at the waves of black, rippling stone and crumbled raw edges.

"Well, Timothy made the food, and the papaya salad is supposedly hot enough to melt its way through your spine. He was prodigiously proud of that."

Vi laughed. "Then, let's eat and enjoy the view."

The table and chairs had been a nightmare to set in place, but on her rare days off, she didn't regret it. Getting it here had been a treat, but she had cheated and used her other form to haul the furniture across the field. It might have blown her cover, but she counted on no one looking for her yet. A little shifted shape and cargo transport never hurt anyone.

She settled across from him, and he laid out the food, carefully arranging the papaya salad next to her. It was as amusing as it was strategic.

They enjoyed a meal in the sunshine with the rippling black stone surrounding them on all sides. When they sat back with the dishes cleared, they both sighed in unison.

"This is definitely a magical place." Xander looked around them and shook his head in wonder.

"It is. And when I leave, it will disappear and be absorbed by the next lava flow. It will be gone in a matter of hours."

He looked around again. "That is rather sad."

"I know, but that is life on an island with an active volcano. It takes what it wants."

"That is a good idea." Xander got to his feet and came around the table, hauling her to her feet.

She grinned and wrapped her arms around his neck. "It sounds like an excellent idea. I don't need to check on the images from last night until after nine."

"That leaves me with four hours."

She stroked her hand through his hair. "I am sure that we can find something to occupy our time until the night is upon us."

He didn't let her continue her chattering. His mouth came down on hers, and he wrapped her against him until only a sandwich of fabric separated them.

Vi held tight to him, and he started to move his hands over her back until he cupped her butt and pulled her against him. Her time in the human world was short, and she didn't want to miss out on what was appearing to be the build up to some interesting sex just because she wanted more foreplay.

The heat from his mouth and the cinnamon taste of him quickly became all the foreplay she needed when he bent her back against the railing and the sky spun above her.

He moved her robe aside and sucked on her left breast through her clothing.

Vi let out a hot moan and threaded her fingers into his hair, holding him there when he would have moved to the other side.

When she was shaking, she let him move. He moved to the right side, and the heat of the sun warmed the damp spot on her dress.

Violette sighed and pressed her breast firmly into his mouth. He pulled her dress up to her hip, and his hand clenched when his touch wasn't impeded by underwear.

She smiled and tugged on his head to bring his mouth to hers again while she slid a hand along the front of his jeans to unsnap and unzip them. His cock sprang into her hand, and she stroked the hot and throbbing length as his kiss turned feral and he worked a finger into her.

She knew she was wet. She had felt soaked since he had driven up on the bike. The effort he was making on her behalf touched her deeply, in several ways. Right now, she was interested in getting touched by something more than a finger.

He stepped back, his chest working heavily, and he turned her to face the expanse of glittering black. He tucked her skirt up around her hips.

Xander couldn't see her grin, but when he pressed into her, her moan carried out and over the horizon.

She arched and pushed back, using the handrail to get the balance point that let her work against him in an equal reaction to his inward thrusts.

She shivered as he filled her and kept his cock working against the sensitive interior of her channel. Her breath came in gasps while her body bucked in rhythm. Sweat coated her skin, dripping down her face to land between her palms. She was on fire, and she loved every minute of it.

Her fever rose to a pitch that culminated when she locked in place and let out a low, rattling moan.

The air left her in a rush, and she heard the hardwood under her hands crack.

Xander held her hips and drove himself into her, pressing tight while he groaned through gritted teeth.

She panted in the heavy tropical air, the sweat and scent of sex was just as earthy as the wilderness surrounding her little house. It fit right in.

Xander wrapped his arms around her. "That happened a little faster than I anticipated."

She turned her head and spoke over her shoulder. "It seemed just right to me."

He chuckled and withdrew from her. Her dress fell around her with a decorum that belied the activities of the previous minutes.

"I suppose that a shower is too much to ask?"

She chuckled and turned to face him, grunting lightly as he pulled her against him. "I have a shower. Come on, it is downstairs."

She led him down the stairs and out of her house.

"I thought we were having a shower."

Vi looked at him. "You have come to the island for months at a time and you haven't showered outdoors?"

"No."

"Wow. This will be a treat." She led him around to the back of her home, and she removed the layers of clothing that she had on.

He blinked at her, and she gestured. "Don't wait. Strip."

She hung her clothing over a rack attached to the wall, and she stepped onto the raised stones of her shower stall. It wasn't really a stall, it was a showerhead extruding from her house with a box filled with soaps and shampoos attached underneath it.

She started the shower and brought it up to a comfortable temperature.

She let the water run over her, and when she turned her head, Xander stepped into the wide spray, gloriously naked.

He was all golden. No tan lines. He was lovely to behold.

As he stepped into the water and the sunlight sparkled down onto him, he caught fire. The water droplets caught the sun and shattered into a thousand minuscule shards that turned into mist.

Eventually, she cleared her throat. "You are hogging all the tepid water."

He grinned. "You are right. It does feel wonderful though. Definitely not something that you can do at the workshop."

She laughed and changed places with him, wriggling with the feel of the water on her skin. She delved into the soapbox and slid the bar over her breasts and down her belly. Vi watched his eyes on her as she soaped all the spots that had felt sweaty, and she rinsed out her hair under the spray.

When she was done, she switched places with him again. He wriggled happily, and she stepped aside as he took full advantage of the height of the cascading water.

He started to hum a bright tune as he turned from side to side and confiscated her soap. He scrubbed front and back, enjoying himself in the extreme.

Chuckling, Vi stepped back and let the sun dry her. It was nice to see him enjoying something that had escaped him, though he was free to come and go as he pleased.

She left him to the shower and the happy noises he was making, heading inside with her clothing and his. She gave it a quick rinse with some water and brought the clothing back outside to hang on the line.

He finished his shower and looked around for a towel.

"Is there a way to dry off?"

She chortled. "Stand in the sunlight. The stars aren't just for looking at."

He took a few steps away from the house and extended his arms to take in the light. His skin dried quickly.

She checked on their clothing and nodded when they were already on their way to mildly damp. "If you want to cover up, we can, but if not, we can have some lemonade on the upper deck."

"That sounds delightful. After you, m'lady."

"You just want to stare at my ass."

"It is a lovely view; who wouldn't enjoy it?"

She chuckled and led the way into her home once again. The rest of the afternoon was suddenly filled with promise.

They were curled in her bed, and she was working on the images that had been forwarded.

"What are you doing?" He rubbed his chin against her temple.

"I am verifying the results that the team has calculated. It may just be Christmas magic, but I am in charge of the team and its discoveries."

"I noticed that there was a bit of tinsel around the office."

"A bit? They used so much, they were in danger of compromising the telescope." She laughed and leaned against his chest, her breasts flattening with the pressure. The snowflake that he wore was front and centre, between his pecs. She felt the prickle of magic on her skin as they snuggled.

A thought occurred to her. "Hey, don't you have to be running security at the observatory?"

"Well, there is a team in place, but since I am the one who hired my company to watch over it, I think I deserve a day off."

She smiled and kept working. "I thought it must be something like that. You were far too comfortable in your tux the other day. It only makes sense, I suppose, that you would have a long-term persona."

"All of the elves of the naughty-or-nice list have a life that they can step into."

"Lucky you." She sighed and finished her correspondence.

"What do you do in the off time?"

She snorted. "We file your reports and try to keep ourselves from going insane. Some years we succeed, some years we don't."

He stroked her hair and caressed her arms. "How did you enter the workshop?"

"I was recruited. There aren't a lot of reindeer shifters born in the world, but Santa can sense it when each one of us appears."

"Rudolph is the youngest."

"Well, yes, but she was the first. It used to be just her pulling the sleigh, but as the population expanded, more reindeer were needed. He pulled us out from across space and time. Ru has been with Santa since Mrs. Claus was still around. I think they were friends. The rest of us came in the order of the song. I was the fifth reindeer. I appeared in the sixteenth century. I was sold to Santa as a toddler and raised at the workshop."

"Huh. Here, we thought you were all more like sisters."

"Nope. We are a family. Ru is firmly in charge, no matter what we choose to do."

He was quiet for a moment. "On another semi-related subject, will you come home with me?"

She snorted and put her laptop aside. "I will, on the twenty-third. Until then, I have things to do here."

He paused. "Just like that?"

"Just like that." She didn't tell him that it was always their intent to get home on time. Ru wasn't going to fly alone.

It had been a clever plot. Scare Santa into paying attention to his team and get them some social interaction. It was a simple plan, but it had taken nearly a decade to complete.

Santa had stopped harvesting the snowflakes of Christmas, so when Ru had come up with the plan, she had been able to sneak the snowflakes into her safekeeping until she had enough for all of the team. She had worked out the method to get their collars off so that the monitoring situation would show them all in the archive. Ru wore each band on her own body as the team left. They owed her a debt they could never repay, so they had tried to make it up for her in their letters to Santa. Santa couldn't reject a plea from the pure of heart, and who had more Christmas in their hearts than Santa's own reindeer?

Xander held her in his arms. "Why do I think that I have just been played?"

She twisted until they were facing each other. "Because I am guessing that you are a very smart elf." She softened it with a kiss.

He wrinkled his nose. "That sounded patronizing."

She grinned. "Very smart."

He sighed. "Will I ever know the truth?"

"You will. I will say this. I didn't look for you, but once I saw you, I knew that we would be a good match. Santa has skills."

"You knew I was an elf?"

"No, not until the lava fries. I just knew that I asked for someone who could love the stars as much as I could, and here you are."

"How do you know I love the stars?"

She stroked his cheek. "I see them in your eyes."

He got a bashful expression on his face, and she kissed him softly. "Let's get some actual sleep. Tomorrow, I have to prep for the meteor gala that the director signed me up for. Looks like I will have to play in fancy dress and explain a falling star."

"Is that what was in the email?"

"One of them. Weren't you reading over my shoulder?"

"I was too busy staring at the love bite I left on your breast to read anything."

Violette chuckled and settled in his arms. The night was good for something other than stars after all.

The gala was underway, and everyone was waiting.

"Ladies and gentlemen, we are about to witness the Cor-Tin-Xen meteor shower. Please join me out on the deck and take turns at the telescopes. You will all know when the event begins. Feel free to ask the staff any questions you have, and enjoy the show that the universe has provided."

Her gown rustled as she led the way out of the auditorium and onto the observation deck where the small telescopes were mounted and waiting. The donors were excited, and they milled out into the night, ready to watch the stars fall.

Violette was on duty, so Xander kept his distance until the rocks skidded across the atmosphere and caught fire. The moment that everyone was fixated on the shower, he wrapped an arm around her, and she leaned against him.

They watched the stars fall, and she felt a profound sense of peace. She had gotten what she wanted, had gotten what she wished for. As a Christmas wish, it was early, but it had arrived just in time to fill her with the holiday spirit.

The childlike delight and wonder on the faces of those around her fed her own soul. It made her envy the elves who got to see this every year.

When a falling meteor split, the crowd gasped in shock and applauded like it was a firework.

One piece continued on its original path to the ocean, but the smaller piece broke off and streaked past the observatory.

The thud of the impact sent ripples of excitement through the gathering.

Violette looked up at Xander and said, "How much do you want to bet that it struck a volcanic pocket?"

Xander smirked. "I am thinking that I will not take that bet."

"You are catching on."

"I am a slow study, but even I can learn." He grinned and squeezed her to his side.

"I am getting a feeling about the impact point. Do you want to stop there on our way to the workshop?"

"I think that would be an excellent way to bid a temporary farewell to Violette Xenic."

She winked. "Excellent. You have the collar?"

"In my car. When you say the word, we will go."

She smiled softly, and they watched the stars fall and wink out, becoming part of the earth.

It was a wonderful last look at humanity and what even the most jaded of them could become when they were shown a bit of wonder.

When the guests were gone and the grounds were quiet, they walked to his car, and he took out the collar. "Are you ready for this?"

"Oh, please. This is the uniform of my day job. It becomes a necklace on my throat no matter what form I wear."

She stood there in her evening gown and waited for him to put on the mark of her service to the workshop. When he buckled the cool leather against her skin, the magic wrapped around her and let her know it was there to call on when she needed it.

His car would disappear when he did, so it was up to her to peel off the snowflake and return it to its box. Once that was done, her reindeer form and instinct to run home would take over.

She pried it off and set it in the small box that she fished from her purse. She handed both to him when she was clear of the protective snowflake.

"Are you ready, Xander?"

He nodded and patted the pocket with the flash drive she wanted him to carry. "Ready when you are."

Violette grinned and shifted into her Christmas reindeer form.

Despite the warning, Xander looked shocked as she took a few steps before kneeling down so that he could climb on.

Having him on her back was rather fun. He gripped her horns, as instructed, and she activated her cloaking magic and took off.

She ran to her home and saw what she had expected to see. The impact point of the meteor was a few dozen metres from her home. An orange worm of lava was flowing toward her erstwhile home, and there was nothing to be done.

Be careful what you wish for, it could come back to bite you in the ass.

After watching for a few minutes, she took to the skies again and began her northward journey to bring them both home. She didn't know if she counted as naughty or nice, but she was willing to submit to Xander's judgment. He may be a little slow, but he definitely got to the right conclusion in the end.

It was his own brand of Christmas magic.

Prologue to Twisting the Pole

Comet looked around the archive and twisted her lips. "I don't want to go."

Ru hugged her. "I know, but you don't have to worry about the modern age. The snowflake will tell you what you need to know."

Comet fidgeted. "So, it is all right that I am not looking forward to the human world?"

"It is fine. Santa pulled you from your time when you were nearly an adult. You had every expectation of living your life as a human and milking cows, having babies and plowing fields. This was not a life you could have imagined."

Comet ran a hand through her hair. "How can the snowflake give me what I want when I don't know what I want?"

"Trust the magic. It will keep you safe and put you where you can be happy."

Comet stepped back and held out her hand, extending the envelope to Ru. "Here it is."

"Thank you. Here is the snowflake. Put it on you and think of what you want, what you really want. When it is time to return, remove it."

"Do I really have to go?"

"It is the only way to make our point. Come on. A few weeks is a nice change of pace. When you come home, you won't have to leave again unless you want to. I promise." Ru stroked her hair.

Comet nodded. "Right. I can do this. The humans aren't really that scary."

"You may even come to enjoy their company."

Comet opened the small box and lifted her tunic to press the snowflake below her navel.

She closed her eyes and concentrated on what she wanted.

She wanted her familiar world back and a man to call her own.

When she opened her eyes, her surprise was genuine. She was home again.

Twisting the Pole

Cora Metzger worked in the front of the silver shop, melting and pouring metal with a skill that her father had possessed.

Her skirt brushed against her legs as she moved around the shop, and she smiled at the familiar feel. It had taken her less than five minutes to put the information in her mind together to realize that she was inside a renaissance festival, but she was content to be in familiar surroundings, even if it was fake.

For this one moment in time, she was back where she knew how to do things, knew what techniques and materials were needed and all communication was done face to face.

She had a shop girl named Vivienne with a pierced nose and anachronistic hairstyle, but she was a whiz at answering the questions from the public while deftly parting them from their money.

Cora was left with her work and her metal.

She listened as Viv sold another of her stylized reindeer pendants. Next to the snowflakes, it was the bestseller in her booth and had already paid for the rental of space and materials for a year.

She finished pouring another casting, and the faces around the open workshop window were fascinated as she set the cast to one side and she poured another.

The wood of the carved mold smoked as the liquid metal touched the surface. The leather straps buckled the two-part mold tightly together.

It wasn't the best mold she had ever carved, but the folks here seemed to enjoy it. Growing up in her father's workshop, she had carved molds out of any material she could find. Stone was always good, but for speed, wood was definitely easier. Cuttlefish bone was fine, but they were trying to stay within the confines of a historical period that no one could define, so she stuck with wood. For those making the purchase, it meant that only twenty or less of the pendants would ever be made.

So, she was going through the different reindeer and snowflakes that were definitely different from those sold in other shops at the faire.

With her metal hardening, she took her seat at the workbench and started carving her next design.

After about an hour, Viv came up to her, "Well, we have sold out today's castings and gotten a hold on the two you just poured. What are you putting in those things?"

Cora chuckled and kept working with picks and files. "Holiday magic."

Viv snorted. "You know I don't believe in religious holidays."

Cora smiled. "Did you know that in the old days, the solstice celebrations were essential to survival? The food that was brought forth gave a much needed calorie boost to get through the coldest days of winter, it was completely consumed. Lords gave their servants a set of clothing and gifts of preserved food. Everyone focused on survival and getting to the next year, but they shared what they had so that they would survive as a community. Now, this wasn't the case everywhere, but in some places, it took on heady significance. It meant crossing the line between life and death and moving into the future. If that isn't magical, I don't know what is."

Viv stared at her with wide eyes. "Wow. That was... intense."

Cora grinned. "The holidays usually are. All this gift giving is a serious matter. Folks forget that it used to be about survival."

"I never thought of it that way. What are you working on?"

"Oh, the baron asked for some charms to give to the new knights entering the barony. Each one is slightly different."

Viv chuckled. "Freaky snowflakes."

"You betcha."

More patrons came to the shop, and Viv showed them their wares. Cora's ears perked up when the woman wanted to see the elven coronet.

This was either going to be a sale or an attempted theft. Sadly, Cora didn't know which one she was pulling for.

She finished her mold and blew the shavings out of the design before using a fine brush to remove all small bits of wood from the design.

When Viv's voice called out a panicked, "Cora!" Cora was on her feet and over the workbench in a flash.

She sprinted after the thief with her skirts kicking up around her legs. She didn't shout, she simply drew close until she was next to the thief. Without saying a word, she plucked the coronet from the woman's grip and the startled thief fell.

The coronet buckled between them, and Cora sighed. "I will have to fix that, you know."

The woman in jeans and a t-shirt looked up at her. "How did you catch me in *that?*"

Security was running in, and they were prepared to take her into their care.

Cora smiled. "It is a matter of practice. If I ever see you near my booth again, you will be on your ass so fast you won't even have a chance to look around."

The security officer handed her a form, so she slipped the coronet over one arm as she filled it out. A minute later, she handed it back with a smile. "Thanks, Antoine the Stunning."

He grinned at her with his two gold teeth gleaming in his tanned face. "A pleasure as always, Mistress Metzger."

She held up the coronet for him to take a photo and then slipped it back on her arm as she returned to her booth. Several bystanders applauded her as she walked back with a swing in her hips.

Viv was tearful as Cora sauntered up. "Did you..."

Cora held up the coronet. "Got it. Will have it fixed by morning."

"How did she bend it?"

"She was holding it when I caught up to her. She went down and tried to take it with her. My grip was stronger, but we pulled it out of shape."

The torches were being lit, and it was nearly time to close shop. Cora returned to her workbench, and she held the coronet in her hands. She glanced at Viv.

Viv suddenly got enthusiastic. "Are you going to do the thing?"

Cora looked around, turned her back to the walkway where patrons were moving in the distance and she held the coronet up to her lips. With a low, slow breath, she exhaled magic on the metal, and it formed back into its proper shape of woven strands of metal wire in intricate patterns.

Viv shook her head. "How do you do that?"

"Practice." Cora quirked her lips. It was a safe piece of magic to use. Viv was interested in the magic of the natural world, so when Cora hired her, she showed her minor magic, and Viv took to it like a duck to water. She couldn't properly use it herself, but she respected Cora's mastery of it.

By the time Cora and Viv parted ways, the human would know how to bend metal, just a little. It would be Cora's gift to her for the friendship that she extended.

She handed the coronet to Viv. "Back on the display."

Viv took it and juggled it. "It is still hot."

"Bending metal gets it hot." Cora lit some candles on her worktable and finished the carving on the last of the medallions.

"I don't know how you can do that by candlelight." Viv watched her work.

How could Cora explain that she had learned how to carve at her father's knee? She had been going to marry a nice silversmith from the next village and work with her husband. That had been her plan until she turned thirteen and she shifted for the first time. She was lucky that it had just been her and her parents who witnessed the transformation, but her fate had changed in that moment.

Two days later, a very handsome man with very pale hair and a young woman with a ruby necklace had come to the village. They had knocked on her father's door, and the man had spoken with her parents. While they talked, the young woman had walked outside with Cora, and they had spoken about life, silver smithing and the future. Cora had outlined her hopes and dreams, and the woman had smiled sadly, asking, "What if your future isn't yours to choose?"

"I suppose I will do what my father tells me to." Her faith in her father had been absolute.

To her horror, her father gave her to the pretty man, and the young woman turned into her mentor and friend. Her parents got security and health for the rest of their lives, and they would die together knowing that their daughter was alive, healthy and safe. She could be what she was and not die for it. It was—by their estimation—a better life.

They didn't understand. Life without them hadn't meant a thing.

Cora shook her head and continued her work. Modern candles were way better than anything they had had while she was growing up.

She worked until the design was complete, and she set the mold aside. She would pour in the morning.

Cora stretched and smiled. "Time to call it a night."

Viv went about locking up the displays in the anachronistic safe and locking down the front of the shop. Cora touched the hidden light switch, and as the shop was sealed up, the light came on.

She helped pack away all of the stock, and when everything was clean and tidy, they opened the rear door of the shop, turned off the lights and locked up.

They walked together to where the music was ringing and the drums were pounding.

Viv was dancing before they arrived in the pool of light.

Cora laughed and bid her friend farewell for the night.

She stood and watched the dancers for a while. She swayed in place, and it was that small bit of movement that must have caught someone's attention.

A man with a new tunic in rich burgundy with silver piping came over to her, and he bowed low. "Mistress, may I have this dance?"

He stood and extended his hand to her.

"Well, sir knight, I think we might be able to share it."

She gathered her skirts with one hand and placed the other hand in his. He led her into the whirl of dancers, and they skipped, turned and jumped to the music.

For one moment, Cora forgot when she was and imagined that her parents were watching her dance. It was impossible, of course. They died in a plague ten years after she left them.

She shook off the memory and focused on the smiling faces until the music ceased.

She curtsied to her partner and smiled. "Thank you, sir knight."

He grinned. "It was an honour to escort you through the dance, Mistress. You are quite skilled."

He offered her his hand, and they left the dancing area.

"You are one of the new knights?"

He nodded. "Sir Salk Arthwait."

She smiled. "Artisan Cora Metzger."

"Pleased to meet you, lady. Are you staying for the festivities?"

She shook her head. "No. I am not a member of the local barony. It is for them and their people only."

He scowled. "We are allowed to invite guests."

Cora smiled. "I have made other plans already. It was pleasant to meet you, Sir Arthwait."

He nodded. "You as well, Lady Cora."

She left him and kept herself from looking back. She really wanted to, but it wasn't a good idea to start something when her trip home was just a few days away.

Clever. So, that was how the reindeer had hidden. They obeyed the laws of Christmas magic and kept it honest. The ladies were using names that were composed of their actual designations as reindeer.

Salk shook his head as he watched her go, her skirts swaying slightly as she made her way through the crowd. She moved with the grace of someone who grew up in clothing similar to what she was wearing now. She didn't check her feet or tug at the skirt.

So, Comet had come to rest at a holiday Ren Faire. He smiled and moved away from the dancers and into the shadows.

He darkened his skin and moved away from the festivities. His were not the only eyes following Cora Metzger.

Salk slipped through the shadows, watching the man who was following Cora.

The man who was stalking the reindeer was wearing standard street clothing.

They walked out of the fenced-in area and past security. Cora waved cheerfully, and the man acted casual as he passed the on-duty guards a few moments later.

Salk slipped past them without them noticing him. Cora walked toward the campers that were lined up, and her stalker followed.

Salk watched and moved closer to the man who appeared to be up to no good.

When the youth pulled a blade, Salk grabbed him and held him by the throat. With his voice low in the shadows, he whispered every evil deed that the youth had committed, how punishment was meted out in the karmic universe and what he would face when the wheel of life ceased spinning.

The youth's face was streaked with tears when Salk let him go. He crawled away from Salk and got to his feet to run back toward the parking lot.

Cora disappeared into a tiny house on wheels, and Salk listened for the latch, nodding when it clicked into place. With Cora safe inside, he walked back to the party and the welcoming feast for the new arrivals.

Cora settled into her loft for the night. Her money was safely tucked away, and she was nearly done with the eBook that she had purchased the night before. After learning that the hero and heroine lived happily ever after on a space station, she turned off the glowing screen and snuggled in for a good night's sleep.

She had casting to do in the morning.

Cora sat at her workbench and worked on the medallions for the knight ceremony. The barony had gotten several new knights in for the holiday faire. Many of the regulars wanted their time with family or weren't able to get out of their regular work duties. Apparently, day jobs were the bane of the faires.

Today was Friday. Tonight, there would be a huge ceremony for the knights who were pitching in, and the baron and baroness would acknowledge their efforts to the barony.

The casting had been the work of an hour. Now, she was polishing and scraping manually, using an agate burnisher to bring out the glittering details.

It took her hours of Viv answering questions about the work, but eventually, she was able to look up from the final finished medallion.

She threaded it onto a chain before settling it onto a small velvet pillow in a hand-carved wooden box.

Cora stood and stretched, flexing her fingers as well as twisting her back.

Viv finished with a customer and smiled. "Did you want to go for a walk?"

Cora nodded. "Sure. I will take the medallions and deliver them to the baron."

Viv chuckled. "I was thinking more of you going to get some lunch."

Cora winked. "I will do that on the way back."

"Good. I could go for a meat pie and lemonade."

"I will see what I can do." Cora gathered the medallions in a leather bag, and she left her shop to walk through the bustling pathways where holiday shoppers wanted gifts with a twist.

She greeted the familiar faces as she passed and waved to a few that were too far to speak to.

Over a dozen courtiers occupied the pavilion that housed the baron and baroness. Cora joined the line and waited her turn.

She had to admit, she could see the appeal in playing dress-up and enjoying modern hygiene with the prettiest parts of the past. It was far more fun than staying indoors.

When she got to the front of the line, she was announced.

"Artisan and silversmith, Mistress Cora."

Cora curtsied and inclined her head.

"What do you have for us, Mistress Cora?" The baroness, Lily Hogarth, smiled brightly.

"I have brought the commission that you ordered for the knights. They are completed and ready for when you wish to disperse them."

Baroness Hogarth smiled. "Excellent. May I see them?"

Cora stepped forward, and the baroness and her ladies oohed and ahhed over the designs on the medallions.

"You have outdone yourself. These are amazing."

Cora smiled and watched the ladies as they tucked the boxes back into the bag.

"I hope that the knights enjoy them. Thank you for your patronage." She had already been paid, so her link to the silver craft was complete.

"We are delighted to have such a talented artisan in our barony."

She nodded again. "I will return to my shop now. My poor assistant is keeping up with the public demand. Have a bright day."

She bowed and backed away until she was swallowed in the crowd, and then, she turned her back and walked out of the pavilion and back into the throng.

Cora headed to the meat-pie vendor and got Viv her fix. Viv was easier to work with if she was kept fed and watered at regular intervals.

As soon as she got back to the shop she handed Viv the warm pie and the tankard of lemonade. "Here you go."

"So, how much did they love them?" Viv tucked into her meal while perched on a high stool.

Cora brushed the crumbs from her lips that were testament to her own hasty meal. "There was a lot of squealing."

She settled some stone molds on the edge of the small forge to warm.

Viv mumbled, "I can imagine. When are they going to give them out?"

Cora shrugged. "There is the jousting this weekend. Probably there."

"You don't want to be there?"

"Not particularly. My part of it is done."

Viv shook her head. "You are so odd. One would think that you would want the praise that comes with the artistry."

Cora shrugged and started to melt some silver. "I like making things."

Viv sighed and finished her meal, taking a break to drop off the lemonade tankard and flirt with the pie man or, possibly, his wife. Cora didn't know which Viv preferred, but that was her business.

The slight scrape of someone touching her counter brought Cora around. She turned and smiled. "Yes?"

It was the knight from the previous night.

"Oh, hello, Sir Salk."

"Mistress Cora, it is good to see you in the light of day."

She walked up to the counter and leaned against it. Yes, she was showcasing her breasts, but in the laced-up bodice that the faire goers preferred, it was impossible not to show off her cleavage to anyone taller than she was.

He smiled. "It is very good to see you."

She took in his loose laced-up shirt and the snug fit of his leggings. "You look downright casual this shining day."

He grinned. "It is much better for the afternoon. When we do the fight demo, I will gear up."

"And sweat through the fighting."

He shrugged. "The price of employment."

"I am sure that you enjoy it."

Salk inclined his head. "I definitely do. That brings me to the reason that I am here."

She inclined her head. "Do tell."

"I am asking you to be my lady at the fights. I am asking for your favour and will win for your honour."

Cora cocked her head. "If you lose, will I lose my honour?"

Salk drew himself up to his full height, and she felt a strange ripple of recognition. There was something familiar about the way he moved.

"I will not lose."

She shook herself out of the déjà vu and smiled. "I will have to come up with a favour. Just a moment while I check my stock."

She walked to the rear of the shop and opened a few drawers when she found what she was looking for.

She pulled the leather necklace with the small charm on it out of the box and brought it with her. "When do you need it?"

He glanced down at it. "Just before the fight. I will pledge myself to fight for you, and you can put it on me then."

Cora nodded. "When is the fight?"

"At four."

She sighed. "I will see you there."

He lifted her hand to his lips, and he pressed a kiss to it. "I look forward to it."

Her skin tingled, and she stared after him as he disappeared as quietly as he had arrived.

Viv returned and took one look at Cora before gasping, "What the hell happened to you?"

Cora blinked. "What?"

"You are smiling. It is a really wide smile. I almost didn't recognize you."

Cora shrugged. "I think I just got a date... kinda."

"Really? Tell all." Viv came behind the counter and settled on her stool.

"I am going to the fights at four, and I get to be one of the ladies. It sounds a bit boring but fun at the same time."

Viv grinned. "Who is your knight?"

"Sir Salk Arthwait."

Viv gasped. "Oh, he is really hot."

"He is rather pretty in a dark, broody kind of way." Cora shrugged.

"Sure, we can go with that. Frankly, I wasn't sure if you were into boys or girls. None of my business." Viv grinned. "So, is that what you are wearing to the fights?"

Cora nodded. "It is. I am not changing into something fancy just to be seen."

"At least change into the leather bodice with the silver trim. It doesn't look like you were putting cigarettes out on it."

Cora looked down and acknowledged the burn marks. "I will concede that point. How long do I have?"

Viv fished into her bodice and pulled out her cellphone. "You have two hours."

"Good. Tell me when I am down to thirty minutes so I can change. I still have work to do."

A few small beeps and Viv nodded. "Done. Alarm is set."

"Excellent. Now, off to work."

Cora spent the next ninety minutes melting, pouring and polishing, as she did every day, in full view of the public.

When Viv's timer went off, she faked a coughing fit and went to the back of the shop to turn it off.

Cora seamlessly finished the transaction that she was in the middle of, and when Viv had recovered from her technological fit, she wrapped the earrings in soft suede and tied them with a leather tie before sending the purchaser on his way.

Cora went to the back of the shop and took out her fancy bodice, unlacing the stained and burned leather that she was wearing and replacing it with the black and silver.

She fluffed out her hair and stroked her hands down her dark skirts. Scowling, she poured some water into a basin, and she took the scrub brush to her hands. The black crescents under her nails were part of working with silver. Corrosion set in quickly when you were dealing with shavings.

The charm was safely tucked in her cleavage, and she ran her hands down her skirts one more time. "How do I look?"

Viv smirked. "Nervous as hell, but you look good."

Cora scowled. "I shouldn't be nervous."

"You can be. It is fine, natural and rather endearing."

Cora made another face, triple checked the favour and nodded to Viv. "I will see you when this is over."

"You aren't going to the firing squad. You will just get to sit there and look ladylike."

Cora elevated her middle finger before she left their shop and followed the crowd to the four o'clock fight demonstration. It was times like this that Cora wished she had a grip on modern watches. It seemed like a much better alternative than having Viv constantly check her cleavage.

At the gathering, she settled in the bleachers with the onlookers. The chairs set out for the ladies were empty, so she guessed that the knights would have to come get them.

When the knights clanked out in their armour and colourful silks, the crowd cheered. Cora had to admit it was impressive, if nothing like the reality of the medieval times.

The baron and baroness greeted everyone and then called upon the knights to ask a lady for their favour.

The crowd shifted with excitement, and many of the ladies clutched ribbons that they had gotten in the favour shop. Apparently, the advertising said that the ribbons turned any man into their own personal knight.

Cora watched as Salk came toward her, but to her shock, another knight locked eyes with her and grinned. She had met him before, and Sir Tahnk was not a person she enjoyed socializing with.

Salk moved with surprising speed, and he grabbed Tahnk, spun him around and made it to Cora with a few long strides.

"Lady, may I carry your favour into battle?" His lips were twisted in a smile.

She reached into her cleavage and pulled out the silver medallion with the flying reindeer on it. "Sir knight, you may."

She leaned forward and tied the leather around his neck. His lips were inches from hers, but she pulled back when it was firmly fastened.

He touched the medallion and tucked it against his neck.

"From your breast to mine."

He took her hand and led her to the chairs, seating her in the one that had his coat of arms on it.

A page brought the ten women and two men goblets of lemonade. The knights bowed to the baron and baroness, they bowed to their ladies and paired off as directed for the first fights.

The first few minutes were about the dance of the battles. At some unspoken signal, the fight turned serious.

Salk's opponent went flying. He skidded across the dusty ground and ended up leaning against a support post. Salk raised his helmet and confirmed that he was out.

His lady sighed in disappointment.

Cora sat and sipped at her lemonade as Salk waited at the side for his next round.

She spent the next hour watching fight after fight with Salk always coming out ahead.

Finally, it was down to Salk and Tahnk.

Both men were tired, but they faced off with their swords, and the clash was tremendous. They weren't playing for the crowds; they had some issues to work out.

The metal-on-metal sound was incredible. Cora clenched her fists together and leaned her body forward as she watched Salk take down the leering idiot who had been following her around since the first day she had turned up at the faire.

When Tahnk was finally disarmed, the crowd was up on their feet and cheering. Sir Salk came up to her, and he knelt in front of her again. "I have upheld your honour, Mistress."

She stood and offered him her hand. "You have done me proud, Sir Salk."

He kissed her knuckles, and he got to his feet. The smell of male and sweat mixed with metal was coming from him in waves, but in the heat of the afternoon, it seemed completely right and proper.

The baron called him forward, and he took her hand in his gauntleted one, walking her toward the dais.

"Sir Arthwait, you have defeated our greatest knights, and for that, we offer an invitation to the solstice ball for your lady."

Cora blinked. "That's tomorrow."

The baron grinned. "It is indeed. I look forward to seeing

your skills in the dance, Artisan Metzger."

She curtsied and looked at Salk with suspicious eyes. "Did you know about this?"

He grinned. "Yes, but this was the only way I could figure out to get you to the party."

One of the ladies of the court came and gave her a ribbon that would act as her ticket to the party the next night.

Cora turned to Salk, "Now, what am I to give you for acting so ably as my champion?"

He opened his mouth, but she pulled him down to her and kissed him quickly, to the hoots of some of the bystanders.

He seemed shocked when she let him go, but she smiled, curtsied and left the fight grounds without looking back.

Her grin faded as she entered the kiosks and vendor stalls. She needed a dress.

When she outlined what was going on, to the amusement Viv, she saw the gleam in her assistant's eyes. She was in good hands.

Viv left her for a few minutes, sprinted through the stalls and came back with a handful of business cards. "Go to each one of these places. I have told them what you need, and they just need to take measurements."

Two hours later, the components of a spectacular outfit had been accumulated and each vendor had offered her a steep discount. It was now a community event.

Cora was able to concentrate on her work for the rest of the day until it was time to close shop for the evening.

Down the lanes, she could hear the music starting up, and Viv was hopping up and down in her leather slippers as she waited for official dismissal.

"Go, Viv. I will be fine."

Cora folded the wooden cover over the front of the shop, locked up with hasps and padlocks from the inside and headed out the back. Viv was long gone when Cora was heading down the lane toward the music.

Music had always drawn her. Even as a child, she had delighted in any song, rhythm or steady gust of wind that she could colour in her mind with the idea of music.

She walked up to the back of the crowd and watched the dancers.

Twisting the Pole

The patterns of the dance were amazing to see. The visitors had been taught the steps and faltered a little, but eventually, they were laughing, stepping and hopping with the rest of the crowd.

Cora smiled and clapped to the beat with the rest of the watchers.

Salk was in the midst of the dancers. The young woman who was partnering him looked like she was either going to pass out or hump his leg.

Cora watched for another two dances, and then, she faded back and headed for her tiny house.

She passed through security and headed for the camping lot. Her tiny house was parked in one of the spots and hooked up to electricity and water. It amused her every time she walked up to it. The snowflake magic had given her a tiny, portable castle.

She walked up her steps and slipped inside her home on wheels.

Cora kept the lights on as she worked on designs inspired by the music and dance. She might never have a chance to make the jewellery, but she was happy to have it down where she could see it.

A knock at the door pulled her out of creativity and into the real world.

She moved the small shield that covered the face port and blinked in surprise. "Salk. What are you doing here?"

He lifted a basket. "I have been told that you often skip dinner. I am prepared to keep your strength up so that you don't miss the party tomorrow."

Cora smiled. "Come in."

She opened the door, and he entered the small space.

Salk looked around. "Interesting. There is every comfort of home."

"Which is fortunate, because it *is* my home." She took the basket from him and folded a table down from the wall. When it locked in place, she set her burden down and gestured for him to unpack his offering.

He opened the basket, and she grinned as hamburgers and fries emerged. At the faire, the food he had with him was contraband.

"I won't ask how you got that, just like you will forget that you saw this." She turned to her small kitchen and knelt, pulling the small hatch in the floor open to retrieve two imported beers.

As she set them down on the table, they frosted over.

He grinned. "Cooler in the floor?"

"Something like that." She gestured for him to take a seat, and she scooted her stool over to the table. "Thank you for the food."

"You are welcome. Thank you for the medallion. I was only expecting a ribbon." He grinned and fished the medal out of his shirt.

The flying reindeer was one of her favourite designs. She hadn't wanted to sell it, but she wanted someone to have it. The impulse to give it to him had been intense.

"It looks good on you." She bit into the burger and stifled a moan. Cora tried to keep herself calm as she ate, but she was fighting the urge to stuff it all in her face at once.

Halfway through the meal, she cocked her head. "So, why did you provide me with this luxurious feast?"

He grinned. "I like you. You were not what I was expecting, and I am pleasantly surprised."

She chuckled. The rumour mill at the faires was notorious. It was a community that stretched from sea to sea and across the oceans. Now with the internet, the rumours and gossip could streak along as soon as someone got out of the public eye so they could text.

Some faires were stricter on the rules of modern conveniences than others, but using a cell phone while in garb was universally frowned upon.

Salk gestured to the tiny house. "So, how long do you live in here?"

She shrugged. "Anytime I am away from home."

"Where is home?"

"Up north." She kept it nice and vague. "You?"

"The same. I just came here because I was requested to, but I am very glad I did." He wiped his lips with his napkin, balled it up and tossed it into the basket.

She tried to change the subject, because his gaze was suddenly intense. "How did you know I like burgers?"

"I asked your assistant. Vivienne was very forthcoming."

Cora rolled her eyes. "She would be. She is a sucker for a guy in armour, or a girl for that matter."

"Is Cora your real name?"

"You mean away from the faire? Yes. That is the name on my credit card." She chuckled. "How about you?"

"Oddly enough, my name was exotic enough for this purpose. Salk Arthwait is my actual name."

She finished her burger and wedged the last of the fries into her mouth. When she cleared her mouth, she sipped at her beer. "It is a nice name."

"Thank you."

Silence hung between them. It wasn't awkward, but it did give her a chance to finish her beer. He drank his and raised his brows at the flavour, pausing after to read the label. "Where did you get this?"

"At the local vendor. It took a bit of trial and error, but I finally found one that I consider palatable."

"You did very well."

She chuckled. It was definitely a change from apple cider, mulled cider, hot cider, cold cider. There was not a lot of variety at the archive of Santa's workshop. It felt like Santa had forgotten that they were even there on days other than Christmas Eve.

He shifted on his chair, and she got up to clear the bag and fold the cloth in the basket. When it was clear, she set it on the floor and folded the table away.

"Pivot, take a step and we can sit in the living room."

She walked past him and sat on the couch built into one end of the tiny space.

"How big is this place?" He wandered over and sat next to her at an angle so that their knees touched.

"Two hundred and eighty square feet."

"Wow. It seems that you have everything you need in here."

She looked at him and considered her answer. "Yeah, I do seem to have what I need at my fingertips."

"Was it a custom build?"

Cora laughed, "No, I got it at *Tiny Castles R Us*."

He snickered. "Fair enough."

They sat and drank their beer in silence.

Cora asked, "What drove you to the fights?"

"The exercise was entertaining. I am used to having a bit

more activity in my life, and this was a chance to reclaim it."

She nodded as if she understood.

"What about you? How did you come to work with silver?"

She answered honestly. "I learned it at my father's knee. My mother was a designer, and my father made her sketches come to life."

"Are they still living?"

"No, they passed on years ago. It still feels like just yesterday." The truth of the pain was in her voice.

He reached out and put his hand on hers. "I am sorry for your loss."

She shrugged. "It is fine. I just haven't had much ability to deal with it."

Salk nodded, paused for a moment and then asked. "What were you doing when I arrived?"

"I was working on designs. I draw far more than I could ever create."

"May I see them?"

She grinned. "Of course."

She got up and went to the small cubby where she had tucked her sketchbook. She turned and brought it back to the couch, sitting closer than she had before, ostensibly to show him the drawings.

She inhaled the scent of him and enjoyed the masculine touch to her quarters. There was something familiar in his scent that she couldn't put her finger on, and it made her want to investigate further.

He flipped through the designs with intense focus. "These are amazing. Hey, here is the pattern for my medallion."

She snorted and then fought the urge to grab the book and pull it back. The medallion he was wearing was one of nine designs and the only one she had created. The word Comet was written quite clearly beneath the pattern.

"You drew one for all of Santa's reindeer?"

She cleared her throat. "I thought that if anyone needed a little Christmas treat, it would be the reindeer."

"Why did you make Comet?"

Cora licked her lips. "I don't know. I suppose it was just the design that I wanted to make first."

He smiled slightly and closed the book. "Well, I have imposed on your hospitality enough for one night. I will see you tomorrow."

She got to her feet as he stood. "You don't have to go yet."

His eyes gleamed. "I think it is for the best. I do have one thing to leave you with..."

She stared up at him, and he kissed her softly, gradually deepening the contact until she was leaning up toward him and clutching at his shirt for balance.

Her heart was pounding in her chest when she finally realized that he was gone. As suddenly as he had appeared at her door, he had removed himself and his basket while she was focused on that small point of contact.

"How the hell did he move that fast?" She scowled at the door and was bemused by the fact that it had been latched. It only latched from the inside, but Salk was definitely gone. She could feel the loss of his company in every inch of her.

Salk's cock was screaming silently at him to return to take what Comet was so obviously offering.

He had never thought that the woman he was sent to seduce could strike at his heart with her creativity, her grace and her spirit, but here he was, in the shadows and watching over her castle.

She smelled of heat and starry skies. He didn't know how it could be possible, but when he touched her, kissed her, he saw the stars and heavy bands of colour.

Tomorrow, they would have a proper date, and he would be able to escort her home at the end of the night. What happened after that was up to her, but he was hoping to experience more of that heat.

He dispersed himself into the shadows and engaged in his normal occupation of finding the naughty and whispering in their ears details of all their crimes in order to seed nightmares of recriminations. It wasn't fair, but neither was preying on other members of their species.

Administering shadows was not a job for the weak at heart, and it had been a relief when he no longer had to haul coal around. Salk enjoyed his position with the naughty-or-nice list, even if it took him to the dark places of the human mind. A moment with Comet made up for an entire year of shadows.

Comet fidgeted with her silk skirts and touched her hair. The braiding was elaborate, and it was twisted up on top of her head, held in place with her own elven coronet.

The gown was a blue so deep it was almost black. The silk was rich, but it floated around her as she moved. The floor-length vest was embroidered with fantastical creatures, and the latches fastened it at her waist. The black slippers were comfortable, and she felt like she was wearing a costume at long last. Others could put on garb and play a part. She had been putting it on and reliving the past. Now, in these obviously modern clothes, she could enjoy the feast, the dancing and spending more time with Salk.

Viv gave her a serious and assessing look before she nodded. "Amazing. If you weren't my friend, I would be jealous."

Cora grinned. "Nothing to be jealous of. You were the one who picked this all out."

"Yes, but I had no idea how natural it would look on you."

She took the favour that would get her access to the event, and she scowled at it. "You could still go instead of me."

"Not a chance. Salk has been by here twice today to make sure that you haven't gotten cold feet. I don't want you to miss this chance to have a good time. And speak of the devil."

Cora looked, and Salk was striding toward them in Ren Faire formal wear. He was wearing the same black and silver that she was, but on him, it looked intimidating.

Viv was amazed. "Hey, you match!"

Cora gave her an evil look, and she lifted the folding counter to step out into the lane.

Salk stopped ten feet away, and he stared at her. He approached slowly, as if afraid to startle her. "Mistress, you would make the very stars in the sky jealous. Your beauty shines in the darkness, and the celestial lights look dim in comparison."

Cora blushed. "I am unable to match your flattery, Sir Salk. You are the epitome of a knight of this realm; all others are mere pages in your presence."

He grinned. "Very nicely done. Are you ready to leave?"

He extended his arm.

She placed her hand on his wrist.

He looked back at Viv. "Don't wait up."

The cackle from the shop faded as he led her through the lanes of shops and over toward the area that had been separated for the feast and party.

"You do look lovely, Cora."

"You are stepping out of your role, Salk." She turned her head and winked at him before looking forward again.

The centre of the green space held a huge pole that had to have been erected earlier in the day. "What the hell is that?"

"They have decided that they wanted a special symbol for the solstice, so they have instituted a type of maypole for tonight. The dancers have been practicing all afternoon."

She squeezed his hand. "Are you one of the dancers?"

"I am on standby in case of a turkey leg-related injury."

She laughed and he took her to the spot reserved for them and he helped her settle into place at the high table.

She spoke to the knight on her left, and Salk was on her right. The feast began, and the entertainment started as well. She had never seen jugglers up close without trying to get past them, so she was forced to sit still and enjoy the show.

Acrobats, dancers, a few singers and each one was accompanied by another course delivered from the kitchens.

Cora nibbled at each course and tried not to laugh at how wrong some of the dishes were. There was something to be said for knowing what the herbs actually were and not what they were called in modern times. Ancient names were a lot less precise, but you had to be there to know the differences.

Salk leaned in. "You are making a face."

She chuckled. "I am sorry. I just had a thought about what would improve the recipe."

"I am sure that the cooks would take suggestions, just do it from a distance." He chuckled.

She laughed. "Yeah, that is what I figured."

When the room fell quiet, the baron stood. "During this festive season, we have had this faire to see if it could be done, and if it was not for the generous travel of several excellent knights, it would not have been done. So, we are here tonight to honour those knights who have come from far and wide to help us."

He called out the names of the knights, and each rose to their feet and came forward for their medallion.

"Sir Salk Arthwait, our champion, and he has had the good fortune to escort the artisan who crafted these amazing medallions. Mistress Cora Metzger."

She got to her feet at the urging of the baroness, and she quickly sat as soon as the applause faded.

Salk got his medallion, and it was around his neck when he returned to her side. She looked at it and smiled. "Another of my favourites."

He chuckled. "I guess I am lucky."

"I suppose you are." She gave him a sly look. "So, what happens next?"

"The torches are lit, and we head out to watch the dancers weave magic around the pole. If this goes well, we will be here until the morning."

She blinked. "Really? I didn't ask Viv if she could open up early."

"She agreed when I spoke to her earlier. She is surprisingly excited to have you out and about."

Cora made a face, and he laughed and brought her hand to his lips.

"It appears that everyone is plotting against me."

He smirked. "I prefer that it is plotting for your best interests."

She was about to comment when the gathering began to drift outside. Music started, and she sighed as her own impulses pulled at her.

"Mistress, will you do me the honour of joining me in the dance?"

She wrinkled her nose again. "Fine, but only because I love dancing."

"Ah, an enthusiastic partner. What more could I ask for?" He winked and got to his feet, offering his hand to her.

She walked with him into the night air and enjoyed the cool caress of the wind on her face. The baron and baroness took to the dance area and went through the first dance of the night together.

Cora waited next to Salk until the dance was opened to everyone. In moments, they were stepping, turning; he lifted her and spun her around before setting her back on her feet.

They moved easily together, and Cora found that was completely right. Salk felt like a man who would be able to understand her past if she could tell him and if he could remember it. No human could keep the knowledge of a reindeer after they parted ways. It was part of the Christmas magic. All they would know is that they had been touched by joy.

Hours passed, Cora drank water and lemonade. She danced with Salk and even did one turn with Tahnk. He was surprisingly light on his feet for someone built like an ox.

Finally, eight forty-nine approached, and the dancers formed up around the maypole. The red and white ribbons were taken up, and the dancers were in place. Music started and they skipped and turned around the pole in a pattern reminiscent of a snowflake.

Cora felt something building under her skin. Shock rippled through her as magic began to gather as the solstice crept closer.

She held onto Salk's hand and glanced up at him as she fought for control over her form. Her horns wanted out.

To her surprise, pointed ears and silvery skin were obvious on Salk's face. Even the hand she was holding had changed in hue. He was made of smoke and shadow.

"Cora, is something wrong?" He looked down at her, and instead of dark-chocolate eyes, swirling shadow took their place.

"You were sent after me." She bit her lip. Her disappointment was obvious.

He blinked and stared at her head. "I think we need to leave the space before others notice your horns."

She shrugged. "I can just say I put them on. Your skin is harder to explain."

He looked down at his hands and cursed. "Definitely need to get somewhere else."

He put his hand around her waist, they bustled through the crowd, watching the dancers and they heard the countdown to winter solstice as they rushed toward the exit.

The wave of power smacked into them, and he was suddenly made of shadows, and her energy, vision and horns were all reindeer.

He wrapped her in his arms and swept her to her home, through the door and into the safety of her house on wheels.

He stepped away, and she looked at the tendrils of darkness.

"What are you?"

"I am one of the coal elves, though now, we call ourselves shadows or nightmares. We punish the naughty by making them dwell on their actions."

She touched her horns and sighed. They were firmly wedged in with her coronet. They weren't going anywhere until the morning was here and the crowd that had conjured the magic was gone.

He sighed. "I had hoped to ease you into the idea of what I am."

She wrinkled her nose. "I should have guessed. You are too good looking for a human, plus you smell better, even when you sweat."

He grinned. It looked odd on such a serious face.

She sighed and took a seat, unlatching the vest so she could slouch. "Well, you were sent to bring me home?"

"I was, but only in time for Christmas Eve. You have a few days left."

"A day and a half. I have a day and a half left. Tonight is the twenty-first. I have to be on my way on the afternoon of the twenty-third at the latest."

He sighed. "I meant to get to you earlier, but you hid yourself very well. The magic was only able to get me close to you, not tell me who you were. The name thing is very clever."

She grimaced. "Well, at least I got to dance before I am hauled home."

"I am not going to haul you. I would like you to come willingly."

She raised her eyebrows. "You are joking."

"I am not."

"What could possibly entice me to go back?" She didn't tell him that she was going to go anyway. He didn't deserve to know that.

"Me."

"What?"

"Santa has offered all of the reindeer an elf of their own. He didn't say it in those words, but the elves of the naughty-or-nice list were all assigned to one of your team, and the matches made appear to be solid. I, for one, would enjoy spending much more time with you, in any location."

She quirked her lips. "Are you just saying that to get me to go back?"

"No. I could reach in your mind and bring your dreams to life in that effort. I will not. It is your choice."

He sat next to her and took her hand.

She leaned up and kissed him. His skin tasted of cinnamon and mint. Cora pressed him to the back of the couch, and she straddled him.

With her horns out, she felt more aggressive, as she always did. In the blink of a second, she ran her hands down him to free his cock and stripped off her gown and shoes.

His eyes widened in shock, and he mumbled against her lips. "When did that happen?"

She leaned back and grinned. "I am not called Comet because I run across the sky. Speed has always been my gift."

"I am amazed your dress didn't get caught on your horns."

"It did. I just untangled it and hung it up." She pressed her lips together.

"I am guessing by your state of undress that you are willing to let me stay the night."

She smirked. "And by your state of undress if you care to check."

He leaned up to kiss her. "I thought I felt a cool breeze. You have skills with laces."

She whispered against his lips. "This was my time, so I know it very well indeed."

His shadows crept around her to hold her and stroke her skin. They were both exposing their true natures tonight. There was no hiding what they were or what they could do for this one point in time. Why shouldn't they just enjoy it?

Her breath came faster as his touch roamed over her. She reached between them to stroke his cock with a slow and careful beat. He tensed and pried her hand away, rising without standing and pressing her back to the ladder that led to her loft.

He lifted her hands and pressed them to the highest rung, raising her body with his shadows until she was suspended and supported.

Under his command, Salk's clothing slid completely from his body and folded in the corner. To her surprise, his clothing had actually made him smaller. The broad shoulders, narrow hips and powerful neck were definitely not what she had expected.

She had thought elves were delicate, but he was all strength and focus, and it was directed at her.

His mouth was hot as he tasted her skin. She shivered and tossed her head when he scraped his teeth along her neck. His shadows held her legs apart, and he moved between them, rubbing his cock against her as he worked at her neck, and she shook violently at the combination of sensation.

Her hands clenched, and she moaned while he began to inch into her.

The supports of her tiny castle were tested as he lay siege to her, pressing her back against the rungs of the ladder with each heavy thrust.

He kept his attention on her neck, and at another time, she would have laughed at his awareness of her most sensitive spot. He had picked up on it immediately.

She was held in place as her body rushed with heat and pleasure. When her release hit her, it swept her away and Salk kissed her, taking in her cries and pressing against her while his hips shoved upward, and he shivered wildly.

From his lips, he breathed a cascade of magic into her. Cora held onto him tightly as her body reacted with another wave of release.

She was dazed and felt like she was floating. When she was settled in her bed, she realized that it wasn't her imagination, she was definitely floating.

Salk folded back the sheets and tucked her into bed, joining her and holding her against him, careful of her horns.

"Get some rest, Cora. You have a bit of a trek ahead of you."

She chuckled against his chest. "I travel the world in a night, having an evening of sex won't come close to tiring me out."

"Is that a challenge?"

She laughed. "No, but I am one of the reindeer. Our team is still alive in myth and legend because no one else can do what we do."

"You have me there."

Cora snickered and sighed, snuggling down for a nap.

Salk held her as her breath fanned across his chest. Her right horn was pressing into his arm, but his shadows kept it from puncturing him. He exhaled quietly and shifted so she was held securely and comfortably.

Having her give him authorization in the very basic way of stripping down and crawling into his lap had been a bit of a surprise, but he hadn't hesitated. This was his one chance to get on her good side, and now that he had, he wanted to do it all over again.

Her hand on his chest was rough with callouses from her metal work. She worked hard, and she was definitely a master of her art. It may have been contributed to by the magical snowflake somewhere on her body, but the initial skill was hers. She really was an excellent designer and metalsmith. She needed to be able to continue that interest when she was back at the workshop, or she needed to be able to leave as the elves did.

He was going to speak with Santa when they returned. The idea that she had been stuck in the archive all year round with no outlet for her creativity was enough to boil his blood.

He looked down, and Cora's hand was circling his cock, moving slowly. Her eyes were closed, but her lips were curved in a smile that made his toes curl. He exhaled and waited to see how far she would take it and hoped that this was the start to a very long night.

Cora made breakfast and dodged Salk's hands while she did it. "Hey, do you want something to eat or not?"

He grinned. "I do."

"Good. Put the table down and get some plates." Cora chuckled as he wandered around the tiny space with ease. It was amazing that such a large man could get around in her tiny house.

He smiled. "What do you have on your agenda today?"

"Working where the folks can see me and enjoying my last day with Viv. You?"

"More fight demos. I like it. I haven't had a chance to swing a sword in centuries." He grinned.

"So, were you all shadowy before Santa?" She slid the scrambled eggs onto their plates and grabbed plate of toast a moment later.

"No, just a dark elf who had no family. You?"

"I had just learned what I was and Santa came to ask my parents for me. They knew that I would be ostracised from my community and sent me with him. There isn't a day that passes that I don't miss them. They sent me away for my own good, but I wasn't ready to go."

"How old were you?"

"I was still a teenager. I grew up at the workshop." She settled down and ate her breakfast.

Salk was staring at her in shock. "You grew up there?"

"Yeah, it was fine for the first while, but when Mrs. Claus died, we were forgotten about."

"It was different before?"

Cora laughed. "Sure. We went out with her, had *girls' days*. We dressed for the human world and watched them. It wasn't much, but we got to leave, even if we didn't communicate with the humans."

"I had no idea."

"There was no reason you should have, but we still went into heat every single year and had no outlet. Can you imagine nine women all desperate at the same time? It is amazing that the wounds healed by the time Christmas came around." She chuckled. "Some years were a little more violent than other."

"Why don't we know any of this?"

Cora finished her food. "I am guessing that while Santa grieved, he couldn't stand to see anyone happy, and then, he just forgot that we weren't animals."

"So, you decided to remind him."

"Ru did. She was there when he met his wife, and Ru was there when she aged and died as humans do." Cora smiled. "She was responsible for this entire breakout. I am guessing it was to snap Santa out of his personal involvement."

She brushed the crumbs off the table and onto her plate before she got up and washed the dishes.

"So, what were you going to do this Christmas?"

Cora sighed and glanced at him. "I am guessing that this is the right time to tell you that we were all coming back on the day before Christmas Eve. There was never a plan to let Santa go it alone."

He looked at her in stunned silence before he started laughing. "So, I was sent to retrieve someone who was coming back anyway?"

"Yup. Nice outfit by the way." She gestured to his change of clothing.

"I snuck out while you were sleeping." He grinned.

She was back in her normal garb of skirt and blouse with leather bodice.

With the dishes done, they locked up and made their way to the stirring faire.

Cora had to set Viv up to take over the business. It was probably going to be the hardest part of the entire visit to the human world.

Viv's eyes filled with tears. "Why didn't you mention you were leaving?"

"I didn't want it to be hanging in front of you every time we spoke. I have a contract to sign over the entire shop to you, and I will make as much stock as I can today."

Viv wailed. "I don't understand."

"Be confused later. For now, we have a pre-Christmas rush to deal with." Cora reached inside her and blurred Viv's memory. Viv could still remember the conversation, but it wasn't going to haunt her.

It was time to get on with their day.

At the end of the afternoon, Cora looked around. She had gone as fast as she could during the day, but metal melted, poured and cooled at its own speed. She had no input once she had completed her pour until it was time to finish.

Viv was off getting a meal before the evening party started, so Cora signed the contract and left it at Viv's station.

They had gotten through the day without any problem, but Cora wanted to hug Viv and go. Leaving was never her favourite part of a relationship.

Viv returned, and they chatted for a few minutes.

Cora cleared her throat. "I have to get going. Can you lock up?"

"Sure. Hot date?"

As if summoned by the word *hot,* Salk appeared.

Viv grinned. "You two have fun."

Cora gave her a hug. "Take care, Viv. Have a blast tonight."

Salk watched, and he nodded to Vivienne. "Have a merry evening."

Viv grinned. "That is the idea."

Cora left her shop, placed her hand on Salk's and they walked through the small, temporary town until they got to the security office.

"So, we are leaving at dawn?" Salk asked her in a quiet voice.

"Yes. I mean, we could take off tonight if you like." Cora shrugged. "It makes no difference to me."

"Would you mind?"

"Nope. I have a small pack with presents for the girls, but if you hold onto that, we can be on our way around three in the morning when there aren't many folks awake. It is better that way for takeoff."

"I will agree to your expertise in that matter. What did you want for dinner?"

She bit her lip and looked around. "Can we order Chinese food? I don't have a cell phone or a computer, so I haven't been able to spot a menu, but I would love to try it just once."

Salk grinned, and he pulled a cell phone out of his belt pouch. "I believe we can manage that."

Cora rubbed her hands with excitement, and once inside the small castle, he scrolled through the menu options on the tiny phone.

The bemused delivery driver arrived an hour later, and Salk tipped him lavishly and brought the giant pile of bags inside.

"Are you sure you can do this?" He gestured at the food as he set it on the counter.

She grinned. "I am a nine-foot-tall deer. I am capable of eating most of this house if I am peckish."

"Well, then, Mistress. I present your feast."

Cora spent the first ten minutes working out chopsticks, but when her hand finally knew what it was supposed to do, there was no stopping her.

She plowed her way through some of everything that Salk had ordered, and then, she returned for her favourites.

"I have to say, I am amazed by your appetite."

She chortled. "It isn't appetite. It is capacity. They are very different things."

Salk cocked his head. "Would you be interested in sharing my quarters at the workshop?"

She paused with noodles dangling from her mouth. "Sharing?" She quickly chewed and swallowed. "I don't understand."

"I don't want you to be locked in the workshop again. My quarters are about twice the size of this tiny palace, but I am sure we can also get you some workspace in one of the shops, if you want to continue your designs and metal work."

Cora put her hand on his. "We will see what kind of strides Ru has made when we arrive. When we get back from our rounds, there will be an entire year to figure out what happens next."

He jerked his head. "Fine, but if I have to wait for you, I will not be happy."

Cora laughed. "I look forward to seeing what happens."

She sat and realized that she was looking forward to something. For the first time in centuries, she was anticipating the future. It was definitely worth the effort it had taken to get here.

In the dark of the night, Cora stepped out of the hatch on her roof. Salk crawled up behind her.

Naked, she looked at him and peeled the snowflake off her belly, setting it back in the tiny box he was holding for her, and he tucked it in with the bag of gifts she had picked up.

"Are you ready to hop on up?"

He grinned. "I could do it now, but someone might call the police."

She snorted and shifted into her hoofed form. Her rack was large and wide, but as Salk used his shadows to get him into position, they made a perfect set of handles for him.

When he had a hold, she called on her own magic and stepped off the roof, galloping across the sky with increasing speed until she was the streak of her namesake.

Next stop, the workshop.

Prologue to Blizzard of Heat

"Well, you have gotten rid of nearly all of us." Cupid looked up from her filing, and she smiled at Ru.

"You know that that isn't what is going on. Change requires leaps of faith. I am trusting him to do the right thing."

"It is a big chance."

Ru sighed. "I know, but something has to change. He has been locked in his pattern for too long, which has locked us up. Both things need alteration."

Cupid nodded and finished her filing, making notes on how far she had gotten. She was meticulous.

Rudolph chuckled. "So, have you figured out what you want to do?"

"I think I would like an office with actual people and a chance to help folks through the stress of this holiday. Since I can't do it for you, I would like to do it for someone."

Ru smiled slightly and gave her a quick hug. "You have always been there for folks that need it. Your team depends on you, and you never let them down."

Cupid sighed. "I know. I just want to try it with others and see how things work with humans. I have heard things, and I want to see for myself how horrible the holidays can be for some."

Ru put her hand on Cupid's shoulder. "That is going to be rough on you."

"I can take it."

"I know you can, but seeing pain changes you. It either makes you colder or increases your empathy."

"I will welcome the change. I have had too much of my life be static and immobile. Change is growth, for good or other."

"Just don't lose yourself in their pain. You are not human; you can never be human. All you have is a moment to share with them and to be with them."

Cupid blinked at the bald statement. "If I can ease one person's cold and hostile winter, I will do it."

Ru grinned. "That's the attitude I expect from you. Here is your transport."

Ru extended her hand, and a small box was in her palm.

"Did you have that with you the whole time?" Cupid blinked.

Ru snickered and opened the box. A small and elegant snowflake was sitting and glittering against dark velvet.

Cupid took the snowflake and pressed it to her shoulder. The rush of magic made the hair on the back of her neck stand up.

Ru handed her the box and smiled. "Think about where you want to be and go there. The magic will do the rest."

Cupid closed her eyes, and she was swept away in a blur of magic and snowflakes.

She opened her eyes to the knowledge that she was Cwen Uma Piderson and she was the office manager for Legal Aid. It was time to face the holidays with those who had little to celebrate.

Blizzard of Heat

Cwen hung up the phone and massaged the back of her neck. Four weeks of being the office manager and getting the supplies she needed never got easier.

Fighting her way through bureaucracy was a challenge that exhausted her, and keeping the supplies flowing and the files in their proper places was her contribution to what was going on at Legal Aid.

She kept snacks and everything else well stocked for the clients. The stunned expression on most of their faces was more than enough for her. Their faces were those of people who had lost everything or who had everything hanging in the balance.

The cheerful decorations in the office weren't Cwen's idea. She frankly thought they were in bad taste, but the children who came in with their parents loved them.

The lawyers often chided Cwen for being too serious. She just wanted to keep things running smoothly.

One of the lawyers came into her office. "Cwen, we just got a new hire. Can you show him around and get him set up?"

"Sure, Anthony." She smiled and got to her feet, rotating her shoulders.

She came around her desk and walked into the lobby. It wasn't hard to spot the new recruit; he was the only one wearing a coat that cost more than most of the occupants of the room made in a month.

He smiled at her approach, and the breath left her lungs. *Oh, my.* He was going to be very good for their win rates.

"Hello. I am Cwen. I manage the office."

His smile warmed. "I am Tyr Westerson, here to take some of the burden off the rest of the crew."

"Excellent. Please, come this way." She shook his hand and gestured for him to follow her down the hall.

She showed him the receptionists. "This is Deanne, and this is Dana. They will be your hands and feet. Feel free to call on them if you need anything, and they will do what they can."

Tyr stepped over and shook the hands of the dazed women. "Pleased to meet you."

The ladies looked like they were scrambling for something else to say, but the phones rang and they had to turn away.

She led the way through the maze of hallways, pausing to point out the breakroom before she showed him his office.

"Here you go."

Tyr poked his head in and sighed. "I was terrified that the room was being used for storage."

"Not on my watch. We keep our records clear and filed. Nothing gets wadded up in a corner." She nodded and crossed her arms.

Tyr grinned. "You run a tight ship."

She shrugged. "I try. I will get you a computer and link it to the network. There is a pad and pencil in the top drawer of the desk. You can give me a list of what you need to get comfortable."

He looked around. "I guess I will start that list."

He unbuttoned his costly coat and hung it up on the coatrack in the corner. Cwen left him alone, and she headed to the storage room.

Ten minutes later, she knocked on his door with her knuckles, juggling the laptop and the other basics that she had brought with her.

Tyr opened the door and looked down at her in surprise. "That was quick."

He reached for and took her burden from her. "Wow, it looks like you got everything on my list."

She chuckled and lifted the notepad as he settled the pile on his desk. "I have already connected the computer to our system, and your temporary password is *workload*. The charger is there and the printer is down the hall to your left. The coffee cups are available in the breakroom. You are welcome to bring in your own. We encourage the folks here to use a little polite whimsy on their desks. It keeps you grounded."

She flicked her hair over her shoulder, and he focused on her with the sharp gaze of a predator.

Uncertain of what to do next and unwilling to run, she stood there and scowled. "Anything else?"

Anthony came around the corner, and he grinned. "Well, I have heard a lot about you, Tyr. Welcome to our little corner of Legal Aid. This time of year, we are dealing with a lot of illegal evictions and discontinuation of services. I have a stack of cases for you to start going over if you are ready."

Tyr grinned. "Bring it on. It is why I am here after all."

Cwen nodded and left them to talk about cases. She checked on the printers, toner, paper and the coffee. The essentials had to be maintained to keep things running smoothly.

It was her job here to keep those around her as comfortable as circumstances would allow. She comforted mothers and children, held the hands of despondent fathers who were losing their homes before Christmas. The season of joy put extra stress on those around her, and she felt it when she looked into every face in the waiting room.

Every night, she went home to her apartment a few blocks away, and she baked treats for the office. Keeping morale up during all of the litigation, restraining orders and visitation arrangements was the least she could do.

There were one set of cookies or brownies for the lawyers and one for the clients. She knew all of the allergies in those working in the building, so she was free to bake within those guidelines. For the clients, she stuck to shortbread.

She returned to her desk and got to paying the bills again. She made sure that the caseloads were evenly balanced and sent notes to Anthony if they weren't. Cwen never confronted him, she simply did what women always did—she nudged him in the direction she wanted him to go.

She dived into her work and stayed there until she was able to surface again. Her stomach was a remarkable alarm clock, but it had a tendency to let her focus until after the building was quiet.

Cwen got to her feet and stretched, snorting and grunting as she loosened the muscles that hours at the computer had tightened up.

She froze in mid-stretch when she heard the scrape of a shoe in her doorway. Tyr was watching her.

"I thought I was the last one here." He looked like he had

been working hard. His hair was ruffled, and his tie and shirt had been loosened at the neck.

She shook her head. "No, I was doing payroll. It is always engrossing. You don't want to leave it half done. Folks get irritated."

He chuckled. "You are correct. I have a personal question to ask you."

"Ask away."

"Where can I get some good takeout? I have a few more hours of catching up to do."

Cwen reached into her desk and flicked through a handful of menus. "What do you prefer? Italian, Chinese, sandwiches or barbeque?"

"Tonight, I think I need Chinese."

She brandished a menu and handed it to him. "I was going to place an order myself if you want to split the delivery charge."

He looked at the menu and grinned. "I am guessing these marks are your favourites?"

"They are. I order from them twice a week."

Tyr chuckled. "I will call in an order. Can I try a few of your selections?"

"Of course."

"Wonderful. If you aren't occupied, I wouldn't mind some company."

She nodded. "I will be there after I get the handoff for the takeout. You do the ordering; I will bring it to you."

Tyr nodded and headed for his office, leaving the door open.

Cwen walked around the waiting room and all the meeting rooms, gathering cups, plates, napkins and the tissues left behind by those in shock or grief.

It wasn't strictly part of her duties, but the cleaners didn't come in until after ten, so she tried to give them a leg up when she could.

She loaded the dishwasher and heard the afterhours bell as it chimed the arrival of dinner. She nearly skipped to the door and buzzed in the delivery guy after verifying his identity.

She grabbed the first bag and then was handed a second. "Let me get my wallet."

Rob shook his head. "Nope, it is all paid for. Have a nice night, Ms. Piderson."

She peeped above the bags. "You too, Rob."

He left, and she waited until the security door swung shut. Once it was secure, she headed through the building and to Tyr's office.

She wandered in and found the edge of the desk with her hip. "You must be hungry."

He chuckled and helped her put the bags down on the desk. "I always shotgun new places. I try everything and narrow down what I want to eat."

"Well, you can't go wrong with Heaven's Garden."

She identified her cartons by scent, and she settled them. "Hang on, I will get some chopsticks."

She sprinted to her office, and when she returned with chopsticks and napkins, he was opening her soda for her and gesturing for her to sit in the client chair on the other side of his desk.

She scooted the extra chair over, angled her chair and she settled down with the chopsticks and one of the cartons. Kung Pao chicken was always a favourite.

Cwen looked at him and cocked her head as he dug into the first box he grabbed. "Why are you here?"

Tyr paused with a wad of noodles firmly in his sticks. "I am eating."

"I mean at Legal Aid. You are a little fancy for this place."

He grinned and took a bite. When he had cleared enough of it to speak, he said, "I am on loan. I am a trouble-shooter for when the workload gets too high. My organization lends me out when necessary."

"What is your speciality?"

"Criminal law. I will be working with cases that are marked as requiring criminal defense."

She blinked. "Like what?"

"Shoplifting, vandalism, drunken assaults. That kind of thing."

Cwen appreciated that he was dumbing it down for her. "So, a jolly holiday all around."

"Pretty much. My goal is to get those free that I can and to have them serve public service instead of time away from their families during the holidays."

"Well, that is something at least. How long will you be here?"

He shrugged and opened a pack containing sweet and sour chicken balls. "As long as I am needed, and then, it is back to the normal grind."

"No rest for the wicked?"

Tyr chuckled. "Something like that. I have gotten folks off the naughty list to a certain extent. I can't keep them there, but I can help them get a leg up on getting themselves out of the hole they are in. When it comes down to it, we are all responsible for ourselves."

Cwen nodded. "For better or worse."

He opened his soda and slurped. "For naughty or nice."

Her senses went into high alert. "What did you say?"

"For naughty or nice. Isn't it the season for it?" There was a challenge in his gaze.

"I suppose." She found her pack of spring rolls and grabbed the packets of plum sauce. She squirted the first packet onto the rolls and fished one out with her chopsticks.

"So, why did you come here? I have heard glowing reports of you from the other lawyers. You could get a job as an office manager anywhere."

"I like it here. I feel needed."

He nodded. "You are definitely that. I had one of those cookies earlier. You should open a bakery."

Cwen shook her head. "I like baking cookies at the end of a long day. It relaxes me and gives me a reason to show up for work the next day."

"Why?"

"So that I can bring something that will lighten someone's mood. Even if that just lasts for a moment."

"Is a moment worth all that effort?" He raised his brows.

"I think it is, and it is my offering to those around me." She worked her way through the spring rolls and returned to her Kung Pao, dipping her chopsticks into the white rice and dropping a serving of it into the space she now had in her carton.

"What do you think a moment can do?"

Cwen grinned and poked around in her carton. "A moment can stop the escalation of fear, can break the concentration needed to get angry. A kindness can stop panic in its tracks, and eating a cookie can give you a moment to reflect. It is a tiny thing, kindness. In the right moment, it can move mountains, but few people give it the credit because it starts by moving one pebble."

Tyr blinked. "Wow. That is just... Wow. I don't say this often, but I think you just inspired me."

She chuckled and settled more firmly in the chair. "See? A moment has had an impact already."

He laughed, and they sat and ate as much of the food as they were able.

When they were done, they packed up and stored the food in the fridge. It was a lot less than they had started with, and Cwen was a little embarrassed at how much they had cleared.

During their meal, he had quizzed her about the others in the building and what he should be on the lookout for. He even got her opinion on a few of the cases where the client had come into the building. Apparently, he valued opinions.

She grabbed her jacket from her office, fished her keys out of her pocket and got dressed to face a stormy and cold night. She was happy that her journey was only two blocks.

The final part of her winter gear was the heavy and hideous winter boots that she was fond of. When she was barely recognizable as human, she stomped toward the front door. Tyr was waiting for her.

She grinned, but he couldn't see it. Her scarf was in the way.

His leather gloves and long coat were perfectly suitable for someone getting in a car, but he was staring at her in shock. "Why are you dressed like that?"

"I am walking home. You head out, and I will turn off the lights behind me."

He frowned. "I can't let you walk home."

"Tough. I am walking. You can either go your own way or walk with me, but then, you would have to turn around and walk back to your car."

He scowled again. "I don't like either of your options."

She pushed him lightly, and he stepped out the door. She lunged to the side and hit the lights. The lockup was automatic, so they continued on until they were in the lobby and facing their reflections in the glass with the night behind the protective layer.

"Well, I suppose I will see you tomorrow, Tyr. Welcome to the team." She smiled and checked all the closures on her clothing before heading out into the blustery night.

A dark sedan pulled up as she crossed the street and scuttled across the icy sidewalk. Tyr got into the back seat, and Cwen shook her head. Of course, he would have a car service at his beck and call.

She moved briskly through streets that few folks were willing to traverse; she entered her building with a relieved sigh. The shadow of the sedan as it drove past her proved that there had been a third option she hadn't mentioned. Tyr had followed her home while snug and warm in his car.

Cwen chuckled and headed up to her third-floor apartment; she had cookies to make.

Two weeks and three late-night takeouts later, Cwen finished confirming the numbers for the Christmas party and prepared to lock up for the weekend.

The party would be on Saturday night, and spouses and significant others were invited.

Tyr had responded to the invitation in the affirmative, so she had adjusted the head count by one.

In all, thirty people were going from their particular branch of the legal-aid organization to a dinner and dance at a restaurant that had sponsored the meal. It wasn't a standard arrangement, but they had gone through a month of paperwork to authorize the gift of food to their department. The confirmation had come through two weeks earlier, and it had caused a stir of excitement in the office. They weren't going to have stale fried chicken again.

Cwen couldn't imagine what the previous year's meal had been like, but she was hopeful that the party would go off without a hitch.

She had put a lot of effort into making the arrangements as easy for everyone as she could. Cab vouchers had been acquired, and they were ready for a pleasant night.

The intercom chirped, and Dana's voice came through, "Cwen, the office order is here."

Cwen got up and came out to the reception desk, checking that everything she had ordered was present and accounted for. It was the last delivery before Christmas, and who knew what the new year would bring. Cwen would be long gone by then, and her time at the office would be a dim memory. The magic of the snowflake would find someone else to fill her shoes.

Once the delivery guy was dismissed, she carried the boxes back to the storage area, one by one. She was going to leave them fully stocked and ready for the new year.

It seemed surreal to her that she had enjoyed her time here and it was nearly over. Wednesday of the following week, she would be on her way back to the workshop and her moment of life in the human world would be over.

By this point, Santa would know that they were gone and Ru would be applying their demands, handing him their letters and obligating him to change their circumstances.

Hopefully, when Santa looked over the issue, he would agree that they were entitled to the same freedoms as the elves that worked for him and could come and go as they pleased. If he didn't agree, the reindeer were willing to take off again.

Cwen moved the boxes of photocopy paper easily, but she had to pretend that they weighed a ton. She was setting the last box into place when Tyr's voice came from behind her.

"Need a hand?"

She shoved the box onto the shelf and turned with a smile. "Nope. All done. Excellent timing. How was court?"

He smiled. "Probation and community service."

"Excellent. Well, tomorrow is the company party, so we can all celebrate together."

"Are you bringing an escort?"

She snorted. "No, I have enough men in my life simply by working here. I don't have time to shop around."

He grinned and came in, his suit jacket folded over his arm. "I see you are stocking up."

"Well, after the holidays, things get even worse than they are now. The extra supplies are going to come in handy."

He cocked his head. "You have this note in your voice like you are trying to make things easier for someone else."

She wrinkled her nose. He had been paying attention while they shared takeout in the evenings if he could detect that.

"I have some time off booked. I just don't talk about it."

"Going home to spend time with loved ones?"

She chuckled. "The closest thing to family that I have ever had."

He blinked at the vehemence in her tone. "I... Well, I hope

you enjoy your visit."

She sighed. "Just the same old routine, but this time, we will all have stories to share. It will make for something different when we get together."

She smiled and shook her head at the scenarios in her imagination. "We get up to some hinkie stuff when there is no one looking. I can only imagine how their time away has gone."

Tyr came closer. "Would you like to go out for dinner with me tonight?"

She blinked in surprise. "Like, a date?"

He grinned. "Something like that."

"Um, I suppose so."

"Good. Would you like to leave from work?"

She was bemused, but she nodded. "Sure. I guess I have a few more hours to go. So, don't pick anywhere fancy. I am not dressed for it."

He inclined his head. "Of course. I will choose something appropriate."

Cwen nodded. "Right. Uh, I need to get past you to return to my desk."

He backed out of the storage room and watched her as she headed to her office. She knew he was watching, because she looked behind her on two separate occasions. He was still watching with a smile on his face.

Cwen scuttled back into her office, and she breathed slowly. This was the closest to a relationship that she had had during her weeks in the human world. If she played her cards right, she might get her first kiss by the end of the night.

The car ride had been done in nervous silence, at least on her part. The next week was off time for the office and the local courts. All would be quiet.

The driver was a silent shadow, but he seemed to know where he was going. It was nice that one of them did.

She sat with her hands in her lap as the car moved through crowded streets. Cwen tended to walk where she needed to go, so being in a vehicle was freaking her out a little.

Tyr reached over and held her hand. He didn't say a word, but the contact calmed her.

They were in the car for half an hour when it glided to a halt in front of a subtle awning. Tyr got out of the car, and he opened her door, taking her hand to help her out.

The patch of ice on the ground made her lose her footing, and she ended up plastered against him. "Sorry."

He chuckled. "I consider it a good start to the evening."

His hands were on her lower back and supporting her. With a quick move, he turned so that she was on the scraped sidewalk and her feet were steady again.

He released her and offered her his arm. Not being a fool, she wrapped her mitten around his arm and walked with him to the restaurant.

A courteous doorman let them in, and Tyr walked around as if he owned the place. He wasn't looking around him with condescension; he simply had an expression that everything in his vicinity was his actual territory.

She was helped out of her coat, and Tyr got the small numbered slip from the coat check and tucked it into his shirt pocket with his own.

They were escorted through the restaurant, and several of the patrons looked at her with surprise. A few even managed disdain through their botoxed faces.

Cwen shrugged and kept walking as the attentive host led them to a quiet and private dining room.

Tyr held her chair out, and she sat down, a little surprised by the effort he had expended.

"When did you arrange this?"

Tyr grinned. "I have a standing reservation. Antoine would be scandalized to know that the nights I wasn't here I was eating tacos behind my desk."

The host returned, and he had a slim set of menus in his hands. He gave her the first and Tyr the second.

She didn't know what to choose. She stared at the menu until she found something that appealed to her. Chicken and mushrooms with pasta and sauce. It was just what she was in the mood for.

"Did you want an appetizer?" Tyr smiled at her over the top of his menu.

"Um, sure. When have I ever turned down food?" She chuckled.

"Well, you are a bottomless pit. That is certain. Do you mind if I pick something for you?"

"Feel free as long as I get my main course." She smiled brightly and set her menu down.

He laughed and nudged her knee with his. "Of course you will. I am sure that we will have an excellent time tonight. It is good to see you away from the office."

She snorted. "Aw, you have followed me home three times. You have already seen me away from the office."

Tyr sighed. "Well, you wouldn't let me drive you, and my dress shoes are unsuitable for walking in the snow."

A server came in, and Tyr ordered a bottle of wine, a pitcher of lemon water and a glass of soda for Cwen. The server didn't even bat an eye as he left with the order.

She quirked her lips. "Do you own this place?"

"No, but I have defended the owner a few times. We have never lost a defense against a spurious suit." He smiled.

"What kind of suits?"

"Everything from paternity to slip and falls. There was even a tooth broken off in one of the desserts. It is amazing what folks will think to sue about."

She smirked. "Not amazing. Sad. Personal responsibility seems to have launched itself out a window. Let me guess. The broken tooth was already broken, the owner is gay and has never been near a woman, and the slip and fall was a setup."

He shook his head. "The broken tooth wasn't human; it belonged to the man's dog. The slip and fall was as a result of a patron over-imbibing at the bar. He couldn't stand up on his own and wondered about why he was bruised the next day. That was security footage worth its weight in gold. As for the paternity suit, the owner used to be a woman, so there is no testicular activity to start a child. It was his brother that participated, and she thought that the connection would be close enough to pass the testing."

"Was it for a share of the business?"

"That is correct. This is a very exclusive and very successful enterprise. Also, Antoine is very handsome, but few folks know about the transition."

"If few people know, then why tell me?"

"You won't tell anyone else; you value secrets." Tyr smiled.

The server returned with the drinks, and when Cwen had her

selection in front of her, he smiled slightly.

She smiled back and said, "I am a heavy drinker."

He chuckled and asked, "What can I get for you?"

Tyr ordered something French and complicated for an appetizer.

Cwen ordered her chicken, and Tyr got something with slices of beef. Her French wasn't great, but it could make out that much.

When he had taken their orders, he disappeared.

"This is rather surreal. So, what are your plans for the holidays?" It was a topic that she was used to fielding and hearing around the office.

He shrugged. "I had hoped to spend it with a special someone, but now, I will be travelling on the twenty-third so that is out of the question."

She looked at him and cocked her head. "Really? Me too."

He looked genuinely surprised. "You are?"

"Sure. Time to go home again. I have enjoyed my time out and about, but there is no place like home. Besides, I have obligations."

"At Christmas?"

"Christmas Eve, actually. It is a tradition going back a very long time, and I have no intention of breaking it now." She snorted and sipped her soda. The sugar hit helped her wake up, and when the soda was gone, she felt moderately better.

She cleared her pallet with some water, and she looked at Tyr as he rubbed his forehead.

"You look like you are in pain, elf."

He jerked in shock. "What?"

"Oh, don't be an ass. I know what you are. I have known since I looked into your win rate. You have huge gaps of time when you simply ceased to exist and your department went on without you, as if you weren't even there. I only know of one type of person who could have that effect on the human world and it is an elf. So, did Santa send you?" Her smile was genuinely amused.

He scowled. "So, you have known all along?"

"More or less. I had my doubts, but now that I have eaten with you a few times, I am very sure. Your manners give it away. Human males, for the most part, would have begun pressuring for intimacy after spending all that money on takeout. Sad but true."

He blushed. "I never thought having good manners would have been a giveaway."

"Well, that, and when you were arguing with Anthony, your ears peeked out. That sort of finalized it for me." She wagged her eyebrows.

He laughed. "Fair enough. So, you wanted to come home anyway?"

"It was always the plan. We just needed to shake him into doing something different."

Tyr cocked his head. "Do you think it worked?"

She put her right hand on his left and gave it a squeeze. "Pretty sure."

"Me?"

"Yup. He had us segregated from anyone else, but we don't age. We were all born to humans and taken away. When we joined the workshop, we became part of Christmas the same way Santa is. Everyone knows our names. By now, we are a form of demigods, the same as he is."

Tyr raised his brows, but as he would speak, he paused. The server came back in and set a stuffed-mushroom appetizer in front of them.

He took a spoon and a wide fork, scooping up a serving and setting it in the smallest plate and placing it back on the stack of graduated plates in front of them.

When Tyr had been served, she watched his hands and mimicked the selection of cutlery.

As the server left, he raised his brows and said, "Demigods?"

"Our power used to come from Santa, but since humanity has acknowledged us, the children watch for us, sing of us, wait for us. We have icons in yards, in schools, lit up in tiny lights on the darkest, coldest nights. The elves used to hold that position until they faded in the eyes of humans. Now, they think you are tiny and cute. Your energy comes from the ancient world and Santa."

He paused. "I have never thought about it like that."

She shrugged. "There is no reason you should. He won't make a fuss about it, because you are his kind, but you are now powered by Christmas."

Tyr blinked, and he sat frozen in time.

Cwen ate the appetizer and smiled. "It's good; you should eat yours before it gets cold."

He mechanically ate the mushroom and slowly came back to life.

"How do you know all of this?"

She snorted and set her cutlery down. "Well, you see, the team and I have three hundred and sixty-four days a year to look into this kind of thing. About fifty or sixty years ago, they started chanting our names and our blind work ethic went out the window. We started to want to know more about the human world for the first time since we had been taken out of our times and trained to pull the sleigh."

"Do you miss your home?"

She shrugged. "I was born in the eighteenth century, and my father made harpsichords. He made a good living, but he tithed me to the church. I was on my way to join the abbey when Santa and Ru appeared, asking me to help them."

"How old were you?"

"Eleven. I had shifted once, but our local priest said I was possessed by a forest spirit, and he did an exorcism. Nothing happened after that, so I thought it was over until I ran into the two on the road. My escort froze in place just as you did, and I was whisked away on Ru's back." She smiled at the memory.

"Why are you smiling?"

"Because until that moment, I never realized that the reindeer magic made them bigger than horses."

"Seriously?"

"Oh yeah. We are freaking huge. We have to be to keep our bodies warm as we fly above the cities, through the cloud layers. Magic only goes so far and then a solid circulatory system has to kick in."

He chuckled, and the server returned to whisk away the appetizer plates, and then, he was back a moment later with their meals.

The next hour was spent eating, enjoying each other's company and finally discussing the details of what Tyr did in the human world.

He sighed. "I really do help to get folks off the naughty list. Everyone can have a moment of bad judgment. If they are genuinely remorseful and want to change, I can help them do it. If not, they have to pay. They need to have someone actually see them for what they can be and believe in what they are."

She swallowed to stop the tears that wanted to appear. "So, that is why you hit Legal Aid during the season."

"All around the world, I find my way into the court system using the magic and I work on freeing those who deserve to be home with their families. I can't do it for everyone, but I do it for those that I can."

Cwen smiled. "And here, I have just been baking cookies."

"Do not undersell the meaning of that small gesture to those who are in danger of losing everything. They have come in to sit with me with crumbs on their lips, and I have my own crumbs on mine, so we meet as equals. They are being treated as someone who matters and that is conveyed by that one small cookie."

She blinked rapidly to clear the tears that were forming. "That is a heavy burden for one cookie."

He chuckled and squeezed her hand. "Those are really good cookies."

She laughed. "Thanks. They are team recipes. With nothing else to do, bake-offs are common."

They were offered dessert, and she declined. She might make sweets, but she didn't like to eat them.

Tyr ate a confection with ice cream, poached fruit and a glossy sugar cage.

Cwen sat and sipped at a nice cup of coffee while he had dessert.

She sighed. "Well, we have covered a number of topics. I am guessing that you have my collar?"

He nodded. "I do. I didn't expect Cupid to be a redhead."

She snorted. "I am no cherub, and I was born with the red hair. The nuns were planning on shaving my head to let out the devil."

He frowned. "That would have been a crime."

"I think so. It is hard enough to keep it under control. It wants to curl, and it drives me nuts." She grinned.

His dessert was finished, and a new face appeared in the doorway, approaching them with a smile. "Tyr, you are looking well."

"Antoine. Everything was delightful, as always."

Antoine and Tyr shook hands.

When the newcomers gaze settled on her, Cwen raised her brow. "Good evening."

Antoine came around and bowed over her hand with a flourish. "Dear lady. Did you not find something on the dessert menu to tempt you? Or are you a delicate flower who eschews sweets?"

"Sweets are not my vice. Point a loaf of bread at me, hand me butter and stand back."

Antoine stood up and chuckled. "You should have said something. It could have been arranged."

"Everything was wonderful. I am quite satisfied." She smiled.

"Too bad for you, Tyr. I have managed to satisfy your lady friend, and I wasn't even in the room."

Tyr rolled his eyes.

Cwen smirked. "It is true talent that he will never achieve. We can only mourn for him."

Antoine cackled, kissed the back of her hand and left them alone.

"I am fairly sure you have won yourself a table here whenever you want one." Tyr smirked.

"Too bad I won't be here to take advantage of it. I don't know what will happen next year, but I doubt I will be able to get free again in this way."

"Why?"

"Because I am pretty sure that Santa freaked and he won't want to experience that again."

"There will be an entire year to get through before you need to worry about it. I am sure that there will be something we can do."

Cwen blinked. "We?"

"Yes. I am always willing to work with those who deserve a chance at justice. You are definitely one of them." He leaned over and kissed her.

Her heart thumped in her chest, and she kissed him back, leaning in until she heard the cutlery on the table clink.

He tasted like apples, cinnamon and ice cream. It was definitely a dessert she wouldn't mind sampling again. All the flavour, none of the calories.

He was moving his head against hers, and she leaned further

over until her chair tilted under her and she yelped. He caught her and righted her chair.

"I think that we should call it a night. I will see you tomorrow at the Christmas party, and if you are still interested then, we will pick things up from there."

She wanted to pout, but she was still dazed. "Well, I guess that is all for tonight. Can your driver give me a lift home?"

He sighed and stood, helping her to her feet. "Of course."

He opened his wallet and pried off several large bills. He dropped them on the table and offered her his arm again.

She took his arm, and they walked together to the coat check where their coats were waiting and he just had to hand over the tags to claim them.

He held her coat for her, and she wrapped herself up as she normally did. Her first kiss was still occupying her mind, and her thoughts were spinning.

The town car pulled up as they left the building, and she had to ask, "Is he one of you?"

Tyr chuckled. "He sort of is and sort of isn't. You are not the only odd thing to come out of this world."

She wanted to ask him for more details, but he opened the door for her and politeness meant she had to scoot into the seat.

The drive home was quiet but different. Tyr held her hand as they drove back to her home, and it was as if her mitten wasn't even there.

When they pulled up outside her apartment building, she moved to get the door, but he pulled her back for another kiss. Her soul melted a little at the touch of his lips moving over hers, and she was in a cloud when he released her, got out of the car and opened her door for her. She dug in her coat pocket and fished out her keys.

When she stepped out of the car, she gave him a tight smile and headed for her front door.

"Cwen, I will see you tomorrow night and pick you up here at six thirty."

She wrinkled her nose. "Fine. Six thirty. Good night, Tyr."

She unlocked the door and closed it behind her without looking back. The moment she looked back, she would jump into his arms. That wasn't a good idea.

Cwen leaned back for a moment against the security door, and then, she began the arduous march up the stairs until she got to her apartment. She opened her door and walked into the dark space, shucking her clothing as she went. Her door locked automatically, and she was naked by the time she reached the bedroom.

Her bed called, and she crawled into her cool sheets, reliving her first kiss over and over until sleep claimed her.

Cwen wrapped her shoulders in glittering velvet, and she settled a cloak around her, her gloved hands closed the clasps while the small purse swung from her wrist. Her keys, some cash and a credit card were all that she brought with her. Well, that and some lipstick.

The clock displayed six twenty-seven, so she headed downstairs and waited in the lobby.

At precisely six thirty, the dark car glided up and Tyr got out. He was wearing a dark suit, and she smiled. If she had one day to play fancy dress, she was going all out.

She left her building, and Tyr stopped in place. Her hair was twisted up, and then, it cascaded down over her left shoulder.

Her cloak was a midnight blue that made her cool-blue eyes sparkle and her hair look shades darker.

Tyr looked at her as if he was seeing her for the first time. "Cwen, you look amazing."

She grinned. "Do your thing and open the door. This outfit isn't designed to stand around when it's minus thirty."

He gathered her up and tucked her into the town car, moving around to sit next to her. "You look..."

"Amazing. Yes, you mentioned. Thank you. You look lovely as well, but you always look lovely."

The driver snorted with laughter. It was the first sound that she had heard him make. The odd thing was that the sound wasn't human.

Tyr took her hand and he sighed. "Stop laughing and drive, Arthur."

They sat together in comfortable silence as they drove to the venue.

Tyr blinked. "How did you get this place for the office party?"

"It was ladies' night, and I was there with Deanne and Dana

after my first day at work. There was a guy who was trying to set fire to the place, and I tackled him. He was the ex of one of the servers, and he was trying to punish her for claiming that she always had to work by burning down her only means of income. He was a charming fellow. Anyway, I brought him down and held him for the police. He had kerosene and a barbeque starter, which are not normal accessories for those who want to attend a nightclub."

"Did you have to testify?"

"I made a statement and he confessed, so no."

"What happened to him?"

"Oh, he had to spend a week getting psych evaluations. He swore that I sprouted horns when I took him down."

Tyr laughed and got out of the car, walking around to open her door. She accepted his help getting out, and they stood outside one of the most prestigious nightclubs in town.

A few cabs pulled up and other office staff gathered. With a deep breath, Cwen walked forward, hauling Tyr with her. The familiar face of the owner greeted them, and the doors of *Sparkle* were thrown wide for their private party.

Appetizers were carried through their gathering, and when they were all in, the door was marked with the *closed for private party* sign.

The music started up, and the Legal Aid lawyers and employees began to party into the night.

It was around eleven when phones began to go off around the room. Cwen didn't carry her phone with her, so she had to look over Dana's shoulder. "What is it?"

"Weather warning. We need to get home right now. There is a blizzard coming in."

Cwen groaned. "Right."

Everyone had been drinking, so they started calling their cab companies. Every single one had several hours of waiting lists.

Cwen looked to Tyr, but he was already in action. "My driver can take four of you at a time. Cwen and I will stay until the last."

The crowd bunched together into sets of four and began to evacuate. Arthur was going to be busy.

The mood was dampened, but Cwen hauled Tyr to the dance floor. "That was generous of you."

He swayed with her and smiled. "It was an excuse to be the last one to leave with you."

"We will have to help the manager and staff get home."

"Arthur will take care of it."

"What is he?"

"He is my assistant. He comes when I call and I don't need to use a phone."

She smiled as he pulled her tightly to him. "I see. So... magic?"

"Yes. Would you expect anything else?"

She sighed and continued dancing. Behind them, the others were tense and nervous, babysitters were being contacted and arrangements were being made for the next few days.

It was a disappointing end to a great party, but Cwen kept dancing.

When a dark figure appeared at the edge of the dance floor, Cwen realized that everyone else was gone. "Hello, Arthur."

He bowed, and she caught the gleam of the lights on his cheeks. He was made of snow.

Tyr was swaying with her, slowly and with great attention to keeping her pressed against him.

"Tyr, I believe everyone else has gone home."

He sighed. "I know. I am just enjoying this."

"Arthur is waiting."

"He came inside?"

"He did. We don't want to let him melt, so we should be going."

Tyr grinned. "He really is in here, isn't he?"

"He really is."

She snorted and cool air rushed in between them as he released her.

Arthur looked at Tyr and frowned.

"Arthur says we won't make it far. There is already a foot of snow on the streets. My place is close, but we would not be able to make it to your home. Will you stay the night with me?"

Cwen scowled at him. "Is this a ploy to get me into your bed?"

"The invitation, yes. The snowstorm, not my doing." He grinned.

"Fine. Whatever keeps Arthur safe." She winked at the driver.

He grinned.

They got ready, and the manager came to them. "Sorry that it ended up this way, Cwen."

"You did a great job, and this will be a party to remember. Everyone is home safely. Did you need a ride anywhere?"

She shook her head. "No, I am fine. I live two buildings over. I will just lock up after you, and everyone can hunker in until the snow is over."

Cwen shook her hand and then pulled on her gloves. Arthur settled her cloak on her, and she used the velvet wrap over it all to keep the breezes out. Tyr got his coat on, and they were soon ready.

"Merry Christmas." Cwen winked at the manager and headed out with her two-man escort.

The night was lit with the fat flecks of snow that were blowing down around them. Tyr tucked her into the car, and Arthur slid into the driver's seat. When Tyr was next to her, his arm around her holding her close, they began to creep forward into the snow-covered night filled with skidding cars and stumbling pedestrians.

It took ten minutes to move six blocks but that was enough to get them to Tyr's home. The brownstone was on a quiet street that seemed to be obscurely tucked into the bustling downtown area.

"Somehow, I pictured you in a high rise."

Tyr grinned. "I am an old-fashioned kind of guy."

He got out and walked around the car, opening her door and helping her out and into the teeth of the blizzard. He sheltered her with his body as they approached the door. The moment that she glanced back at Arthur, both he and the car were gone.

Tyr opened the door and bustled her inside. The cessation of the press of wind nearly made her fall over. She swayed violently before she got herself under control.

She removed her wrap and cloak before bending over to get her boots off her feet.

Tyr removed his coat and footwear before taking her outerwear. "Boots?"

She grinned. "I am practical if nothing else. No one looks under a gown this long. They saw silvery toes and assumed that

I was wearing pumps."

"How did you enjoy your time with the humans?"

It was the first time they were truly alone. He dropped his human glamour, and she checked out the points of his ears and the gleam of his skin.

She reciprocated with her horns and the tawny cast of her own skin.

"Wow, I didn't think that you actually had horns."

Cwen smirked. "And I always thought that pointed ears were a rumour. See, we are both learning."

He snorted. "Can I get you some coffee or tea before the power goes out?"

"Coffee. I don't get enough of it at the workshop." She wrinkled her nose. "We have to ration it."

"Won't it keep you awake?"

She grinned. "That is what I am hoping."

He smiled and led the way to the kitchen where he put a cup and a puck in a single-cup coffeemaker and pushed a button.

She watched as the dark, steaming liquid filled the mug, and when it was done, she took the mug with a happy sigh.

"Cream or sugar?"

"Sure, but I will drink it any way I can get it." Cwen waited while he pulled out the accessories from the refrigerator and cabinet, respectively.

She put a teaspoon of sugar into the coffee and a few splashes of cream.

He prepped a cup of coffee for himself, and they waited until the machine stopped pumping and snorting. With his own mug in his hand, he smiled. "So, do you want to start a fire or did you want a tour?"

"Tour and then fire." She smiled.

So, he took her by the hand, and he showed her the uppermost level with the small deck that looked out over the white-whipped city.

He showed her the bedrooms, the small study, and then, they were back on the main floor, settling in the living room next to the huge fireplace.

Cwen was sitting perched on a huge cushion as she watched Tyr load wood into the fireplace. "When was the last time you lit a fire?"

"It has been over sixty years, but I think I can manage this."

She watched, and the flames slowly curled around the wood until the logs turned black.

Tyr sat back and sighed. "I might be out of practice."

"May I?"

He nodded, so she grabbed a poker and adjusted the logs so that air could move between them. The flames went from struggling to flickering in seconds.

"Well, it seems like you are better at starting a fire than I am." Tyr sat back on his own pillow.

"Everybody has their strengths. Mine is an annoying analysis of the situation coupled with decision-making skills."

"And a lovely pair of horns."

She reached up and patted them. "Yeah, they are cute. I was fortunate that they didn't reach their full size until I turned one hundred. These could have gotten me burned as a demon or a witch."

"Are they gold?"

"No, they are more of a bronze." She sighed and leaned back on one hand.

Tyr shifted and moved toward her, touching her horns and coming in for a kiss. She smiled against his lips and stroked one of his pointed ears.

He shivered, and he bore her back to the floor. Cwen chuckled and dissipated her horns.

"Aw, why did you get rid of them?"

"I am saving your hardwood."

He took her hand and pressed it to his crotch. "You are a hero."

She laughed. "I meant your flooring."

Her fingers took in the shape of his erection through his trousers. It jerked a little at her touch, and she focused on how she felt about sleeping with an elf.

It all boiled down to she was tired of being alone in a crowd. This was her moment to have a connection that went beyond the superficial.

She settled under him and gave herself up to his kiss, his touch and the hand that was dragging her skirt upward.

When he found her wet and slick, his head jerked back in surprise. "You aren't wearing any underwear."

"I am a reindeer, of course not. I don't age, nothing sags, so why bother?"

"I am not complaining." He grinned and leaned back, pulling away from her to remove his clothing.

She leaned up on her elbows to watch him as his skin was exposed inch by inch.

His dark-gold hair gleamed in the firelight. The darker hair that led a trail down his abdomen widened into a thatch of silk that framed his erection. She could see scars on his torso and arms, and it led her to believe that he had not always been a lawyer.

He extended his hand to her, and she took it. Standing up sent her head spinning, so she leaned against him and he held her tight.

Tyr slid a hand to the back of her neck, and he pulled her head back so she was tilted upward for his kiss. His other hand unzipped her dress, and he pried it off her shoulders.

She helped, and soon, the fabric was in a heap around her feet. He eased her onto the wide sofa and came down on top of her.

She slid her knees to either side of his hips, and she waited.

He cocked his head. "You haven't had sex before." It wasn't a question.

"Nope. No pressure." She gave him a wry smile.

He sighed. "This won't be like I have been imagining it, but that can happen later."

"You are planning on a later? We won't be out in this world much longer."

As they spoke, he was pressing into her with the utmost care. Her body might be ready, but it wasn't used to this activity, and he was taking the care needed to spare her injury.

"I don't think that a return to the workshop should necessitate a return to the status quo. I am sure that the other elves who have been sent out and have located their reindeer are thinking the same thing. We had no idea what you were. I do not know if that was for your benefit or for ours."

He moved into her with careful thrusts, and she lost interest in the conversation. There was an ache, a sharp twinge, but then, pleasure began to increase when their dance truly began.

Each cascade of pleasure ran through her and registered in

her memory. She had no idea where the sensations were taking her, but she let them lead the way.

The sense of urgency was familiar to her. Every season that she went into heat, the urgency took over. She had no idea that this was the desired treatment for that instinct. It was definitely effective if frustrating.

Tyr went up on one arm while his hips continued to rock into her. He caressed her breasts with his free hand before sliding his hand between them to stroke her clit. The urgency built suddenly, and she wrapped her legs around his hips, arching into his thrusts.

After several minutes of struggle, her urgency snapped and waves of hot pleasure ran through her limbs making her twitch and jerk under him. Her channel clasped at his cock, and he shoved into her hard and fast until he groaned in his own release of tension.

He relaxed onto her, and she caught him, holding him tight.

Sweat stuck them together. She drew designs on his back.

When Tyr finally lifted his head, he blinked. "I think you killed me."

"No. Wounded at best. I didn't even leave a mark."

He smiled. "I don't mind marks."

"As you said, we can leave that for later."

He nipped her lips and grinned. "Shall we retire for the night?"

She sighed. "No."

"What then?"

"I need to go out in the storm. I can hear folks calling, and I can do something to help them, but I need help. Will you come with me?"

He leaned up on both arms. "You want me to go out in the storm?"

"I need you to talk for me. I can get those in need to hospitals, to homes, to work in emergency services, and I can do it all without being seen, but only this one night. Only when the blizzard will hide me."

He got off her and helped her to her feet. "You are serious."

"I am very serious. If the streets are impassable, women in labour can't get to hospital, folks having heart attacks and emergency services people need to get to a place where they can do some good."

"How will you find them?"

She rubbed her head. "I can hear them. I can hear them all. I need to help them, and I need you to help me."

He sighed. "Let me wash up and get some clothing. If we are dressing as the spirits of winter, I need to get into something more appropriate than a tux."

"You do that. Where is the bathroom? I feel a little sticky." She wrinkled her nose.

He moved and swept her into his arms, and he carried her up the stairs to his bedroom and the ensuite bath. A dampened cloth took the semen and spots of blood from between her thighs.

She sat on the edge of his bed and waited, grinning as he came out in a white tunic, blue hood, black leggings and boots. "Oh, perfect."

"I am ready if you are. Do you wish to leave from the roof or the front door?"

"Oh, the roof. There is nothing like a flying takeoff."

The voices in her mind were wild, but she had heard them before. She would get to them all, or at least as many as she could while the storm raged.

Cwen was unable to speak, but she carried Tyr to one stranded car after another. They attended accidents, women in labour, heart attack victims, brought stunned hospital workers in to where they could relieve those who had already been on duty too long.

Cwen ran all night and into the morning until the whipping winds eased up. With the blizzard clearing, she ran back to Tyr's home and the rooftop from which she had first taken off.

Tyr dismounted, and she changed back into human form, walking through the doorway with a swing in her step.

"Aren't you exhausted?"

"One night in a blizzard is nothing. I am used to a bit more of a workout, and it is usually under severely urgent circumstances. This was a light jog." She smiled and swayed.

"You are tired."

"Of course I am tired. I have just enough time to get a full day's sleep before I have to head home."

"You will sleep for a day?"

"Yeah, sorry. I will be up tomorrow morning and ready to head home shortly after."

"That is early."

"There is nothing else for me to do here."

Tyr wrapped his arms around her. "Stay with me until the twenty-third. I promise to make it worth your while. There is a lot in the human world that you haven't seen."

She chuckled. "This city is locked in snow. Nothing will be open before it is time to leave."

"In that case, we can spend the time in bed, watching movies and cuddling. Either way, it is not something you have had access to at home."

She yawned. "Okay. You know the deadline as much as I do."

"I do, and I know you would stomp me into goo if I made you miss it. Relax and rest. You have earned it."

She entered his bedroom and crawled into his bed, tucking herself between the sheets. "We leave on the twenty-third."

"Guaranteed, now sleep, Cupid. You had a helluva night."

As she prepared to leave, Cupid couldn't stop grinning. All those people that she had retrieved and helped were talking about being rescued by one of the reindeer and an elf. It was sending people into a frenzy of donating to holiday charities and soup kitchens.

Cupid removed her snowflake, and she returned it to the box. Tyr put it with all the other stuff she was bringing back, including a selection of cookbooks. If he was going to ride, he was going to carry cargo.

She kissed him one last time. "Okay, see you at the workshop."

He kissed her back. "Things are going to change, Cupid. If they don't, I will sneak into the archive and we can run away for another year."

"I will hold you to that. I have always wanted to see Antarctica."

"I have heard that they don't want tourists. They leave foot prints in the ancient moss."

She grinned. "Who says that I will land?"

She settled her collar around her neck and shifted into her

four-hoofed form. It was time for the flight home.

Her Christmas spirit was back and actually at an all-time high. It might just have something to do with the rider settling on her back, or it might have to do with interacting with humans. She had an entire year to analyze why. For now, it was time to take to the skies.

Prologue to Bells and Chains

Donder finished her sprint around the archive, and she took one final look at her room. It was perfect and precise. Just what she always strived for.

Ru sauntered up, wearing her customary uniform of dark-brown leather tunic and trousers. It was definitely a look.

"Are you ready, Doni?"

Donder nodded. "I am. Are you? After Blitz leaves, you are going to have to deal with the fallout."

"I will be fine. There isn't anything that can be done to me. He needs at least one of us for the sleigh. Are you ready to hand over your collar?"

"I am." Donder quickly unbuckled it, and Ru strapped it to her arm. Ru winced and fastened the buckle.

Donder asked, "Are you all right?"

"I am. The weight of it is getting heavy. That much power focused on me is a little hard to bear. At least I only have Blitz to send off. I can manage that."

Ru fished the box out of her pocket. "This will hide you from casual searching. Stick to the name you selected and keep it in your mind. Do you know what you want to do?"

Donder grinned. "I want to plan parties and decorate for the holidays. Doniyka Derger will be enjoying herself this holiday season."

Ru chuckled and hugged her. "Have fun, watch the humans and find out what makes the holiday special for them."

"Why?"

"Because you know what makes it special to you. You have to find things that remind you of why folk still believe in magic."

Doni put the snowflake above her navel and took a deep breath. "Take care, Ru. Here I go."

A blur of snow and magic swept her across the world and dropped her squarely into Doniyka Derger.

Bells and Chains

"Doni, can you come in here, please?"

Doni looked up at her co-worker and winced. "Uh-oh, he said please."

Lisa nodded. "It bodes ill."

"Very ill."

Doni got up and took her notepad and files with her. "Yes, Jake?"

Jake Lerot had a blush on his cheeks. "I have a tremendous favour to ask of you."

Doni took a seat and smiled brightly. "What do you need and what kind of bonus is in it for me?"

He wrinkled his nose. "Won't you just help me because it is the holidays?"

"Nope."

He grinned. "That is what I thought you would say. This job pays double, has a non-disclosure agreement and successful completion has a thousand-dollar bonus. You have to start this afternoon."

"Non-disclosure?"

"Yup. All I know about them is that this is extremely sensitive and there is some urgency. They are planning a Christmas party and can't find a decorator to come in and work with them. We are their last resort." Jake looked a little miffed at that.

Doni snorted. "Give me the address, oh, and slide over the contract."

Jake slumped with relief. "Thanks for agreeing to this. As far as I know, it is a private club and no cameras are allowed. You will have to leave your phone in your car."

"I will ask them to check it in when I get there. I am not going anywhere without it."

"I am sure if they have an issue, they will let you know."

She read the contract for the *High Bern Social Club* and signed the bottom. The budget was huge, the bonus would make a local charity very happy and so, Doni was content to do her utmost for the sake of the company.

"Can I get a contact number?"

Jake slid the card over and that is when Doni knew something was up.

"Jake, you said that you didn't know these folks."

"That's right."

"And yet, you not only had the non-disclosure contract on thick vellum, but you have the business card of Bern McVee, proprietor of the social club?"

Jake blushed again. "I might have been there once or twice."

"Well, whatever I see is going to be under client privilege. I will call this guy and be on my way. I will bring a notepad and my measuring tape. My laptop will remain here."

"I knew I could count on you."

Doni grinned. "And I knew I could make you pay. See you later."

She got up and went to her desk, dialling the number and waiting for the response.

"Hello."

"Hello, is this Bern McVee?"

"It is." The voice was a dark, slow rumble.

"This is Doni Derger at Cross Decorating. I have been assigned to your contract and would like to meet with you so that we can go from planning to execution with all possible speed."

"It sounds like a plan. When can you be here?"

"I can be on my way as soon as I get an address."

He laughed. "I suppose that would help. Sixty-four Artemis Drive. You can't miss it. The gate will be notified of your arrival."

"Thank you; see you soon."

Jake gave her the original contract after assuring her that he had a copy, and she took it with her to the client's business.

She assumed it was a business, but after driving for half an hour, humming along with Christmas carols on the radio, she pulled into the drive of a gated property.

The guard at the gate raised his brows as she lowered her window. "Miss Derger?"

She smiled. "Doni, please."

He gave her an amused smile. "Miss Derger, you are expected. Take the main drive and continue to the rotunda near the main entrance. Mr. McVee will meet you there."

The gate opened, and she drove through. Her window hummed as it closed, but she needn't have rushed it. The drive to the main house took five minutes.

She followed the directions and parked near the large doors of the long manor house. It was an impressive structure. Stables, a pool and other amenities had been visible during her drive, so this was a fairly extensive home.

As she emerged from her car and approached the house, a man came out wearing black from head to toe. His blood-red hair was tied neatly into a long ponytail that cascaded down his right shoulder and reached his hip. His eyes were icy grey. It was definitely a startling combination.

"Miss Derger? Welcome." He smiled and extended his hand. "I am Bern."

"Call me Doni, please." She gripped his hand and released it with a businesslike movement.

"Doni. Did Jake tell you about what we need?"

She shook her head. "No, I am afraid that he simply turned red and tried to look anywhere else. Oh, here is the non-disclosure agreement."

She got the folded parchment out of her bag, and he took it with a smile.

"Excellent. Please, come inside, and I will tell you what we are looking for."

"You do realize that it is very close to the holidays? This might not be practical."

"Those who frequent this club felt that a little holiday cheer was required. I listen to my clients, and so, I would like you to work your magic. Jake speaks very highly of you."

Inside the door of the manor were a young woman and a young man wearing masks, collars and skin-tight latex.

The young man helped Doni off with her coat, and she barely managed to grab her notebook and pencil before he whisked everything away.

The young woman knelt and dried her shoes with a towel.

Doni was getting the idea of why the manor needed the gag

order. It was a sex club.

Bern looked at her with his brows arched as if surprised by her lack of reaction.

"Please, come this way, and I will explain what we are looking for." He offered her his arm, and she took it, not wanting to stumble into the wrong room at the wrong time.

"Around the holidays, many folks experience an increase in stress, so they come here to work it off. We want you to inject a little holiday cheer into a few of the rooms."

"If the holidays are causing the stress, are you sure you want to bring the decorations in?"

"I am certain. We have a few voyeuristic areas where the exhibitionists enjoy themselves. There are also some conversation areas where I believe a little judicious decorating could be a boon."

They walked through the halls, and he led her to a room that had elaborate lettering proclaiming it the *Spanking Room*.

"This is one of the rooms we want decked out for Christmas." His smile was more of a smirk.

The reason he was so amused was that the room was in use. There was a young woman whipping an older man, and she was wearing a few strategic straps in lieu of clothing.

Doni shrugged, unclipped her tape measure from her belt and went to work.

She looked at the racks that held the whip assortments, the floggers that were lined on one wall and the stand of paddles. She needed to find ways to make them festive while remaining useful.

Doni finished her notes on the size of the room and the necessary supplies. She nodded at Bern, and he grinned, leading her out.

The man getting the carefully administered beating was getting closer to whatever goal he was focused on achieving, so she left him to his focus and followed Bern out the door.

She exhaled in relief and took Bern's arm once again. "You are testing me."

He grinned. "I am. I confess to thinking that you would be slightly more prudish. You are proving me wrong."

She shrugged. "I am considering this a challenge to make everything festive and yet functional. It is going to be a rush, and I am going to have to get in touch with some very alternative vendors, but I think I can get into the swing of this."

"Ah, swings. That leads us to one of our exhibitionist rooms. We have a set of swings and some ribbons."

"Lead on." Her mind was cycling, and she was frantically making mental lists that she couldn't confirm until measurements were taken.

The swing room was going to present a challenge, so she was going to have to make do with some non-flammable accessories and pillows.

"I am assuming that you want to have us remove the holiday effects at your request?"

"No, once we have them, I can have the subs take them and put them away. We have plenty of storage."

She nodded, and they continued on the tour. There was a chamber filled with shelves that had a countless number of sex toys. She was going to have to set up a special holiday section. She was pretty sure she could manage a few glitter vibrators.

Doni was constantly amazed at the memories that swam up when she needed them. The sheer variety of sexually related information surprised her. There was a reason that she wasn't freaked out by this; part of her mind considered it completely natural.

They went through the house, room by room.

Bern turned to her. "Now, we are heading out to the stables."

She flipped to a fresh page; half of her notebook was already gone to ideas and small lists.

"Excellent. Lead on."

One of the latex-clad subs brought them wraps. To her surprise, Bern settled her wrap around her before putting on his own. He offered his arm once again, and they headed out into the brisk wind and walked on the immaculately cleaned stone path.

"So, how long do the subs volunteer as subs?"

Bern smiled. "They are on holiday break from their studies. Everyone here is a consenting adult, vetted by our membership council, and they are all bound by behavioural and non-disclosure agreements. The subs will be on house-servant duty until the new year."

"So, everyone here simply agrees to indulge in the fantasy?"

"Precisely. The rules indicate that they can only play with others who want to indulge in the same fantasy. We have monitors who make sure that everyone in a scene is willing to participate."

"You are speaking as if you are often called upon to defend this club."

He chuckled. "Is it that obvious?"

"Only slightly. You are on private property, everyone here is consenting and you have panic buttons in all the rooms. What is not to understand?"

Bern paused and stared at her. "How did you know what those were?"

"It made sense to me. You just confirmed it." Her grin caught him off guard.

He rubbed the back of his neck. "The safety of our members is our biggest concern."

She held up a hand. "This is an alternative sex club. Please avoid the use of the term *members*."

His snort was loud enough to make the horses in the nearby paddock lift their heads.

"Fair enough. Well, consultant, are you willing to check out our stables and consider something more suitable for the upcoming season?"

"Lead the way. I am here to do a job."

He sighed. "Too bad. I would love to find out what lurks beneath that prim exterior."

She laughed. "Few, if any, would call me prim. I prefer controlled."

"Why?"

"Because sloppy emotions lead to bad decisions. If you keep everything controlled and planned, you can focus on what you want the outcome to be."

Bern smiled. "How long do your relationships last?"

"Just as long as I want them to." She wrinkled her nose. "So, longer than tinder, but I am not looking for anything long term."

"Have you played games before?" He opened the door to the stable, and several long horseboxes were obviously set up for human use.

"Not really. I am not into games." She looked around and

made more notes, stroking the soft nose of one of the horses that was still inside. The tag on his stall door indicated that his name was Titan, and he was in for a sprain.

She looked into his soft brown eye, and her beast spoke to his. He lifted his head and rubbed his cheek against hers.

"That is amazing. Titan hates everyone."

"He's a sweetie. He is just cranky because the folks that are usually on his back are trying to show off for their sex partners."

"Are you a horse whisperer as well as a decorator?"

She looked at Bern. "I prefer holiday designer, and no, I just listen."

Titan reached out and accepted a petting from Bern. His dark gaze focused on her as he smiled. "You listen very well."

"I have to. I have to know what a client wants, regardless of what they say. Sometimes the two things are in conflict, and I have to figure out what will make them happy, despite what they are asking me for."

Bern chuckled. "So, we are in the same business."

"In the abstract, yes." She smirked. She stepped away from Titan and made a few notes. "Now, a specific question. Is there an arbour or a forest where I can have something a little special set up?"

He blinked. "I think we have something like that. It is off the cleared pathway."

"I am good for a hike through the snow if you are."

He grinned. "Let's get one of the horses and go for a ride."

She stood with Titan as Bern strode away. The horse nudged her, asking why she wouldn't ride him.

"You are sore, Titan. If you get better, I promise to spend some time with you if I am allowed to." Doni chuckled as he nudged her shoulder. "Don't be jealous. I am just here to visit and do a job."

She heard his thoughts and emotions. He was delighted to have one of her kind next to him. So much better than boring humans.

"The humans have their part in the world. We get to be extraordinary. It makes them a background against which we shine."

She stroked Titan's nose and neck, scratching his jaw with her fingers. Finally, Bern returned with a large chestnut female.

He settled her in her stall and nodded to Doni. "Just a minute while I head to the tack room."

She spent time with Titan while her new buddy chatted with the lady who had returned to the stable.

The chestnut looked over at them, and she snorted at the unlikelihood that the woman who was stroking Titan's chin was a reindeer.

Doni grinned. Animals knew her the moment she touched them. When she was on the chestnut's back, the horse would know what she was.

Bern passed her with armloads of leather. The saddle had a number of small holes in it, and she had the sneaking suspicion that those holes had a purpose she didn't want to know about.

He put on the saddle blanket and moved around the horse with competence. The lady he was putting the saddle on remained steady and held her head high. She glanced over at Titan.

Doni caught what passed between them, and her knees buckled. Apparently, the chestnut was going to be carrying the elf lord and his woman. She was very proud of herself. Normally, Titan did that particular job.

Doni leaned against Titan and breathed magic into him. His pain receded, and he pranced in his stall.

"Easy, lad. You will have to get your clean bill of health from the vet. I just want you to have a pain-free day." She spoke softly and pressed her forehead to his.

He gently pressed back, and she smiled as she stroked his neck one last time.

"Good, Titan. Behave."

Bern looked toward her. "Are you ready to leave your lover?"

She winked at the horse and swayed toward Bern. "Yes, but you had better make the parting worth the while."

Her mind was startled at her sudden playful tone, but it was the exposure to beasts. They brought her impulses closer to the surface.

Bern led the horse out of the stable, and the moment they were outside, he paused the horse and offered her a hand up into the saddle.

She looked at his hand, and she bent her knee. He lifted her up with one hand, and she settled on the saddle.

"What is this lady's name?"

"Artemis. She and Titan are slated to bring a new foal into the world the next time she goes into heat. I believe they will be an excellent match."

He swung up behind her and settled against her, wrapping his arm around her waist.

She could feel the hard muscle of his thighs bracketing hers as he flexed and Artemis stepped forward.

Doni reached out and touched the horse's neck. She felt the jerk in response. She silently confirmed that Titan had not just been trying to impress her; Artemis did have a reindeer on her back.

"What did you do?" Bern's arm was around her waist as Artemis walked through the snow and headed into a forested area.

"I simply touched her neck. Perhaps my hands were cold."

"You have ridden before?"

She held in her snicker. "Once or twice. It really is like riding a bike that moves on its own and eats shrubs."

He chuckled, and Artemis moved with more speed.

Elf lord. What the hell was an elf doing running a sex club in the middle of nowhere? Doni kept her back ramrod straight as they trotted through a natural archway and into exactly what she had in mind.

The trees bent and arched together into a separate world that could very well hold elves as well as any number of magical creatures.

"How long have you been running this establishment?"

"It has been in my family in one way or another for generations."

She tried not to grin. For an elf, that could be one lifetime or even less.

They continued until they were in what Doni could only think of as a snow globe. The trees were heavy with snow and everything gleamed and glittered.

"I can definitely work with this." She chuckled, and the thick blanket of snow absorbed the sound.

"Well, I had a feeling that this would be your element." He tightened the arm he had wrapped around her waist and pulled her tightly against his torso.

Doni smiled. "Are you calling me an ice queen?"

"No, I just think that you have been around your share of snow." His breath was warm against her ear. "You have a plan for this location?"

"I think it can make a rather fun destination for your club participants. I have a plan."

"Excellent. Why don't we discuss what is plausible and what is not over some tea?"

"It sounds nice."

"Good." He turned the horse and Artemis took the hint from her rider and thundered back toward the stable at a slow gallop.

Bern held her, but as she couldn't brace herself in the stirrups, she was ground and slammed against him with every thudding step. Her butt had intimate knowledge of the dimensions of his groin and thighs by the time they stopped in the yard outside the stable.

He dismounted gracefully and held his arms up to her. She gave in to her impulse, and after she lifted her leg up and over Artemis's neck, she slid into his embrace. He set her on her feet and appeared to be in no hurry to release her.

Doni looked up at him and finally cleared her throat. "I think you need to take care of Artemis and then you did promise me tea?"

His grin was unmistakable as one of a male who had been slightly diverted, but would remember where he had left off.

Doni smirked and stepped away the moment he let her go.

Artemis tried to butt her with her head, but Doni merely gave her a light stroke on her neck and told her to be nice to Titan. The bit of magic that Doni had offered him would make something impressive in his offspring. Artemis wanted to be his next mate.

Doni followed Bern and the horse into the barn, and she paid court to Titan as he watched the master of the property take care of Artemis.

"I am guessing that the subs come by and brush them down?"

"And feed them. There are six household volunteers at any time. The stable is a rather choice assignment." He pulled the saddle and all the strapping from Artemis.

When he left the stall, Doni took his place and brushed the horse down, thanking her for her service with every stroke.

Artemis was gleaming when she finished and Bern was watching.

"I am thinking that you have been around horses more than just once or twice."

She shrugged and set the brush and curry comb back on their shelf. "You would probably be right."

She dusted her hands off and smiled, picking up her notepad again. "Back to the house?"

"Yes. We will go over some of the ideas that you have, and I will try to answer any questions that might have come up."

She nodded, checked her wrap and took his arm again. "Lead on."

Bern walked her back through the stable, she waved at Titan as she passed and, as she glanced back, Artemis was staring at her with wide eyes.

"What did you say to Artemis while you were grooming her?" Bern asked it quietly.

"Oh, we just had a girl-to-girl chat." She smiled.

"With a horse?"

"Oh, yes. Horses are exceptionally chatty. She is very proud of being your backup mount when Titan is off duty."

They were halfway to the manor when she said, "Artemis enjoys carrying the elf lord of the manor around."

Bern stumbled and then righted himself. "You are joking."

"No. I am very serious. Titan agreed. You are their elf lord, and they are proud to carry you."

He turned to look at her. "Do you believe in elves?"

She grinned. "I do. I also believe in magic and Santa and the joy of the season."

Bern raised his hand, as if to touch her face, and then, he seemed to recall that they were working together. "Right. Well, if you trust what comes from a horse's mouth, you have more faith in whispers and rumours than I do."

He turned, and they resumed their walk to the manor. The subs engaged in the same routine, taking their outerwear and cleaning their footwear.

"We will have tea in the morning room." Bern spoke absently, as if completely used to the human furniture that was bustling around them.

Bern led the way once again, and soon, she was being offered a chair and a view of the grounds through a huge bay window.

The horses were playing tag in a distant field, and the light was relentlessly making its way across the snow.

"This is quite the establishment." She smiled and looked out over the grounds. "You don't fence in the horses?"

"They are enclosed by the same wall that keeps out the curious."

"About that, is that a legal wall?"

He grinned. "The wall has been around a lot longer than the zoning. This club is necessary to many, and it is protected by those who value it."

"That makes sense. Well, I have a few questions for you."

He inclined his head. "Proceed."

The subs came in; one carried a bowl, a water pitcher and had folded linen over her arm. The male carried a wide tray and a plate tower covered with treats.

He moved with precision and set out the tea on the table, while the young woman put the bowl on the counter, tucked Doni's hands into the bowl and poured the warm water over her palms. Doni scrubbed the flecks of hay and bits of grime off her palms and out from under her nails. Another surge of water and she was clean. The sub blotted her hands and smiled shyly. "All done, Mistress."

The sub moved to Bern, and his hands were treated to the same ablutions.

When they were both clean and dry, the tea was set and the cups had been poured.

The subs retreated; the young woman removed the basin and pitcher and the young man knelt next to the door.

Doni lifted her tea and sipped. She smiled, and the young man's shoulders relaxed.

"So, he guessed correctly. Excellent. Alec has a skill for gauging the way a client would enjoy their tea."

"He guessed very well. I don't normally take milk in my tea, but it suits this blend." Doni took another small sip before eyeing the tower of sandwiches.

"So, Bern, am I allowed to bring in assistants to help me set up?"

He smiled and shook his head. "No, but I have access to up to eight subs that will do exactly what you want, when you want and how you want it. They can be here with an hour's notice for as long as you need."

"Will meals be arranged for them?"

"Of course, and for you as well."

"If I give you an equipment list, can you have it here?"

"We probably already do, but I can have it ready for you to work with. I just need an email and you can send me a list of what you need and where you want to work." He reached into a shirt pocket and provided her with a crisp and heavy business card. It had his name embossed, his email address and his direct line.

"Here is everything you need to get in touch with me. You already know where to find me."

She tucked the card into her notebook. "Are you interested in my plans so far?"

He nodded his head. "You have the budget and you know the timeline. The sooner that we get this started, the better. I can tell by the gleam in your eyes that there is something special planned, so I am giving you free rein to do so."

She picked a sandwich and nibbled at it. "I just have one additional request."

"Name it."

"When the subs work with me, can they wear something a bit more practical? If we put down any pine boughs, they will get all scratched up and rashy."

There was a slight exhalation from the corner where Alec was still kneeling.

"We can't have that. Yes, they will be in jeans and t-shirts while they are assisting you."

"Excellent. Well, in that case, I guess I have seen everything I need to see."

"Good. Sit back, relax and have something to eat. You are looking a little pale."

She grinned. "I always look pale. My team and I rarely get to hang out and tan."

She finished her sandwich and waited for her host to take a few of them.

He stared at her, she stared at him and finally he asked, "Aren't you going to have any more?"

"Not until you do. Eating the entire tower is a possibility, and I don't want to insult my host."

He smiled and took his plate, loading on a selection of sandwiches and pastries. "There. Have at it."

She grinned and took three small sandwiches and set them on her plate. Her bites became less delicate and more aggressive as she worked at filling her belly.

The tower was taken down as he asked her polite questions, and she answered every time her mouth was empty.

All too soon, the tray was empty and the last fleck of cream had been licked from her lips. She sipped at her third cup of tea and sighed happily. "Well, thank you very much for the food, Bern. I will be in touch in the morning with a tentative schedule."

He grinned. "You are going to eat and run?"

"Well, I will drive at a safe and moderate pace. Safety is key, after all." She winked.

Bern snorted and set down his cup. "That is our motto."

They got to their feet together and he led the way through the halls once again and she was soon being eased into her coat with her bag being held by the young sub who had first met her at the door.

"Your car is waiting. It was a pleasure meeting you, Doni. I look forward to seeing you soon and hearing your plans for this place."

She reached for his hand, and they gave the time-honoured contact for hello and goodbye. "It was nice meeting you as well. I will be in touch."

He nodded, and the sub handed her her bag. She slipped it over her shoulder and headed outside where cars were being discretely parked by valets in leather and one of them was standing next to her car.

Doni smiled as she came up next to her vehicle, and she said, "Thank you. I guess this beats the servants' exit."

The man opening her door grinned. "That requires a shift in wardrobe."

She still had a smile on her lips as she drove away from the manor. This was going to be a very fun client.

Bern looked at Artemis, and he shook his head. "You certainly were chatty today, weren't you?"

She lowered her head in apology.

"She can talk to you? Directly speak with you?"

Artemis lifted her head and nodded with excitement.

"Well, I can't fault you for that. Just remember, I am only here on Santa's sufferance. He has given me this place and time with the humans in exchange for watching them. I like it here."

Artemis shook her head again.

"Yes, I know I am supposed to seduce her into returning to the workshop, but now that I have met her, seen her, I am not sure that I want that for her."

Titan whinnied from the other stall.

"No, I can't just mount her and convince her that way. It doesn't work that way in the human world. You need agreement first and hormones second."

Titan blew and shook his head.

"Yes, I know it is foolish, but that isn't the way things are done. If she is playing human, she needs to be courted in the human way." He chuckled. "Fortunately, we are surrounded by humans with alternative mating dances. This is going to be fun."

The rest of the horses bobbed their heads in agreement. Bern's excitement was contagious; it was what made him an excellent host for the club.

Doni worked on her plans into the night. She drew up the schematic and started calls for the supplies she needed. Everything was given a rush order.

She kept Bern apprised of her progress, and three days after their first meeting, she was ready to return to the club in order to start the setup.

She called Bern, and he answered with a smile in his voice. "Doni, I have been waiting for your call."

"You have no idea how relieved I am. I have enough supplies here to complete eighty percent of the job, and the rest comes in tonight."

"If you wanted to get started, I can have the subs here in an hour."

"It can wait until morning, but if you can arrange to have them there at nine, we can get started and have you set up in less than forty-eight hours."

He sighed. "As you like. I will have eight of them ready to serve you with all of the ladders that you requested."

"Excellent. I will be there just before nine. See you tomorrow."

"See you tomorrow, Doni."

She hung up and smiled. She was looking forward to this assignment with as much enthusiasm as she had for the gingerbread village she had installed in a mall.

Doni wandered into Jake's office. "Have the bills started coming in?"

Jake had a high blush as was normal when they discussed the club. "Yeah. That was quick work."

"Yeah, I am a master of the google search. I will be out of the office tomorrow. I am going to be on site at the club for the next two days."

"Okay. I will make sure you still get paid." He winked and waved farewell.

"You do that. I am pretty sure that I could arrange something special and none too pleasant with the club, if anything goes wrong with my pay day. What I am planning is going to definitely bring the joy of the winter holidays to the club."

"I have to say, the folks at the club are excited. Nothing like this has ever been done before."

"Well, I hope to do the anticipation justice. With that in mind, I am heading out early to verify the supplies I am loading into the trailer as well as my car."

She gave him a wave and headed out, grabbing her bag and leaving the building, climbing into her car to drive to the climate-controlled storage unit that the company used for just this sort of thing.

Doni took out her clipboard and ran through her supplies, hoping that her bravado was earned. She took a lot of pride in her work, but these arrangements had to be suitable for a wide variety of clientele, all in the same facility. She had her work cut out for her.

It was a warm day for the depths of December. The eight

subs were waiting for her. They finished lining up as she pulled in front of the manor house, and she was laughing as she parked her car.

Doni got out of her vehicle and inclined her head. "Thanks for coming out, number One, Two, Three, Four, Five, Six, Seven and Eight."

They bobbed their heads in turn. Each had a huge number on the front of their shirts, and their open coats provided them with the protection that they needed in the balmy weather.

"In the back of my vehicle are the boxes that we need for the interior of the club. Please begin unpacking and moving the boxes inside into the staging area that Bern arranged."

They nodded, and moments later, the hatch of her SUV was open and a train of numbered subs were walking into the manor with one of the leather-bound subs manning the door.

What followed was a riot of giggles and her shouting numbers as they got into a rhythm. The subs were excited by what they were doing, and after five hours, the house was set up, and it was time to head into the snowy grotto.

Six and Eight ran to get the horses and sleigh to transport the supplies while the others packed the empty boxes into a stack and giggled wildly.

"Mistress?" Three asked shyly.

"Yes, Three?"

"Where did you find those glowing, glittery dildos?"

"I can get you the web address. I will have to check the invoice for that precise supplier." Doni smiled and made a note on her clipboard. "I will get it to you as soon as I am back to my computer. Would you like to give me the email address, or should I send the message through Bern?"

"Through Master Bern, please. It is a rule of the club." Three smiled.

"Not a problem. I am not here to get anyone in trouble."

"Thank you, Mistress. I think that I have someone who might appreciate one of those for Christmas."

"Not a problem. For the record, you guys are so efficient; I wish I could hire you for every job."

The gathering smiled and looked pleased with themselves.

She knew from their quiet conversations that they were all off university for the holidays. One was an accountant, another a med student, a sociology major and a psychology major. The other four were not as chatty.

Their group gathered outside and waited next to her car as the sleigh appeared, pulled by Artemis and another mare nearly as large as she was.

The sleigh pulled up next to the trailer, and the subs sprang into action. Ten minutes of stamping horses later, they clicked into action, and Doni guided them through the woods and into the grotto.

She shared her vision for the trees and the surrounding area, and as the sleigh returned to the manor for the ladders, she arranged the boxes under the trees where they would come to life.

The energy of the subs was amazing. They were excited by the work done in the manor, but now, they were going to make magic.

The dinner that was laid on for them at the manor was amazing.

They sat together in the kitchen and shared tales of near-death experiences on ladders and what they had created in the grotto. The subs were nearly out of their minds, wanting to share it with their masters and hating to have to wait for the reveal.

Bern came into the kitchen at long last, and the subs slipped from their chairs to their knees.

Doni was sipping a glass of lemonade, and she raised her brows. "Dressed for work?" He was wearing skin-tight leather that suited him very well.

Bern came to her and lifted her hand to his lips. "Yes. Yes, I am."

The leather should have made him look smaller, but the snug black covering the width of his chest made her feel tiny.

"Well, I am ready."

It was his turn to raise his brows and her turn to blush.

"I mean that the numbers and I got everything set up. The grotto is ready and the solar panels are set up. By sunset tonight, there should be enough of a glow to make the whole thing magical."

Doni had also caused a small snow flurry as they had ridden away on the sleigh. Their footprints and handprints would be obliterated by now. Even the marks of their snowball fight would be gone.

"I have a few things to attend to, but the rooms in the manor are gaining tremendous popularity. Where did you find those glittering dildos?"

She cleared her throat. "When I find the invoice, I will let you know. Three wanted that information as well, and I told her I would forward it to you."

"Excellent."

She smiled. "Now that my meal is done, I think I will be on my way."

"Please, wait here for half an hour. I will attend to the guests and return so that we can head to the wonderland you have crafted in the woods."

The subs grinned and kept their gazes on the floor.

"Bern, can you tell them to get up? They are missing dessert."

"Subs, rise and resume your meals."

The numbers got back up to their chairs and settled around the table again.

Doni smiled at Bern. "The clock is ticking. You have half an hour."

He leaned down and kissed her, slowly moving his mouth over hers in front of their very attentive audience. He pulled back and smiled. "Thirty minutes."

Doni blinked in surprise with her lips throbbing.

The subs grinned, and Five looked impressed. "He rarely makes time for anyone, and I have never seen him kiss someone before. You must have made an impression."

"I don't think so. I think he is just a little affectionate."

Eight shook his head. "Master Bern does not show affection in public. He is the host here; he does not show favouritism. If you have gained his attention, he has some emotional attachment to you."

Doni looked around at the earnest faces. "You all agree?"

Eight heads nodded.

"Wow. That was the only thing you have completely agreed on today."

Laughter rippled around the table.

Doni had really enjoyed her time with the subs. Two and

Four had only tried to manipulate her once before they realized it would just end up with them up a ladder or hanging from a ceiling to wind ribbon around the suspension harnesses.

When the half hour was up, she yawned and got to her feet. "Well, I am assuming that he was distracted elsewhere and I have to get to bed."

She grabbed her bag and clipboard and headed for the door. She was just about to open it when it swung toward her and Bern was standing there.

He blinked. "You were leaving?"

"Time is up and I don't wait."

"Good to know. Now, please, lead me to the stables."

His aura of command was unmistakable, but his putting her in the role of servant was odd. She scowled, but turned and headed for the back door.

There was no courtly moment here, and something in her rankled at the shift in him from knight to dom.

She stalked to the stables and opened the tack room. "I have gotten eight belled harnesses for those who like pony play. Reindeer antler gear is also available for those who feel whimsical."

He nodded and grabbed Titan's saddle from the named bench, ignoring the myriad attachments that were available for the leather and wood. "Come on then and let's see the rest of the magic that you have wrought."

She followed him to Titan's stall, and the huge beast frisked like a pony at the sight of her again.

"He hadn't seen a reindeer before you arrived. Just a moment while I saddle him."

Doni calmed him while Bern got him ready, and the moment his saddle and bridle were on, they headed for the door.

She cleared her throat. "How did you know?"

"I have been watching for your name in a myriad of combinations. The magic you have wrought is obvious. The horses just reinforced my opinion."

Bern boosted her onto Titan's back, and she settled in the saddle. He landed behind her once again, and they took off into the snow, toward the soft glow in the trees.

As they entered the shelter of the forest, he finally spoke. "We never discussed the horses calling me an elf."

"Elves exist in the world, as do many other things. It was not my concern."

"What if I want it to be your concern?"

"Then, you had better stop giving orders. I don't take well to folks who give me orders." She said it. She was riding with a dom, and she had no intention of hanging around after this contract was done. He hadn't given her a reason to.

"You don't like being told what to do?"

She twisted in his embrace. "Don't be silly. Of course not. If I accept that you aren't human, you can accept that I am not human and I have to act as an obedient part of a process once a year. That is not something I particularly enjoy, but I do it."

"You want to be in charge?"

"No, I want to be an equal. It is shocking, but there it is. Not less than, not more than, but equal." She shrugged.

She turned to face forward, and they entered the beginning of the grotto.

Bern gasped.

Soft lights hung from the trees, powered by the solar panels and battery packs she had hidden deeper in the forest. White leather was everywhere in the trees, as were more of the glittering dildos. It had seemed a little silly, but this was a pervy paradise for those who enjoyed the outdoors. The padded benches were assembled and tucked into the hollows between and under the trees. It was an ideal setting for a snowy orgy or just a cathedral of winter magic for two.

"This is amazing. It is all functional?"

"Of course. I mean, steps will have to be taken not to give someone hypothermia with the dildos. If they are frozen, things could get a little uncomfortable, but there is an insulated chamber with everything that you see on the trees and a discard box underneath for the subs to check on at the end of the evening. They know how it works."

"How does a reindeer know so much about this?"

She shrugged. "I did my research. Some of my sisters wanted sex and nothing else. Others wanted to try to blend in with the humans. I wanted to experience the trappings of Christmas in all their variety. I ended up here."

His hand around her waist tightened. "You are not interested in sex?"

"It was not my sole reason for coming out here. Yes, going

Bells and Chains

into heat is annoying with eight of your closest friends doing it at the same time. But it was the feeling of missing out on something that the humans took for granted. That is what left a hole in my soul." She sighed.

Titan sighed with her.

"Will you return to the workshop?" His voice was low and in her ear.

"Of course. I am not going to punish the world or my team simply because the current rules are not fair. I will go back on the twenty-third, and we will run through the skies on Christmas Eve." She shrugged. "Just like we always do."

The hand on her waist moved lower, pressing between her thighs with a slow rhythm. "Would you stay with me?"

She shook her head. "No. I have to go back. It is a calling as much as a duty."

He kissed her neck. "I can make it worth your while."

"You have other play things. Human ones. I am sure you would tire of just plain old me in no time. I don't want to be tied up, spanked or tortured for your entertainment."

She shivered as his mouth moved across her skin and he stroked the bob of her hair out of the way before he continued his exploration.

"What about what you want? What do you want from a lover?"

The rhythm of his hand over her sex and the pulsing heat that the touch was waking was distracting, but she managed to whisper, "I just want to touch and be touched and wake with them in my arms. Nothing exotic, just plain vanilla as the vernacular has it."

He leaned back, put his hands on her waist and lifted her high, turning her before setting her down with her thighs over his. "What makes you think that I can't give that to you?"

She chuckled and gripped his shoulders. His intense gaze was a little hard to meet. "I think you could, but I think you won't. Elves bore easily from what I understand. I don't want to be a centuries-long regret for you."

His dark-brown gaze bored into hers. "You believe what you are saying."

"I definitely do."

"Then, what if I told you that after catering to the whims of those who were neither naughty nor nice, I wanted something nice in my life, what would you do?"

She blinked. "Um, I have no idea. I wasn't thinking beyond what you obviously represent. I can't turn my preferences off and on. This is me, and I have never been after anything fancy."

He chuckled. "I have never been called fancy before."

Doni had a dozen other things to call him, but he leaned in to kiss her before she could say them.

As he kissed her, a light snow began to fall. Huge, wide flakes came down and landed on their skin and lashes.

Bern lifted his head. "What is this?"

She blushed. "Weather magic. It is my thing. Donder is the reindeer who controls the weather."

"I thought the name was Donner?" He frowned.

"The old name is Donder. Thunder. All of us have our own speciality, and mine is weather. I pull back the storms so that we can fly quickly." She blushed.

"So, you are definitely needed for the team." He looked a little disappointed.

"We all are. That is why we would not skip out on our one day. Santa must have panicked when he called in the elves to send us home."

"Probably. We weren't sent out to send you home; we were sent out to bring you home. The magic that took you from the workshop put you near our long-term assignments. I don't think that was an accident."

Titan was slowly turning under pressure from Bern's thighs.

"I don't think it was an accident either, but I am not sure of the purpose."

He pulled her against him, and Titan surged forward. Her hips slammed against his, and each thundering step of the horse under her drove her against him. Her orgasm didn't creep up on her. Halfway to the stables, she shuddered and clutched at Bern, her body twitching and shivering in the grips of a release she had not anticipated.

Bern kissed her as the aftershocks gripped her and Titan pranced proudly. She wanted to smack the horse for what he had done; the rhythm to his steps had had a definite purpose.

When they reached the barn, one of the subs took Titan, and Bern swept Doni into his arms.

"I can walk perfectly well." Her bag smacked against her side. She had forgotten she had it on.

"I know, and yet, I am enjoying this. You may want to be an equal, but that means you will also have to give in to the desires of your partner."

She scowled. To her surprise, he didn't head for the common areas of the house; instead, he moved into a wing that had been untouched by the decorations and the club in general. It was what the manor house actually seemed to be on the exterior.

Antiques, portraits, couches, even porcelain flower arrangements were all around. He walked her past all of those and into his bedroom.

She smiled. There were no chains, no leather—other than what he was wearing—and no weird assortment of toys. It was a simple bedroom, and she enjoyed the look of it.

He set her on her feet and removed her bag, putting it to one side. Her sweater went next and then the long-sleeved shirt she had been wearing under it.

She was methodically stripped until she was shivering in nothing but her skin and the silvery snowflake tattoo.

He stroked the tattoo, and he obviously felt the magic under the marking. The leather he wore creaked as he admired her.

Reindeer didn't get cold, so the shivering her body was doing had to do with him staring at her. It was a new sensation, to be admired for what she looked like. Normally when folks saw her, she was nine feet tall and pulling a sleigh. The man who had written about eight tiny reindeer had been guessing. He saw what he wanted to see.

Bern worked the leather off, undoing clasps and fasteners that defied description. His skin was a pale gold, all even, and she had to smirk at that. Elves didn't tan. They were the colour they were born to.

His erection was straight, thick and long. The hair that crowned it was the same dark scarlet as the long mane that cascaded down his back.

She pressed a hand to his chest. "Show me what you really look like. Your glamour is good, but I can see bits of you peeking out now and then."

"Only if you engage in that equality that you want so badly."

"You'll show me yours if I show you mine, as the humans

say?" she smirked.

"Exactly."

Doni took a deep breath and let her horns out, let her skin glow and embraced the change in her ears and eyes.

His skin took on a transparent gleam, his hair rippled and glittered like rubies, and his eyes were deep onyx in a golden translucent ocean. It was as if he were made of gems.

His skin was hot, and she looked up at him as he was staring down at her in wonder. He stroked her cheek, and she fought the urge to close her eyes and lean into him.

It seemed like they spent hours just indulging in small caresses, light touches and kisses that were the whisper of a moment. He turned her in front of a mirror and wrapped her in his arms, their contrasting flesh was a stimulation all its own.

He kissed her shoulder, nibbled at her neck and the entire time he caressed her breasts and belly with one hand while the other searched between her thighs.

Doni watched as she licked her lips, her lids drooped and she tilted her head back. It was like watching someone else as her breath came faster, and she moaned when another orgasm swept through her. In slow motion, she watched her skin flush, her knees buckle, and Bern held her against him while she shook.

He moved swiftly and turned her to face him, lifting her high in his arms before lowering her, kissing his way up her belly until she was able to wrap her legs around him.

His cock nudged at her, and she shifted her hips, rocking and twisting until he was inside her. She kissed him wildly and jerked her hips toward him, impaling herself with slow motions.

His kiss matched hers, and she felt him grip her horns to hold her head. Her thighs and his cock were holding her body weight. He really was as hard as he looked.

Bern shifted and pressed her against the wall so he could free up his hands and pin hers. He rocked his hips into her hard and fast. The first slow seduction had been for her; this one was for him.

She clenched her hands against his as he made feral sounds and slammed into her. She could have broken his fingers, but she reined herself in and fought the rise of pleasure in her own body.

The sharp twinges of sensation shook her control. The cool walls gave a counterpoint to the heat of Bern's body, but there was no stopping the spiral of enjoyment that swam upward and pulled her under.

Bern froze against her, his muscles quivering. His voice whispered softly. "Open your eyes, Doni."

She opened her eyes, and he started to move into her in short, hard motions. His eyes glowed and a low, groaning growl broke free of his lips while he held himself inside her.

Doni watched the fire and magic break free of him and swirl around her. The power seared her lungs and settled inside her.

The fire in his gaze slowly faded, and he lowered her to the floor, holding her tight. "That was incredible. I forgot to use protection."

She chuckled and carefully pressed her forehead against his chest. "Don't worry. I am impervious to human disease, and I will not go into heat for another ten months."

He smiled. "Good to know, but I am just shocked that I missed out on what is a rule in this house."

She chuckled. "Can I take my horns down now?"

Bern nuzzled her cheek. "I like them, but I believe that you would be more comfortable blending in for now."

Doni gave him a quick kiss and resumed her human appearance. He sighed and did the same.

She stroked his cheek. "I like you in any seeming."

He grinned. "I agree. You have an elegant charm with or without the horns. However, the horns are a turn on."

She had the feeling back in her legs and looked over at her clothing. "I suppose it is time for me to be on the road."

"Stay."

She blinked. "What?"

"Stay with me. You have executed your contract, and there is no chance for someone else to need you this season. I know Titan would enjoy spending more time with you. Stay."

Doni stared at him and reiterated. "You don't need to keep me in your sights. I am going back to the workshop on the twenty-third."

He seemed surprised. "You are?"

"Of course. We would never jeopardize Christmas. All of us just wanted to go out into the human world and see the people who need us."

"Need you?"

"Need the magic of Christmas. Even those who don't celebrate it need a little magic now and then. We just had no idea why they needed it. From our perspective, Santa and Ru recruited us across time, and now, we are a team, but it has been so long since we were in the human world, the emotions and feelings that they have are all worn off. We don't feel human anymore, so we were suffering from apathy. Oh, and sexual frustration."

He grinned. "I can help with that. I don't even need to put your collar on for that purpose."

"You have my collar?" She raised her brows.

"Of course. I had to find a way to connect with you. It is in my bedside table."

"Next to the condoms?" She couldn't fight her grin.

"And the lube." Bern smacked her butt.

She wobbled over to the bedside table, and she opened the top drawer. There was her collar with the word *Donder* emblazoned in the bronze. When she shifted with it on, it transformed into a wide chest piece that let her be rigged into the harness with the team.

The team. Eight. She turned slowly to him. "That is why the eight subs. You do know that there are nine reindeer, right?"

"I do, but I thought it would be fun for you to lead your own team." He grinned and reached into the drawer to pull out the collar. "Now, we have plenty of women here with collars, but I think that this will look lovely on you."

"Nope. Not until the twenty-third. That is the means by which I am harnessed into the team. I want to keep my freedom as long as I can. That means no collars."

"Too bad; I think you would be fetching in one." He smiled.

"Don't even think about it. I don't need a safe word." She walked over to where there was a discreet rack with crops and paddles. She took one of the paddles in one hand and turned toward him. "Now, I know you elves are strong, but you are not this strong."

She clenched her hand and the paddle snapped into splinters.

Bern looked from her hand to the splinters and back to her

breasts. "You are quite strong."

"Think about what I do on Christmas Eve. You have to be strong for that. Also, the more folks that believe in the reindeer, the stronger we get."

"So, you could have stopped me at any time?" His voice got low, and he approached her with a predatory gait.

"Yes. If I had wanted to, I would have stopped you."

"I must say, that makes this a lot more fun." He rushed her; she leaped over him and landed on the other side of him, grateful for the high ceilings.

She laughed and dodged again as he lunged, but this time, he caught her and pulled her into his embrace.

They wrestled lightly for a few minutes before she let him bend her over the edge of the bed and he was thrusting into her. It seemed she was going to sleep over after all.

The black robe left her shoulders bare and had a wide sash. She sat with Bern as he read the paper in silk pajama bottoms and nothing else. Cara, one of the household subs, was serving them breakfast and kept looking at Doni with awe.

Bern lifted her hand and pressed a kiss to it. "If you don't want her staring at you, we can tell her to stop."

Doni chuckled. "I don't mind. I just can't remember where my bag is."

"Cara will find it. Are you enjoying your eggs benedict?"

"I am. I am always too lazy to make it myself at home. This is excellent." She finished tearing apart one of the English muffins with her knife and fork.

"I have never been a fan of hollandaise sauce." He smirked.

She blushed. He had no restrictions on a number of other substances. They had spent a very long and educational night. She was stronger than he was, but he was sturdier than she was. It was an interesting contrast.

"So, when I travel for business over the holidays, will you accompany me?" Bern asked it with a serious expression on his lovely face.

"Of course. You know we have a destination in common."

Bern grinned. "Good, I will go and make my report, you can have your business trip and, when you are recovered, we will return here."

She blinked. "Is that an option?"

He gave her a slow smile. "It is if you want it to be. I travel for a few weeks a year, and I would love to have you here when I am home."

Doni chuckled. "I will have to let Jake know that I won't be back to the office. He can't get out of paying me. I worked hard on this place."

"You did. A few of the guests are not fans, but the vast majority only spent time in the holiday rooms last night."

She blinked. "When did you learn that?"

He put down his newspaper and held up a tablet. He had been reading the new tech behind the old tech for their whole breakfast. "Guests are asked to provide feedback to curtail issues before they become annoying."

"Fabulous. Can I see?" She bit her lip and batted her lashes at him.

He sighed and handed the screen over. She danced her fingers over the screen and looked at everything from a floor plan to the supply levels in each room. Right now, the subs were cleaning up after the party from the night before.

She flicked her fingers and grinned at the numbers. Four couples of varying genders had used the grotto, and they had left high ratings for the alternative environment.

"It seems you have a future in dungeon interior design." Bern grinned and took the tablet back.

Doni made a face and finished her breakfast. Cara brought her bag, and Doni fished out her phone. A memo to Jake let him know that she wasn't going back to the office. He already knew that she was going to be with family for the holidays. He didn't need to know where she was in the meantime.

Doni kept to the private part of the house and the stables during her time at the club. When the twenty-third dawned, she walked into the field outside the stables where the horses were released to enjoy the moment.

She warned them to return to their stalls when she was gone, and they all agreed. She was going to come back, and there would be distinct lack of apples for anyone who had escaped or disobeyed.

Bern cleared his throat and held out her collar. "Are you

ready?"

"I am. Are you sure of how you need to get on top of me?"

"A glass of wine and a compliment for your design sense." He winked.

"Funny stuff. Hold the horns and don't let go. I could probably catch you, but the horns might do some damage in the process."

She took the collar and put it around her neck. With a sigh, she peeled off the snowflake that made the humans believe she belonged with them. When she returned, she would use it again.

The robe was draped over Titan's back, and he nuzzled her affectionately.

"I think he is in love with you."

"No, I am just his herd master." She gave Bern one last kiss. "Okay, here we go."

She shifted into her beast form, and Bern whistled softly. "Okay, yes, you are their master."

She jerked her head, and he grabbed her horn so she could haul him up to help him mount. When he was on her back, she touched muzzles with the horses before thundering across the snow with her herd and taking flight.

The workshop awaited, but she looked down at the manor and thought of all the things she could learn there. There was always next year, and now, she was willing to fight for her freedom. There would be no sneaking off in the night. She would just go. She had the tools, she had somewhere to be and she wanted a life that was hers alone. That wasn't something she could have at the workshop.

A life was something that Bern was offering her, and she was going to take him up on that offer.

Prologue to Licking His Cane

Blitzen wrapped her arms around herself and looked to Ru. "I have never been alone." Blitzen frowned and shivered.

"Are you sure you want to do this? I think that the others can have the desired effect." Ru looked concerned.

"No. I think that I will stick with the original plan. It won't hurt me to be out in the world for a while, and you know I do love all things mechanical. It will be good for me. I think."

Ru put her hand on Blitzen's shoulder. "I will miss you."

"I will be home soon. The sooner that I leave, the sooner I will be on my way back here."

Ru chuckled. "You can leave and enjoy yourself. There is no harm in it."

"I have never really given enjoyment a try."

Ru rolled her eyes. "I know. You started life as a Quaker, and the simple life has never really left you."

"You know how terrifying this place was when I first arrived."

Ru stroked her cheek. "I remember, but this time, the magic is giving you the knowledge that you need. You won't be pulled out of your time again. If you trust me that this is for the best, I promise you won't regret it."

Blitzen nodded and took her folded envelope from her pocket. "Here is the letter. I hope it does some good."

Ru took it and tucked it into her pocket. "It will. I have a plan for it."

Blitzen smiled with amusement at the grim grin that Ru was giving her. "Santa is not going to like it, is he?"

"Men rarely like to be slapped in the face with the obvious."

"Will it slap him?"

"It is going to knock him backward. Now, if you are ready?"

"I am ready."

Ru unfastened Blitzen's collar, and the air rushed in and caressed her neck for the first time in centuries. There was a moment of panic, and then, Ru handed her the snowflake. Without hesitation, Blitzen hugged her friend and then pressed the snowflake to her naked neck.

Moments later, a swirl of snow and magic swept her up and Belinda Litzen prepared to start her day.

Licking His Cane

Belinda worked inside the mechanism of the cookie-stamping machine while the shop owner looked anxiously at her from his office window.

Calibre Cookies had suffered a failure of their most popular shortbread presses, and Belinda had been called in to fix it.

She moved the heavy plates around with ease, knowing what the whole machine was supposed to look like when it functioned properly.

The snowflake magic of an entire year was working inside her to give her the knowledge she needed to fix industrial baking equipment, and she had really enjoyed being around the scents of the holidays, even if it was on a massive scale.

While dangling in the inner workings of the machine, she found what had set it off. Someone had forked the gears. A thick and heavy steel fork that had been wedged into the rotors. The angle she found it at precluded it being an accidental insertion. She pulled it out and tucked it in her tool belt.

The gears, belts and plates went back into place in under an hour. The evening repairs that she engaged in were definitely in need in this town. The ability to call for repairs in the few hours when there wasn't anyone manning the machines was a boon. She was the only one working off contract at night.

When the machine was ready and the housing was back on, she walked over to the power centre and removed her lockout. She powered up the entire line and started the press. The test batch of dough dumped, was run through the sheeter and, from there, it wedged itself into the mold.

From the mold, it proceeded down to the baking pans until it was ready for the oven. The test batch made six pans with a nice, clear stamp of holiday motifs. The shop owner came out and ran to the line, exhaling a deep sigh of relief at the images on the line.

"I don't know how you did that, but thank you."

"I will email you the invoice. Oh, and this was what caused the problem." She pulled the mangled fork out of her pocket. "I would say you have a morale problem or someone wanted to slow you down."

Harold Derkeson blinked down at the fork in her hand.

Belinda hit the power unit for the cookie press, and she turned the whole thing off. She passed him the fork and continued with the inevitable.

"Well, it is working now, so I will just get my things and get on to my next call." She nodded and gathered her wrenches.

She took out her phone, and she thumbed the screen until the invoice was sent. Belinda smiled brightly. "I arrived quickly, I would appreciate payment quickly."

"Yes. Yes, of course." He looked down at the fork, and he was obviously still stunned.

She grabbed her kit and headed out the back door. It was always painful to see that moment of realization when they suspected that the machines had been killed on purpose.

Every time she had fixed a unit in the last few weeks, she had enjoyed the power of bringing something thought dead back to life.

The energy of Christmas was hope to some, but since she had become embedded in it, she appreciated the power to shift through the darkest days and come out on the other side. It was survival. She wasn't able to extend that to humans, but she could definitely show it to machines. Most of the equipment was far older than the workers who loaded it, and its silent ability to fill the hearts and minds of those who consumed their products with memories from generations past was definitely something worth preserving.

Sweet Repairs was her contribution to preserving that bit of the holidays for the next few generations. Bel felt like she was finally doing something *for* Christmases future instead of just on Christmas Eve.

She started up her vehicle and drove the panel truck off into the false dawn.

Five hours of sleep was not enough, but her phone woke her

with an annoying rendition of *Jingle Bells.*

She cleared her throat and answered with a cheery chirp. "Sweet Repairs. How can I help you?"

"Hello; you have been recommended to me by one of the local bakeries. I have a problem with one of my candy rollers, and we need it back online as quickly as possible."

"Where are you?"

"Rex's Candies on Fourth and Main."

"See you in an hour."

"Thank you. I am Rex by the way."

"Bel. I will be on my way shortly."

She hung up, but she heard him say something in a surprised tone. She would have to ask him about it when she met him. His tone was something she could listen to forever. It rang through the phone like bells in the night.

She ran her hands over her face and smacked her romantic sensibilities. She had a job to do.

The shower wasn't strictly necessary as she had one after she came home, but it helped clear the cobwebs.

She braided her hair tightly against her skull and tucked it under before getting dressed. Her boiler suit was blindingly white, as suited someone working with food. She could see the smallest speck of anything inappropriate on her clothing for her clients.

She listened to the pop of the toaster and rescued the bagel from purgatory before slathering it with cream cheese. It was white and would not show as she left her small apartment near her workshop and got into her truck.

The winter air kissed her skin and tickled the snowflake on her neck. It suited her work with machines to have a silvery snowflake on her skin, visible to all. Most folks mistook it for a gear.

She followed the directions of her GPS and lucked into a parking spot in front of Rex's Candies. It was more than luck to find a spot on this bustling street, and part of her smirked as she settled into place.

She slung her toolkit over one shoulder and forged her way into the shop. Normally, she would have gone around the back, but delivery trucks blocked the lane.

Laughter filled the space, and it was nice to hear it in a place where folks were usually fighting for the last gingerbread house.

It was near eleven and the customers were circulating and moving toward the counter in an orderly manner.

Bel shifted toward one of the staff members, and she waved to get her attention.

The woman looked at her, nodded and let out a sharp whistle. "Rex, here boy!"

A wave of anticipation ran through the room, and out of the back strode a man wearing a flour-spattered black shirt and jeans that were officially what Bel wanted to see on him every Christmas.

Reluctantly, she dragged her gaze up to the sleet-grey eyes that were smiling as he brushed a streak of flour away from his forehead. The silver and black hair was braided back the same way that Bel's was.

He followed the gesture from the woman at the counter to Bel. "May I help you?"

"Sweet Repairs, at your service." Bel inclined her head.

He looked startled and relieved. "Thank goodness you showed up. We ran out of candy canes last night, and then, the machine sheered one of the pins on the rollers."

She looked around at the audience that was smiling foolishly at Rex. "Um, lead the way?"

He nodded and turned. She followed the defined vee of his back and hips through the back of the shop, over the glossy floor and to a cordoned-off area draped with plastic in a weird kind of clean room setup.

"Do you always make candy and bake in the same shop?"

Rex shook his head. "No, we subcontract the gingerbread out to a local bakery, but they had a heat problem in their ovens, and we needed to get the components together for our own orders. Our oven is just fine for small batches, but I have been working on this for hours. We can't do any chocolate in here because it is too hot right now, and I don't want to fall behind any more than we already are."

"Well, I will take a look at the wounded roller and see what I can do." She smiled.

He led her through a prudent three layers of plastic. The layers kept the flour from contaminating the candy roller.

Bel took a look at the machine and nearly wept. It was an antique in beautiful shape with the exception of the dangling roller. "Oh, my darling. Where have you been all my life?"

Rex chuckled. "You seem to have a connection with the roller. I will just leave you two alone."

She nodded and ran her hand over the roller, waiting until Rex had left her alone with it to heave it out of its setting and put it on the worktable. It was natural wear that brought it to this sad state, and when she pulled the remains of the pin free of the machine, she realized she had forgotten to lock it out.

"Damn it!" She quickly set everything aside and found the cable that connected it to the power in the bench, and she put a locking cap on the plug, just to be sure no one tried to plug it in.

It was a foolish mistake, and it could have cost her her hand.

With everything back to her normally safe arrangements, she took a look at the roller and assessed what was needed to make it roll again.

The pin was fused in the roller, and it was going to take welding to get in back into a workable position. To do that, she was going to have to haul it outside.

Now, there were two ways that she could get the roller out of the building. She could carry it herself, or she could ask for help.

It would be unlikely that a human woman could carry the weight, so she would have to ask for help.

She took the rod fragment and slipped it into her pocket, making her way through the curtains to find Rex again. He was her best option.

"Excuse me, Rex?"

He was rolling out gingerbread dough on a sheeter. "Yes? I am sorry. What was your name?"

"Bel. I was wondering if you would be able to help me get the roller to my truck. I have a welding kit in there, and I can manage the repairs that are needed."

"Sure, Bel. Just give me a moment to get these into the oven."

He wielded a large knife and expertly cut out the front, back and sides of a gingerbread house, as well as a wide base. He slid them onto a pan without warping them and tucked a few gingerbread men and women onto the baking sheet. When it was all in the small industrial oven, he turned with a smile. "Lead on."

Bel snickered. "My turn."

She led the way back and pointed to the roller. "You lift, I lead."

Watching his biceps bulge as he scooped the roller into his arms was hypnotic, but he was straining so she held the plastic out of his way and then whisked around him to clear a path and hold the door to the shop open. Again, she moved around him, and she opened her truck workshop door, putting down a tarp to keep the roller clean.

"Leave it here. I have chains and tackle to hold it where I want." Bel smiled. "I promise to have it back as soon as I can."

Rex nodded. "Will you call me when it is time to get it back in position?"

"Sure. If any space opens up in the back, can you let me know so I can stop hogging this parking spot? It makes me feel like I am stealing your client space."

"I will. I will also come by in a few hours with a snack and some hot cocoa."

He grinned, and she turned on the light before rolling down the door.

She picked up the heavy cylinder and set it on her workbench, clamping it down carefully so as not to damage it.

"Now, my poor, worn darling, what can I do to make you feel better?"

She tapped out the broken pin with the utmost care. Bel was going to work on this unit with the focus it deserved.

With the roller free of its broken part, she looked through her available equipment and found the rod she needed. Half an inch thick and three feet long, the rod slid into place, and she checked it for movement. It moved reluctantly and that is what she wanted before she started welding. A few hard taps and it was in place. The protruding ends were perfect. Time to tack them into place.

She was about to use lightning from her fingertips to weld the metal when there was a knock at the rear door. She dissipated the charge between her fingers and her thumb and shook her hand. With a smooth move, she opened the door. Rex stood there with a grin and a covered tray.

"You have been banging away in here for hours. As promised, I have brought you a snack." He stepped up into her workshop and looked around. "Wow. You are geared for anything in here."

She took the tray from him and set it next to the roller on her workbench. She was about to reach for the napkin when he moved around her and whisked it away.

Fresh shortbread was arranged in a fan next to a cup of hot cocoa with marshmallows floating in a smiley face arrangement. Bel couldn't help it; she smiled back.

"You might want to clean your hands."

She looked at her grubby fingers on their way to the plate and scowled. "Right. Sorry. I am not used to stopping in the middle of a job."

"Good to know."

She went over to the pump of hand sanitizer and took a few shop towels, scrubbing down until she could see skin instead of grime.

She took a fresh towel and one more squirt of sanitizer cleared her skin, her hands sparkling and only dark crescents showing that she had been working.

Bel returned to the mug and frowned. The happy face had melted. "Dang. I wanted to suck down his cheerful little grin."

"A little hostile toward cocoa, but understandable." Rex was looking over the roller. "It looks finished."

"Not quite; I have to weld it, cut the length to fit and mount it back in your machine." She took a large bite of one of the cookies and closed her eyes as she leaned back against her bench. It melted in her mouth, buttery, sweet and salty, with just a hint of vanilla.

The cocoa followed and washed the cookie away in a wave of chocolate and sweet melted marshmallow.

"This is really good." She sighed and finished the first cookie, going for the second.

"Thanks. We small batch the cookies. It means more work, but we are just trying to keep our shop up and running."

"Our?"

He grinned. "Rex's Candies is a co-op. We are all about profit sharing. The ladies were delighted when you showed up. They are just waiting for the go ahead to scour out the flour and get the copper kettles warmed up."

"Give me three more hours to get the fit right and do a cleaning on the machine. It will be up and running by six this evening."

He grinned. "How firm is that time?"

"Very firm. I will send you a text when I am ready for help with the roller."

"Oh, if you wanted to move the truck, our spot at the back is clear."

"Great, when I finish the cookies, I will move the truck."

Rex chuckled. "You have already finished them."

She frowned. "Dang. Those were good."

He took the empty cup from her hand and tapped her nose. "There is more where that came from if you get the candy roller running."

She snorted. "Well, let's get out of here so I can move the truck. I am not insured for passengers, and I am not willing to take a chance with that roller back here."

"Fair enough. I will leave so you can get welding."

She watched him go, and he hopped out of the truck. She checked that everything was fastened down and followed him out. She pulled the door down, locked it and headed to the driver's side.

Two vehicles filled the parking spot before she was clear of it, and she really hoped that he hadn't been kidding about the space behind the shop.

She parked behind the shop with relief and slid out of the cab and back around to the rear door. In a moment, she reached her workshop, closed the door and was getting back into the zone of harnessing lightning.

Each of the team had a skill. She had gotten lightning instead of thunder. It was ironic that her folk had eschewed many modern conveniences and she carried nothing but power. Raw, unadulterated power.

Bel went to work on welding the central rod into the roller, and her mind wandered back to her home as it always did. She was the second youngest of nine children, and her job had always been to fix the small things around the house. Her father made the parts, and she fit them together.

She had been putting equipment together since she was little; her fingers were always itching to put things together. It was ironic that she had become the last part of the team. She made them work together. The power of them all was balanced by her place in the team.

Love and lust, ice and heat, battle and comfort, thunder and lightning. Each one of them had a role to create a more balanced team that could be more powerful and get further with every year. Now, the trip around the world was second nature.

Her first trip had been something else entirely.

Her papa and mama set her down and looked at her with kind expressions. "Daughter, this is an excellent offer. You are changing too quickly for us to keep hiding the effects from the gathering. We wish you to soar and be what you are born to be. We know not how you came to us, but we know that you do not belong with us anymore. You have outgrown us, Bella. The lord has a plan for you, and this man will help you to it. Do you believe us?"

Her parents had spoken in nearly identical words and had smiled down at her as they always did when they wanted her to stop working.

"I believe you. I feel what rises inside me; I just acknowledge what it means. No family of my own, no brothers and sisters to laugh with. I will be alone among strangers, and it is the hardest thing to bear. But, I shall bear it. My efforts will move portions of belief along, and that is a worthy result."

The woman named Ru spoke from the far side of the team. "We will step in to become your new community. You will not be alone, Arabella. You will become everything that you were born to be. A symbol of light, hope and generosity."

Her father chuckled. "She will be a symbol of fixing things. Keeping things together and putting things together. She finds the things that bind and puts them into action. We will miss her, but she is not for our world."

Ru walked toward them, and horns sprouted from her head. "She is meant for our world."

Bella's horns came out in response, and she took Ru's hand. Ru tucked her in against her body and hugged her. "You will not be alone, Bella. I promise you that."

Ru looked to her parents and spoke slowly. "She will live with us, be educated and grow into a young woman before she will join the team. She will have a life of contemplation and study before it turns into action."

They nodded, but her father asked, "Will she find love?"

Ru nodded and made her promise. "When the time is right, she will find love. We will not be her family, but we will be her community. We will keep her safe until it is time for her to strike out and seek love."

Bel shook her head and focused on the power that melted metal and made two pieces become one. The arcs of power accomplished her goal in a few motions and a lot of flashbacks. Every time she used the energy, she remembered the past.

She flicked her fingers to cool them and used her free hand to dump water on the steel. The sizzling confirmed her work, and she looked at the melted joint, making sure that she had caught every millimetre of the connection to avoid corrosion inside the roller.

It was perfect, but then, it always was. She moved to the other side of the roller and engaged in the same procedure, once again plunging her mind into the past. It was bizarre to think that she was hundreds of years from her family. It was why she was obsessed with taking the past into the future. Taking her past with her and looking forward made her feel complete.

She had cried over her lost roots, but her parents had given her books to take with her, and her education in mathematics had extended into mechanical engineering. Her focus on keeping machines alive had taken the place of all the ladylike pursuits her mother had tried to instill.

This time, when the light faded, she had a perfectly repaired roller ready to be set into place on its machine.

Bel smiled and wiped the metal down. Well, it was time to slink into the back of the shop and get the candy roller back on duty.

As quietly as she could, she took the roller out of the truck, and after she latched the door with her free hand, she pulled open the door to the candy shop and crept inside.

Licking His Cane

Bel entered the little shroud and set the roller into place with a click. The machine vibrated at the impact as if happy to have its missing limb back.

She returned to her truck for her cleaning kit and crept under the machine to try and clean things up as thoroughly as possible. It was her honour to restore old machines to as close to showroom condition as possible. She worked like hell to keep things up and running in excellent shape. So far, this season, she had no repeat customers for the same machines, but several for different ones. The quality of her work was not in doubt.

She hummed along as she worked on the machine and heard excited exclamations from around her. She heard a burner engage a few feet away and the clang of a copper kettle was right behind it. The sugar was soon on its way to boiling. She had better get herself in gear.

She finished her cleaning and heaved herself to her feet, getting a clean cloth to wipe down the rollers with mineral oil to remove any dust and debris from her housekeeping.

Bel disengaged her lockout and fired up the machine, starting the tiny gas burners that kept the candy from hardening as it compacted it.

The rollers tumbled, settled and were soon churning along at the angle that would take a ball of candy and turn it into a long, thick rope, suitable for candy canes.

With the machine humming away, she wiped down the jigs that were hanging near the pulling hook.

Rex came around and carefully lowered the outermost layer of plastic. "With the elements firing, you should have opened this to the air."

She chuckled. "There is plenty of circulation, and I am watching it for any hiccups. It all looks good."

"And you are getting our equipment ready. Thank you."

"All part of the service. I have never seen anyone pull a candy cane before." She looked at Rex hopefully as the last layer between them came down.

"Is that a hint?"

She shrugged. "I have to stay to make sure that the machine is functioning. It is a matter of professional pride."

"Feel free to stay as long as you like. I love performing for an audience." He winked one of his sparkling grey eyes at her and headed to the copper kettle as one of his staff manned it.

She could imagine a dozen things she would like to watch him do and none of them involved clothing. Her time in the modern world with romance novels and the internet had given her a tremendous grasp of what the masculine body was capable of, in theory and practice. She was always in favour of verifying a good theory.

One of the counter staff came by and parked a stool in the corner. "It will be safe over here. Once he gets moving, you don't want to be in the way. That stuff is hot."

Bel grinned and gathered her tools up. "You mean the candy, right?"

The woman winked. "That, too."

The sounds from the front of the shop indicated that there was a bustling trade going on. The back of the shop had a few women working with chocolate on marble slabs and there was no sign of the baked gingerbread.

Rex was working with the boiling sugar and watching the temperature. When he had judged it to be correct, he turned off the burner and lifted the copper vat onto a wheeled trolley to move it to one of the clean and waiting marble tables.

He hooked the handles to a chain pulley and hoisted the molten sugar up past the edge of the table.

"Well, since I am giving you a lesson, we pour the molten sugar out here to cool. The boiling gets out all water and aligns the molecules so that the resulting crystals have an even texture."

The sugar was disappointingly golden on the table. Oddly enough, it didn't steam.

"So, no water in it at all?"

"No, and it is very thirsty stuff." He moved the copper vessel aside and took a set of long, metal paddles, folding and flipping the sugar as it cooled, keeping it even.

"What are you doing now?"

He laughed. "Letting it set up to the stage where I can pull it. Folding it helps the cooling and gets some air into it. Air is what will turn this from golden to white."

Bel leaned forward and watched him work as the sugar hardened from liquid into toffee-texture. She watched the hard lines of his face as he gauged his progress. When he was certain the time was right, he pulled out a bottle and sprinkled it over the sugary mass.

He glanced at her and smiled. "Peppermint. It is always a classic. We also do spearmint, tuti-fruity and blueberry."

"That is a fairly rounded selection. No cherry?"

He grinned. "I am still looking for a good colour combination for that one. Red gets mixed up with the peppermint. We try new ones every year."

"Nice."

Sure enough, his folding and turning was giving the sugar a paler hue. It took another few minutes before he snipped off sections and coloured them with a dye paste. He put on gloves and started to knead the coloured bits until brilliant red and vivid green were glowing in the candy.

He set the red and green near the heating elements on the roller and returned to the table, grabbing the mass of tumbling sugar and throwing it onto the hook. "Now, I earn my keep."

Bel closed her jaw with a snap as he started to manhandle the mass up and over the hook before pulling it down again. The muscles in his arms, chest and back tightened and rippled with every haul.

She had no idea how much time had passed, but he had a snow-white and gleaming ball of sugar in his arms as he returned to the roller and started to work on the coloured segments. He rolled and flattened them, using the huge snips to cut lengths that would cover the rough cylinder. He positioned them symmetrically around the cylinder and looked at her. "Now to see what your work can stand up to."

He tossed the cylinder onto the rollers, and it tumbled around and around.

"Can I approach?" She wanted to see from a better vantage point.

"Sure. The dangerous stuff is set aside. If you will haul the copper bowl to the sink, you can sit on my shoulders." He grinned and switched out his gloves for clean ones.

The cylinder was slowly narrowing and lengthening. While it tumbled, Rex got the hooked mold down from the wall and set up a station for himself. A sharp knife and a parchment-lined pan completed his setup.

Bel hopped off her perch, and she moved the thick copper

bowl over to the sink. One of the clerks came back, and together, they lifted it in to soak. There were only a few flecks of sugar left on it, but cleanliness was important.

She returned to Rex and stood at his side, but out of the way as he started to press the candy down to narrow it. The rollers kept it smooth, and when the width was right, Rex clipped off a chunk and rolled it in his hands until it matched the outer edge of the form he had. The whole procedure was accomplished in seconds, but when it was done, there was a gleaming, twisted, stripy candy cane. She could hear the click as he placed it on the pan, and by the time she had finished staring at the first, the second was next to it.

It seemed that the candy canes were appearing by magic, but his hands kept working until the pan was full and one of the workers had replaced it with a blank.

The cheer that arose from the shop made Bel grin. She inclined her head. "Well, I have seen what I wanted to see. Very impressive. Thanks for the demonstration. My bill will be emailed to you."

He nodded. "I hope to see you again, Bel."

"Well, we still have a week before Christmas. It could happen." She was about to turn to leave when a warm candy cane appeared in front of her.

"Consider this a tip for your prompt repairs. I don't know what the girls and I would have done if you hadn't shown up." He was holding the cane, and she closed her fingers around it as daintily as she could. The warmth of the candy was still in there.

She looked up at him from between her lashes and licked delicately at the warm peppermint.

His eyes darkened, and he reached out as she stepped back.

"Have a good evening, Rex."

She turned and made her escape with the candy cane clutched in her hand. She held the candy in her teeth as she started up her truck, her bag stowed behind the seat.

She needed a nap in the worst way, and the flashing of her phone told her that the moment she answered it, she would have a call. A little bit of rest was called for and a proper meal. Hopefully not in that order.

Bel woke up with a smile and the taste of peppermint still on her lips. Four hours was all she had gotten, but she levered herself upright and checked her messages.

She had another repeater with a downed oven. The first time he had needed help with his conveyor belt. He was a prompt payer, so she showered and got into her boiler suit.

It was going to be a filthy job, but that is what she was paid for.

She sent out the last of her invoices and headed home after three back-to-back calls that—thankfully—were easy fixes.

Bel used her magic to cleanse her suit of the grime of the concrete floors and the gears that didn't want to stay in place.

She was just settling her truck into the parking spot when her phone went off again. She answered it. "Sweet Repairs."

The voice she had been hoping for was on the other end of the line. "Hello, Bel. I was wondering if you would have time to check on a drop press for me?"

She checked her watch and then remembered she didn't wear one. "How long will you be there, Rex?"

"As long as you want me."

Bel fought the mental images that came with that husky rumble.

"I will see you in half an hour. On my way." She hung up and checked her mirrors before putting the truck in gear.

She liked driving. It wasn't as much fun as when it had involved horses and wagons, but she did enjoy controlling where she went and how fast.

The quiet evening let her get through traffic with relative ease, and when she parked the truck behind the shop, the bar of light let her know that the rear door was open.

She entered with her toolkit in her hand and looked around. The stations were quiet and only the copper pot was in action.

"Where is everyone?"

"It's after nine. They are home with their families, exhausted after a busy day." Rex stirred the sugar with a practiced hand and the wide wooden paddle.

She approached cautiously. "Making more candy canes?"

He nodded. "We sold out of the first three batches. I am trying to get ahead for tomorrow."

A plastic drape showed her where her work was needed. "So,

what happened to the roller press?"

He sighed. "Freak accident. We were running a batch of mints and a pan fell in, dislodging the roller."

Bel grinned at him as she removed the plastic tarp. "It seems to be a theme."

She looked at the patterned roller and winced. The pan had gouged the pattern as well as dislocated the roller from the gear system.

This wasn't an easy fix.

Rex rolled the molten candy to the cooling table and poured it. Thanks to watching earlier, she knew that she would have a chance to work her magic when he was pulling the candy.

She didn't need to lock the machine. It was a hand crank. With focus, she got to work resetting the roller.

"Is there much damage?" Rex folded the sugar and kept an eye on it. His work with the pallet knives was fun to watch.

"I should be able to manage it. How did it happen?"

"Jo was trying to use a pan instead of the gloves to handle the hot candy and Cindy was cranking hard when the pan slipped. There was so much screaming, I thought a finger had gotten jammed into the machine." He shook his head and flipped the candy.

She nodded and kept working, resetting the gearing system and waiting for her moment. It took a few minutes for him to dye the stripes before he pulled the larger mass. From the blueberry scent wafting toward her, she could guess what today's flavour was.

With his back to her, she exhaled magic into the machine and repaired the embossed rollers.

Rex called out casually. "You know, I thought you were just a good mechanic and that you couldn't possibly be a reindeer, but here you are."

She looked up in surprise, and his sparkling grey eyes were aimed directly at her while his body continued to work on the candy on automatic. His neck had to be twisting something awful.

Bel stared at him. "I don't know what you are talking about."

"It was clever, waiting until I turned my back to you and knowing that I would have to. It was hard to catch the wisp of magic used to fix that mangled roller, but it was definitely there."

The candy was ready, and he walked over to the roller that she had fixed earlier that day. Without breaking stride, he put the stripes on the cylinder, and then, he tossed the candy into the rollers.

He now had time to grin at her, and as he watched her, his own appearance shifted.

His eyes tilted and widened, his nose flattened and his neck widened. The ears that extended up and out of his hair had grey tips.

Bel jolted. Myth and legend, even among the reindeer. She was looking at a wolf-fey. She remembered one of the other girls telling her that the wolf-fey would come out to get them if they dared to stray from the workshop. Apparently, that moment had come.

He was smiling, but he obviously read the panic in her eyes. "Bel, what is it?"

"They warned us that you would come for us and tear our throats out."

"Who warned you?"

She rubbed her forehead. "When we first arrived and Ru couldn't watch us, we had fey caretakers. Well, some of us did. Mine warned me of the wolf-fey that hunted reindeer and tore us apart. She said that if I ever tried to leave the workshop, the wolf-fey would be sent to hunt me."

Rex moved quickly, coming around and gripping her arms. She was too surprised to move.

"Tell me her name and I will give her a taste of her own medicine when we get back."

She blinked. "So, you *were* sent to get me."

He sighed and ran his hands along her arms. The gloves he was wearing stuck to her so he peeled them off and discarded them in a bin.

"Of course. We were sent to get all of you, but not like you think. You have to come back willingly or not at all. No one can force Christmas magic. It has to be offered up willingly."

She licked her lips. "So, you aren't going to hurt me?"

"No. Who was your nanny?"

"Loma."

He made a face. "Loma was a bitch. Literally. She was a beta in the workshop fey clan and eventually ended up transferred away. No one knew why, but now, I am getting some ideas. This was right after you arrived?"

She nodded. "Yes. When Ru and Santa were recruiting the others."

"Did you know that a reindeer of Santa's team can destroy a fey with little effort?"

Bel shook her head, swamped in the sweet scent of him. "I have never tried."

He grinned, and she could see the sharp edge of his canines.

"Don't start now on my account. I just wanted you to know that I know so you don't have to hide. I have five more days to convince you to come back with me."

She blinked. "You really mean convince and not coerce?"

"I do."

She looked at the press and blew gently, smiling as the gears settled into place. "Fine. I will watch you make candy canes and you can start convincing."

He pressed a kiss to her lips and then left her, gloved up again and went to work shaping the warm candy.

"Can you man the trays?"

He started to fill the first one with swift motions.

"Um, sure. You might want to put the glamour back on. You look a little feral for a candy maker."

He chuckled. "I do this every year. Rex's Candies has been in operation for over a decade. Before that, I was somewhere else, as someone else. The magic chooses for you, as you know."

She looked down at herself. "I look like me."

"Only because this is your first time in the human world."

Bel moved into position and switched out the pans when the first was filled. There was a rack waiting, and she set it into place.

"So, the wolf-fey face..."

"Is my real face. It doesn't change. The humans here can't see it. The snowflake magic covers my appearance, no matter what I do to myself."

She moved the full tray out of the way; his hands kept working.

"Wow, um, okay. Was it the snowflake that gave it away?"

He chuckled. "It let me know I was on the right track. You could have been anyone, from a customer to a delivery driver. I have been watching for you for weeks."

She nodded. "Should I start the second copper vat?"

He grinned. "Are you willing to help?"

"Of course. I want to see that press in action."

He nodded, "Right. The candy has to be hotter for that."

"I know. I will just get it started. You have to do the actual work."

She set the copper pot on the burner, loaded in the premeasured sugar and turned the flame on.

When the sugar was started, she went and switched out the pans again, leaving him one for the last of the batch.

With that done, she returned to the sugar and watched that the heat was not too high.

When she heard the snap of gloves, she knew that Rex was behind her.

"Well, it seems you have things under control here. I will wash out the last vessel and set it to dry."

She nodded and kept an eye on the sugar. The melt was slow, but when it started to go, it seemed to all get the same idea in a rush. The crystals disappeared and the clear liquid continued to heat.

Rex walked up behind her. "Now, keep an eye on the temperature once the bubbling starts and move the paddle slowly through the sugar."

He wrapped his arms around her and helped her move the paddle in the proper motion.

She grinned and enjoyed the moment.

He taught her how to stir, how to check and, finally, how to shift the dangerous mass to the cooling table. Working with the pallet knives was difficult, but after a little practice, she got the hang of it.

Her phone chirped, but she ignored it.

Rex chuckled. "Don't you have to get that?"

"Nope. I am my own boss. They can leave a message and I will get back to them when I am done here. This is fun." She grinned.

"We are making another batch of blueberry. It is surprisingly popular. So, how did you end up as a mechanic?"

"I was always mechanically inclined and born near the beginning of the industrial revolution. It was a time when new discoveries were everywhere, including my being a shapeshifter."

She worked carefully and folded the sugar over on itself.

"How did that happen?"

She shrugged and kept working. "I don't know. Even Santa was never able to tell us. All he said was that it was fate, that we had a purpose and only we could keep the magic of Christmas going. My family didn't really follow Christmas, but they knew a calling when they heard one, and the horns kind of gave it away." She chuckled. "The first time I met Ru, the horns appeared."

"I thought she was the youngest."

"The most recently born, but she has been with Santa the longest. She was on all our recruitments. She came to us and we changed, some for the first time, others not. When our families gave us up, they took us to the workshop. When we were all grown, we became part of the team and have been for hundreds of years now."

"I thought the team grew over time." He corrected her grip on the knife, and she was able to flip more on the next sweep.

"It did. We didn't all grow up at the same time. You know that time doesn't work properly at the workshop. It is why the reindeer got so bored. It is an eternity of filing reports from the naughty-or-nice list."

She looked to him and pointed to the mass. "I think it is ready for flavouring."

He chuckled. "First, cut the sections to be coloured. Use either the shears or the knives."

He helped her to separate the sections, and she mixed the colours into the hot mass, the gloves barely protected her. She could handle heat, but she didn't know how human hands could get used to it.

The rest of the cane was a little more awkward. It wasn't due to weight but, rather, the necessity of going up on tippy toes to reach the hook.

"Let me guess. You make all the candy canes?"

He chuckled. "The hook will lower when I leave."

She sighed. "Okay, you finish it."

"I will pull the candy. You are going to need to test your repair work on the crank mold. Get the colours."

She retrieved the coloured pieces from near the fire and handed them to him, a few pulls and he had something that was more ivory and purple than anything else.

"You crank and I feed?" She bit her lip.

"Other way around. I trust you not to crush me." He smiled, and the blueberry mass wobbled in his grasp.

She darted over to the machine and started a slow crank. The candy pressed through the molded rollers and came out the bottom, embossed with a reindeer's head.

Rex balanced the still-hot candy, and she kept a steady, strong crank on the handle. She swept the cooling pieces away as the area under the press filled up.

They worked together for five minutes until the mound of candy was huge and the press had proved that it was completely fixed.

Rex dusted the candy with powdered sugar and cracked the small, round pieces apart. He ran his hands over them until the layer was one candy thick.

"Now, we do some packaging. If you have time."

Bel smiled. "In for a penny, in for a pound."

"Don't you have to be getting to your other client?"

She shrugged. "I am due for a break, and this is more fun than napping. It is probably the sugar, but I feel energized."

Rex laughed, and they spent the next hour packaging all the candy he had made that evening.

The fleeting kiss was lost in the banter between them, and it wasn't until he walked her to the door with another candy cane in her grasp that she remembered it.

"Your lips have turned blue." He grinned.

She smiled and licked her lips. "I suppose it is an inevitable side effect."

He moved close and kissed her slowly. "That does taste good."

She blinked and tried to be clever. "You make a good product."

He grinned. "I wasn't talking about the candy cane."

She blushed hotly. "Is this part of the convincing?"

"This whole evening has been about that. The kiss was about what you tasted like." He stroked her cheek with a slightly sticky thumb.

Her phone went off again, and she sighed. "I think that is my cue to run away."

"I won't chase you, Bel, but you know where I am. Come here day or night and I will be here."

"Isn't that a little rough on the system?"

He chuckled. "I sleep above the shop. I know your scent now. When you arrive, I will be down in moments."

Bel nodded and swallowed. "Good to know. I will work on that. Uh, I am still sending an invoice for the press."

He grinned. "Of course."

Right. She turned and scampered into her truck, setting her toolkit down behind her seat. She checked her messages, and one of the calls was desperate. It seemed like a simple repair, and it was on the way home.

If she were wrong about the simplicity, a little bit of magic would soon have her in her own bed. Too bad she was going alone.

You couldn't grow up in times past with not having a passing idea of sex. Families lived in rooms, not bedrooms. Parents cuddled together in winter under the covers. It was wasteful to heat an entire house when only one room was needed to keep everyone safe and healthy for the night. Sex happened.

The odd thing for Bel was that she hadn't thought anything of it. It was part of life. Here, in the modern age, it was something to be alternately hidden and flaunted, but never treated as normal.

With her fascination with Rex's body foremost in her mind, she tried to put thoughts of sex away, but Ru did say that she was supposed to pursue what made her happy. Bedding the wolf definitely belonged in that category.

It was two days before she could get back to Rex's Candies. She was wearing normal street clothes and got in line with the rest of the patrons. Rex came out in three minutes, lifted her up, squealing and protesting, as he hauled her into the back.

The laughter that rippled behind them filled Bel's cheeks with a solid blush.

The heavy scent of chocolate was in the air as he walked through the work area and up a set of well-hidden stairs.

"You weren't kidding. You sleep above the shop."

Licking His Cane

He was silent until he set her down on a chair. "Two days, Bel. You made me wait two days."

She blinked and stifled a laugh. His fangs were out. His words were carefully enunciated. The frustration in his gaze was unmistakable.

Bel smiled and stroked his cheek. "I had to work and sleep. I came when I could."

Rex sighed and knelt on the floor, his head between her breasts.

Bel was startled. She gently wrapped her arms around his head, running her fingers along his hair and gently stroking his ears. She murmured softly, no words, just sounds. He wrapped his arms around her hips and simply breathed her in.

He shuddered. "This is harder than I thought it would be."

There were a number of connotations she could draw from that, but she whispered, "What is?"

"Finding a mate. We get one shot at it. One woman to be ours for eternity. Wolf-fey are highly monogamous." He shuddered again, finally looking up at her.

His pupils were flaring with magic. The snowflakes inside his grey eyes gave it away.

"How did the magic know?" She stroked his cheek again.

"It is what it is, as we are what we are. We are where we are supposed to be, as uncomfortable as it is." He sighed.

The slight touch of her hand seemed to sooth him; he relaxed and his feral demeanour diminished a little.

She leaned in to kiss him, and he pressed her back in her chair.

Bel stroked his tongue with hers and carefully made it past the sharp teeth. His hands tightened on her hips, and he got to his feet, holding her above him as he walked across the loft to his bedroom.

She continued to kiss him, stroking his shoulders and kneading his neck. Her hands plucked at his t-shirt, and she shuddered herself. He gradually lowered her until she was on her feet, and then, he pulled her leather jacket off.

Her clothing disappeared in a swirl of magic, and she didn't know if it was hers or his.

His clothing disappeared a moment later.

She opened her eyes and stared at him. "Oh, wow."

His body was covered with tattoos, marks of swirling snow. It covered his shoulders, the hard furry planes of his chest and cascaded over his belly to swirl in a flurry around his groin.

She grinned. "I think it is trying to tell me something."

She followed the spirals of silver and black down until she caressed the length of his cock and smiled. "Do the marks cover your back as well?"

He gently removed her hand from him and turned. The marks did, indeed, start at his shoulders and narrow toward his tailbone. Wide spirals on his buttocks made her want to trace the pattern with her fingers, so she did.

The muscles flexed, and he shuddered. "Are you teasing me?"

"Exploring. I only have three days left before I head back to the workshop, so I am getting all the experience in that I can."

He froze and turned at a glacial pace. He scowled. "What do you mean?"

"Going back. You know, for Christmas Eve. All of us reindeer are heading back on the twenty-third. It was part of our plan."

"Did Santa know?" He gripped her arms and scowled.

She used magic and snapped their hair down. Two wild things above a candy shop. "I don't know. If he didn't know, he expected you to get us home, and you will. If he did know, he sacrificed his elves to the reindeer. Either way, I get time in the human world and the touch of a man whose voice makes me wet."

Apparently, that was a magic word. She was lifted again and tossed lightly on the bed; the air came out of her when he thumped down on top of her.

He lifted up almost immediately, and he rubbed his lips against her neck, moving down her body and inhaling her scent as he went. He smelled like butter and chocolate today. It was a heady and delightful combination. "Fudge today?"

He parted her legs, and his scenting continued with one thigh draped on his shoulder.

He licked at her skin, and she was as wet as she had promised. His light forays of tasting broke down as he feasted on her, his tongue sliding and jabbing inside while she twisted to take him deeper.

She arched in a bow when her orgasm hit. A tiny squeak left

her lungs.

Rex's lapping slowed, but didn't stop. She breathed heavily as the tension started to build one more time.

He muttered something against her and worked his way back up her body. He nuzzled the side of her neck, and she heard him whisper, "Even better than a kiss."

She knew he was talking about her taste, but she kept herself from saying something snarky. With a slight adjustment to both of them, he pressed between her thighs.

Bel gasped as the length and girth filled her slowly. Rex wove a hand through her hair and held her head so the only place her gaze could go was him.

It was a bit of an effort and a snug fit, but he did fit completely and without any pain.

He kissed her and moved his hips, thrusting and retreating with increasing ferocity. The gentle motions became harder, and soon, she was holding onto the headboard to stop her upward movement.

He nipped her neck and shoulders while she battled with controlling her position on the bed and his position within her.

Wild cascades of pleasure ran between them. She felt her magic rising to the surface, and after a moment of fighting the panic, she let it come.

His markings glowed as sweat coated them. They worked to find release together, and as with the candy making, they achieved it with a bit of effort and sweat.

She gasped and would have cried out, but he put his mouth over hers. She got his groan and felt the sharp jerks into her as he took his turn.

Rex moved his head to her neck, and Bel came back to herself as he slowly lapped at her skin.

"Blitzen, is there any part of you that isn't tasty?"

Rex grinned against her skin before lifting his head, and there was a relaxed and satisfied expression in his eyes. He had gone from wolf to puppy in an orgasm.

"I don't know. I haven't licked myself recently."

"You should. I could spend all day and night doing just that." She grinned. "I was going to ask you out for a burger."

"I think that a little protein would go a long way. My treat."

She looked up at him. "We are going to have to separate if

you want to get dressed. My clothing went into the ether."

"I want to stay here forever, but the thought of a burger is tempting."

Bel sighed. "We can go have a burger and come back and have sex again?"

He was off her in a second, and her body was clean and clothing was back in place a moment later.

Laughing, she got up and went out for a first date with her lover.

With a cheeseburger in front of her, she was content.

"So, what did you do to your repair business?"

"I closed it, and forwarded my number to an alternate repair service that can do a good job and pick up the slack. Generally, bought myself some time off. A last few days in the world."

He looked at her with a small smile. "A last few days with me?"

She sighed and propped her head on her fist. "Yes. That's it exactly."

He reached for her free hand. "That gives me more hope than you walking through my door today. Did you want to help in the shop?"

She shrugged. "Sure. Will it bug anyone?"

"No, and once they are gone, we can do the final candy canes and set up all the gingerbread houses for tomorrow. That will free me up entirely, and we can do something fun, like a date." He grinned.

She laughed. "Sure. If there is no one watching, I can use my hands with the molten sugar."

"You can?"

"Of course, I am impervious to temperature. Did you have any equipment you want me to go over so the girls have a really nice worry-free year?"

Rex started in on his burger. "I will make a list."

Bel chuckled. "Check it twice."

He snorted and they kept eating.

Two more days of fun, frolicking and candy led them to the morning of the twenty-third. They were on top of the sweet shop and ready for launch.

"Are you sure you want to bring all these sweets to your team?"

Bel nodded. "We always have to make our own. These are much better. Now, do you have my collar?"

He held it up. She pried off the snowflake and put it in the box, handing it to him and taking the collar.

"You look a lot different without the snowflake."

She grinned. "Oh, I know. Just wait."

She closed the collar around her neck, and it snapped shut, containing her power into a specific magic.

"Okay, you know how to grab for the horns?"

"Sure; are you sure you can carry me?"

She walked over to him and kissed him quickly. "That is a silly question. Let's get going."

She shifted form. Belinda Litzen became Blitzen. Nine feet of hoofed and horned Christmas magic embodied.

Her wolf blinked for a moment, grinned, and then, he approached her, climbing into position with a little bit of kicking before settling and gripping her horns. A few steps later and they were galloping through the skies in the false hours of dawn.

They had a lot of sky to cover before they were back at the workshop. She had work to do on the morrow after all. *Work, work, work.*

The Letters

Dear Santa,

Get Bent!
For the last few centuries, we have done everything that you asked of us, and we let you shut us up with only the team for company.
You suck!
We go into heat. Every. Single. Year. Do you know what that does to a bunch of women who sprout horns when they get agitated? I have no good shirts left. They have all been shredded.
Now, I am going to tell you what I want for Christmas, because that is the only thing you seem to understand.
For this Christmas, I want a companion that I can keep all year, every year. I want to be with a man who makes me smile and can hold me in the early hours of the morning when I come in and collapse from work.
My wish is to not be alone. To share my life, such as it is, and I wish for my team to have the same chance at companionship. Ru especially. Ru spends every year keeping our spirits up, distracting us during mating season and running interference with you. She needs a man who respects her for what she does, what she is and just for her.

Love,
Dasher

Dear Santa,

Every year, we haul you around and deliver gifts to the good children around the world.

My Christmas wish is that I can meet them. I want to see the excitement building up to Christmas and watch the change in their faces and attitudes.

Doing what we do, we miss that excitement and the anticipation. We never get to see the children that wake up on Christmas morning.

I want to see them before they get the presents. Before Christmas Eve. I need to know who they are.

Now, onto what else I want, I want a chance at love, at a man who can fend for himself so I don't need to keep an eye on him. I want the same thing for Ru. She tries so hard to keep us all in line and make sure that we feel love and affection when we can't get it anywhere else. She needs someone who puts her first.

Love,
Dancer

Dear Santa,

I want to drive one of the big machines that the humans have developed. I have seen them, and I want to drive one.

Every year, I get into the harness and pull along with the others, but I want to be the one directing the path, making the path. I think it will give me a better understanding of everything that Ru does for us.

I am also asking that Ru find someone to take care of her when she isn't on duty. She works hard to keep us together as a team, and she needs someone to pamper her.

As for my love life, it is a little frozen right now. I am not looking for a man, but if one ends up in my path, I wouldn't say no.

Love,
Prancer

Nice and Naughty

Dear Santa,

For Christmas, I want the stars. I want to study the stars and talk to other people who are interested in the sky.

Every year, we run through the sky without being able to really look around. The aurora borealis becomes an obstacle instead of a wonder. It should always be a wonder.

As for mating season, I wouldn't mind someone I can count on, someone who is good at back rubs and who can do a foot massage in a pinch. He also needs to love the stars as much as I do.

As for stars, I want to talk about Ru. You have no idea how hard she works for you each and every year. When we get tired, she pulls us; when we get lost, she leads us. She keeps our spirits up and you lock her up with us for three hundred and sixty-four days a year. She deserves better. We deserve better.

Love,
Vixen

Dear Santa,

I miss the middle ages, but I hear that the humans have created replicas of that time around the world. I want to go to one and make things.

Every year, I run with the group and we streak through the sky, but I want to make something with my own hands and have something to show for my time. Sure, the children enjoy their presents, but we never get to see the faces.

I want to feel metal under my hands and shape it to my will.

We have nothing to show for our lives. We are creatures of myth and legend. I want someone, somewhere to remember me. The real me.

Now, as for remembering folks, Ru is the most deserving person I know, but then, I only actually know nine people, including you. She needs a support team, more help in the administrative details and she needs a love life. You have a ton of elves here; let her date.

Love,
Comet

Dear Santa,

I want to help people. I want to see those at their worst and help them in any way I can. Even if it is something small, I want to ease their burden, just for a moment.

Baking cookies is something I need to practice, so I would like to involve that.

Of course, I need to be in a place where I can control the environment. Ah well, I have seen you do more.

In the love department, I want someone who likes food as much as I do and who doesn't care that I really like food. I have heard that these humans are funny about food. I will have to see for myself.

Love,
Cupid

Dear Santa,

I want to plan a party. I want to plan dozens of parties. I love decorating and making things pretty, engaging the eye and getting folks to lower their guard.

Ru said that we should ask for love, but I want to ask for a companion. I want a man who will simply be with me. He can do his thing, and I will do mine. Occasionally, we can do each other.

My wish is to be able to help folks decorate for the holidays, in ways they would never have thought of themselves. I want light, I want laughter and I want to bring out the little kid in those around me.

Oh, and I want a challenge. Putting up ribbons and bows isn't really too hard for one of us. I want to decorate something no one has thought of before.

Love,
Donder

Dear Santa,

I miss the future.

When I was a child, everything was becoming new. My family encouraged me to fix things, and there were discoveries around every corner. The industrial age was taking off, and I wanted to be taken with it.

Instead of seeing what humanity could create, I was pulled into the life at the workshop. It was a jarring change, and I miss working with my hands.

Now, for Christmas, I want to do something to make folks smile. I want something that can carry Christmas into the future instead of remaining in the present day. I want to be part of the memories of Christmas, even if the humans never see me.

Personally, I would like to get over my fear of wolves. I don't know if you know this, but I have been terrified of them for centuries. If you could make that happen, please let me know.

Love,
Blitzen

Nice and Naughty

Ru sat in the office and watched the gathering below. Santa had rustled up a very handsome selection of elves and was giving them a stern lecture. He was in mid-order when he looked up at her; a bright spark came into his eyes. His whole demeanour changed.

Ru sipped at her tea as he bounded up the stairs.

"How long have they been gone?"

She looked at the tanned face surrounded by the snow-white hair that was his trademark. "Pardon?"

He took her cup from her hands and set it on the table before he lifted her by her arms. "Ru, how long have they been gone?"

She grinned. "Some have been gone since October. You have to figure out where they are. We didn't make it easy."

Santa let her go and sat behind his desk. "Why? Why now?"

"It was time. We have walked around you long enough, trying not to put pressure on you. We know you miss her, but we exist as well." Ru resumed her seat and picked up her tea.

Santa looked surprised. "Of course I miss her, but you could have said something. It has been decades since she was with us. You never said anything."

"You shut us away and tried to pretend we didn't exist. How do you think that made us feel? You are so good at knowing what everyone else wants, why did it fail you with those who depended on you?"

He winced. "I have selected eight good candidates for the team. Will you take a look at them and see if the matches are correct?"

Ru sighed. "You trust my judgment?"

"I always have. We have been together far longer than the team has. I trust you, Ru; that has never changed."

She snorted. "I doubt that. Well, did you want me to examine them now?"

"It would help. They don't know how to find your ladies."

She stayed in her chair, and she lifted her feet up to Santa's desk. "Send 'em in one by one. I will tell you what I think."

"You can't decide if they are in a group?"

"Nope. Send them in with the band of the match you figured out. I will see if it is any good." She set her teacup down. "You will have to send them back through time."

He nodded. "I am willing to expend the energy, but we need that team."

Ru smiled, tapped her teacup and it refilled at her command. "In that case, send in the first offering."

Santa sighed and got to his feet. "Your roots are showing."

She smirked and lifted her cup to his in salute, inhaling the peppermint that she loved so dearly.

She eyed the elf coming through the door with Dasher's collar in his hand, and she narrowed her eyes. The two of them vibrated a lovely golden brown.

"You will do."

He paused. "Don't you need to know my name?"

"Nope. Next." She flapped her hand at the amused elf, and he turned his wide shoulders to leave the office.

The choices that Santa had made went along well for the first six, but when she got to Donder's match, she paused.

"Nope. You won't do. Sorry. She is a little darker on the inside. She needs someone who is a little more anchored."

Ru lifted her hand, used her magic to pull and caught the collar.

"Next!"

When the elf left, the next came in. The smell of candy wafted off him, and he carefully held Blitzen's band in his hand. Her team member would be safe with him.

"Good. You can go. Remember that she likes to be useful. She has always enjoyed having busy hands."

He inclined his head. "Yes, madam."

He left as well, and Santa came in. "Why did you toss Randal out?"

"He isn't stable enough for Donder. She needs a man with a home, a base of operations. A house or something. He also needs to have a dark side. She does, so they need to match and meld that way."

Santa lifted his tablet from his desk, and he flicked his fingers swiftly across the screen. "How about this?"

Ru read the dossier and covered her mouth as she chuckled. "This will do very well. Donder is a holiday decorator; this is going to be perfectly odd."

Santa rolled his eyes and held out his hand. "The collar, please."

She slapped it into his palm, and he left the room for a few minutes.

It was rare that she had a chance to rummage through the elf database, but she did it now, learning about the men that she had just sent out to bring her team back.

She was giggling and tears were running down her cheeks when Santa returned.

"What has tweaked your funny bone, Rudolph?"

"I am desperately glad that I sent them off with the snowflake magic. They would be hopelessly outclassed if there hadn't been an info-dump involved."

Santa sat down and rubbed his forehead. "Is there a cup of tea around for me?"

Ru smiled and waved her hand. A pot appeared between them, just like in the old days.

"I don't understand why, Ru. I don't understand why they chose now?"

"I will tell you later. Well, I suppose that I should return to the archive. Is Rin still around?" She set her cup down and made to get up to her feet.

"You aren't going anywhere. You are staying in the tower for the next week."

That was surprising. "Why?"

"You can pull the sleigh by yourself if you have to. I want to make sure you are where I can find you." Santa scowled.

She leaned back in her chair. "You were a lot more fun before you became a living avatar of Christmas."

He sighed. "And you were much more obliging when you were fresh out of the forest. The world moves and times change."

Ru wrinkled her nose. "Fine. If I am going back to the tower, has it been made ready for me? I am not in the mood for housekeeping."

Santa scowled. "I sent Rin to clean up."

Nice and Naughty

"Is my wardrobe up there?"

Santa smiled slightly. "Just like you left it."

"I thought I was leaving it forever when we collected the others. I am pretty sure I left some laundry on the floor." She dismissed her tea set with a wave of her hand.

She was amazed at how calm he was considering that she had just endangered Christmas.

Santa sighed. "I was enjoying that."

"Tough. Today is a stress point for both of us. If you want to know what is going on, meet me for dinner tomorrow. Oh, and bring an update on how the girls are doing. I want to make sure that my team is enjoying themselves."

She got to her feet and left the office without his dismissal. In the old days, there would have been roaring and yelling, but now, the door swung shut behind her.

She crossed the main floor and headed to an ancient and ornate wooden door on the north side of the building.

The handle of the door tingled as she pulled on the gateway to her old home. Centuries had come and gone since she had been alone in the tower.

Time magic was a fickle thing, but with careful management, it could be manipulated into getting what you wanted. Rudolph had studied the cause and effect of all the possibilities that her team would face. She hoped she had accounted for everything. A life alone was no proper life at all for a reindeer.

It was all exactly where she had left it. Her wardrobe was full of gowns that she and Kresida had chosen over the centuries.

Ru sighed and walked to the window, pushing it open with a hard shove. The icy air swirled in and pulled at her hair, ruffled her bed and cleared the feeling of sadness from the room.

Time had stood still in this chamber. When Dasher was recruited, Ru had moved to the archive to be near her new teammate. Things had been so different then. Kresida was around and laughter rang through the tower daily.

It had been a different time...

She stepped through the winter wonderland of her forest. She knew the name of each and every leaf and the pitch and tone of the brooks burbling under their cover of ice. This was her home, and she enjoyed spending time with the sleeping trees of her domain.

The soft footsteps of a stranger in her home thundered in her ears with the crash of discord. She pressed herself into the trees and used the shadows to conceal herself, and she crept toward the interloper.

Her paws dug into the snow as she crept along, and in a few minutes, her path intersected with that of the invading being.

She could smell the ancient magic on him. He looked nearly human, but the twist of power around him wasn't. She blinked at him from under a heavily snow-bowed pine tree and watched.

He was wearing a tunic and leather leggings. A wide belt held his daggers in place and a thick and furred cloak covered his shoulders. His belt had a heavy red buckle that glowed with a strange light.

The hair on his head denoted age, but his face was youthful and unlined, the sparkling blue eyes showed a wisdom that she was unused to seeing in those who walked on two legs.

His head turned to look at her, and he smiled. "Am I in the presence of the famous wolf who guards these woods?"

Being addressed directly in a language that she could understand was definitely unusual. She crept forward cautiously, and her intruder went down on one knee with peculiar grace.

She stepped forward until she was ten feet from him.

"Forest spirit, I have a boon to ask of you. I would speak to you in a form more conducive to communication."

She sat and cocked her head.

"A form similar to my own would suffice."

Sighing, she shifted from her comfortable and four-footed wolf shape into something he could speak with. Her human shape, kneeling in the snow.

His wise eyes looked surprised. "You are so young!"

She held up her hands and looked at the naked and pink skin that she was wearing. "I do not age as humans age."

He removed his cloak and wrapped it around her.

She smiled at him. "I also do not get cold. Now, who are you, and why are you in my forest?"

"Well, Rudolph, I am in dire need of help."

She cocked her head. "Who are you?"

"Have you heard of the gods of the Norse folk?"

She shook her head. "I cannot say that any have crossed my path."

He looked perplexed, but he continued. "I am Odin. The gods have left this world, but I retain their power. I do not wish to drift off into the ether. I wish to make a place for myself in this world."

She blinked and nodded. "Congratulations. Why have you come here?"

"I have heard of the wolf who walks these woods, the wolf who helps guide travellers home. No matter the weather, you always guide them home. I need you to help me to find a place where the last power of the fading gods has taken refuge."

She rose to her feet. "Is it nearby?"

He cocked his head. "Not really. It is through the sky and nestled between the aurora borealis and the stars."

"I cannot walk there in this form. Certainly, not carry you there. I have another shape for the purpose of carrying those who need help, but I cannot speak to you while in that form."

He smiled slightly. "So, you can take me there? You can sense it?"

"You have described it, and the world is not so full of wonders that such power can hide. I can see it." She looked up toward the distant horizon.

"Will you take me there? I cannot get there alone."

He was standing close to her, and she found his presence calming. "Is it your home?"

"I would like it to be. There are elves here who need a home away from the humans and other species who need to be brought to safety. The first step is to find it."

She nodded. "Why did you call me Rudolph?"

"It means famous wolf. As you have not ventured a name, I had to give you one."

She frowned. "Why?"

He chuckled. "It is a human thing. You will get used to them."

She shrugged. "I doubt it."

She took off the cloak and handed it to him, taking the shape of the best runner she knew that could also carry a rider.

The reindeer she wore stamped its feet, and he didn't hesitate. He put his cloak across her back, and with a tremendous leap, he landed on her back.

She took a few steps and noted that his footprints appeared without any other lead in. Whatever he was, he had not needed her for transport.

She took a few steps and launched herself skyward. The energy he had described was hidden in the moment between night and dawn, so she ran across the arc of the sky, seeking that moment.

Her rider held tight to her horns, and when she finally got to that moment and plunged through, he shouted in surprise.

The light of the aurora wrapped around them and clung to them as they passed from the human world into something that had never seen it.

She landed in a world of snow and light. Her hooves stamped on the ground made of magic and ancient power.

Her rider didn't dismount. He was squirming on her back, and to her shock, he wrapped something around her neck.

She bucked and tried to throw him off. The wrapping around her neck tightened, and the red glow was unmistakably what had been on his belt.

With a tremendous heave, she dislodged her rider and turned on him, her antlers lowered.

She tried to change into her wolf form, and she couldn't. She was trapped. She ran at him, and he moved out of the way. It was the beginning of a very long fight.

Odin sat with his head bloody, and she was lying exhausted on the ground.

"I am sorry, Rudolph. I needed you. I have been looking for someone like you for centuries, over a thousand years, actually."

She huffed, blowing hard against the ground.

He stroked her head and scratched between her ears. "It is a new era, Rudolph. The gods of old are fading and gone, the new ones are full of hope and good will. The humans still need us, but we have to take a new form, reshape us for the new age."

He stroked her muzzle before putting his cloak over her. "You can shift to human now, but your wolf is out of your reach."

Nice and Naughty

She sighed but shifted to her human form. "Why do you need me? I was content in my forest."

"The elves need a place to live. We need to bring them here, and while they have steeds that can lead them here, no one can find the place without you."

She cocked her head. "Elves left the human world centuries ago."

He grinned. "In your time. This place is out of time. We will come and go as we please until we have things the way we want them. Then, we will nest ourselves into the human mythos, watching for those who have been naughty and rewarding those who are nice."

She blinked. "You want to watch the humans that closely?"

Odin shrugged. "I feel it when I look at them. I was not only king of the gods, but the all-seeing. I am willing to share that power with elves as humanity expands."

She touched the heavy collar around her neck. "And so, you bound me to help you?"

"This is an exciting venture, Rudolph. I needed power, guidance and a partner. You fill those requirements. I am sorry for the deception, and I swear to never try and trick you again."

She looked at him and extended her hand. "If you swear it, I will help you. This is completely insane, but I will do it. I am not sure if Rudolph is a proper name for me."

He grinned. "I swear to honour you for your efforts and never take you for granted."

They clasped hands, and a partnership was struck.

"What the hell? How long have you been standing there with the window open, Ru?" Santa came in and shut the window, turning her and bustling toward the table and chairs.

"I don't feel the cold." She brushed the snow off her tunic, and she shrugged.

Santa grabbed a quilt off her bed and wrapped her in it. "Humour me. Can you summon some tea?"

She waved her hand and shaped a tea service out of the magic of the dimensional bubble. She picked up a cup, filled it and sipped the hot peppermint tea.

Ru sat in the bundle of quilt with her breath still frosting the air.

"What had you so lost in thought?" Santa took her hand.

She looked at him with a small smile. "The day we met. I was remembering your promise not to trick me and to never take me for granted."

He blushed. "Ah, I suppose that I broke that promise."

"You did, but she was wonderful."

"She was. Humans are born to flit through life, but this time of year always reminds me of the night you brought her home."

Ru smiled and sipped at her tea, remembering a Christmas long past when folks regularly died in the cold and having family meant surviving.

"What are you doing, Rudolph?" Odin held the reins of the small sleigh that she was pulling.

Ru lifted her head and sensed the fading life in the forest. She pulled the sleigh through the trees, and she paused next to the form huddled against the thick trunk of an oak. The young woman was shivering wildly, and her life was fading.

"It is a human, Rudolph. Humans die."

Ru continued to the woman and touched her with her muzzle, pawing at her clothing.

Odin sighed and grumbled, leaving the sleigh to pick up the woman that Ru was insisting on rescuing.

When they were both in the sleigh, she lifted off and flew them back to the workshop. The elves made clothing and essentials to give to the humans to help them through the winter, and Odin had delivered them. The sleigh was much lighter, even with their rescued woman as ballast.

She cruised through the sky and pulled them all home.

Ru kept her windows closed and a fire going. The woman was in her bed, and she slowly stirred. "Where am I?"

Ru smiled. "My home. I am Ru. What is your name?"

"Kresida. I thought I was going to die." She trembled and tears formed in her eyes.

Ru sat next to her, taking her hand. "You are alive and well.

You will have food and clothing and be safe for the rest of your life."

Kresida sobbed and clung to Ru's hand. It took her nearly an hour to share her story of being cast out of her home when her parents died and the lord of the manor decided to take over their property. He had cast her out in the cold, and her death had been the expected result.

Ru got Kresida a gown to wear, and the woman had cried again at the rich fabric with the elaborate embroidery. Ru summoned a meal for her and watched while she ate.

"When you are feeling up to it, I will show you around your new home."

"I think I need some more rest." Kresida smiled and pushed aside her empty plate. "I appear to have died and you are my angel."

Ru blinked. "What is an angel?"

Odin's voice sounded from the doorway. "An emissary of god. She thinks she has died and this is the afterlife."

Kresida looked at Odin wearing his tight leather tunic and trousers, and a blush formed on her cheeks.

Ru looked between them and frowned. There was a chemistry in the air that she usually sensed when beasts were ready to mate. She was still too young for that sort of thing. She wouldn't be physically mature for four hundred years.

"Odin, this is Kresida. Kresida, this is Odin." Ru made the introductions.

"My dear saint. Thank you for my rescue."

Odin came forward and kissed Kresida's hand. "It was not me who rescued you, but Rudolph in all her glory. She led me to you and insisted that I bring you here."

Kresida smiled. "But it was you who lifted me from the snow. I remember that much."

Ru snorted. They were lost in each other's eyes. This is what her instinct had tried to show her. Kresida belonged to Odin.

Ru sipped at her tea. "You were her saint."

"Yes, though you saved her. I can never thank you enough for that. The time we shared taught me so much about humanity and how it changed. They were more than simple energy sources for us. They needed to believe as much as we needed them to believe it." Santa smiled and sipped at his own tea.

She nodded. "It seems like only yesterday. I wish that time didn't speed by. It feels like she was just with us, but I know it was a long time ago."

"I am not sorry that I moved you through time. It was necessary to get us to this point where the world needs us the most. If I had not come to you then, we would not be here now."

She nodded. "I understand the logic. So, do you have any questions for me?"

He sighed. "Yes, why now?"

She smiled. "Because they are all adults, and a life alone, even an eternal one, is a gloomy prospect. They were not made reindeer by their choice but by mine. The least I could assure them was a mate that would live as long as they did."

"So, this wasn't just about sex?" He smirked.

"Nope. This was about companionship, about finding partners for them. I didn't have one, and I know how much that hurts, so I wanted to make sure that they all had someone they could depend on."

Santa froze. "You are breaking my heart."

She sipped at her tea. "You already broke mine; I just didn't know it at the time."

He sighed. "You brought her into my life."

Ru shook her head and chuckled. "Not Kresida. After she passed on. You treated me like a beast, a means to an end. We were no longer partners. I was your creature, and since I am bound to you, there was not much I could do."

"I never... I didn't mean... I just had to deal with losing someone again." He ran his hand over his face.

"I know that you had just worked through losing the other gods when we first met. You made a plan, and you took action. You were alone, and you found a companion. That was the man I was waiting to see when Kres died. Instead, she faded and you went with her, remaining in limbo while the world turned around you. Yes, you attended to the humans, but you left me behind."

He got to his feet and left her alone. She sighed and rubbed her forehead before drinking more tea.

Nice and Naughty

When she had gotten her despair under control, she walked to the window and let the winter in once again.

Below her, she could see the elf village, the goblin towers, the dwarf warrens glowing under the snow. They had rescued as many as they could from the encroachment of the humans. The ones who lived close by had committed to helping Santa in his rounds.

Kresida had acted as advisor to the elves and had helped select the presents that they were to give to those who deserved and needed.

"Ru, you need to get out. You need to find a man and enjoy life." Kresida grinned, her dark hair already silver at the temples.

"That isn't really in the cards for me. I suppose I am destined to work." Ru smiled and looked over the detailed map of human habitation.

"Well, then, you need some more reindeer. I don't know where you came from, but I am pretty sure that there are more like you somewhere." Kres chuckled.

Ru blinked and looked at the map. The human species was only going to keep increasing. A few more bodies pulling the sleigh wouldn't hurt.

"I need to speak about that with Odin—uh, Santa." She smiled and used the new name that Kres had saddled her husband with.

Of course, there were no others like her, not yet. She hadn't come into being yet. Time travel was tricky.

Ru paced while Santa sat behind his desk. "Kres has a point. It is tiring getting you everywhere you need to go. I need some backup. I have an idea, but it will require the use of some of that Christmas magic you have been hoarding."

He frowned. "I haven't been hoarding it."

"You have, but I need it. I need eight snowflakes and your power to throw them across time. I have very specific folks in mind, but I can't open the gateway on my own." She tapped the ruby collar she still wore.

He nodded. "When did you want to do this?"

"I already know where the girls are. We can do it now and collect them in a few years."

He sighed and went to the wall, pulling out the box that had melded into wood. "If you and Kres think it is a good idea."

Ru smiled, and together, they went to the top of her tower to throw the power of Christmas through time and space to create her team.

Eight baby girls were chosen, each one on the brink of death. A snowflake touched their skin, and each began to thrive and grow.

Ru knew where each and every one of her team were growing up and maturing. She would have to build a home for them before they were brought to the workshop.

Ru walked to the top of the tower and stared at the sky and the portals that opened to thousands of points in time. Somewhere, she was waking and walking for the first time two hundred years in the past. She remembered the woods greeting her and the creatures within it coming to pay her homage. She was a tiny bit of the spirit of the earth itself, and now, she was helping to keep that spirit flourishing in other beings.

"I thought I would find you up here." Santa's voice sounded behind her.

"I thought you had run away to try and ignore me again." She turned and stopped still. He was holding an armload of roses that had a familiar gleam.

"I have brought you a peace offering. These are flowers crafted by the dwarves. They can withstand any temperature as they are made of ruby and emerald." He offered them to her.

She chuckled and took them. They even smelled like roses somehow. "Thank you. I suppose I don't have to put them in water."

He nodded. "You are correct. So, would you care to adjourn to your rooms where I can be more comfortable?"

She laughed. He was resistant to the cold as well. "Fine. I need to change clothing anyway."

"It was a bad habit that she got you in to."

Ru grinned. "It is the only fun one."

She led the way down the stairs, cradling her precious flowers.

In her quarters, she summoned a vase and set the flowers in it.

"I still don't know how you do that."

"Well, I don't do it around my team. It would freak them out, but since I am bonded to this pocket dimension, it does what I ask."

Santa asked softly, "Is that why she was alive so long?"

Ru glanced at him. "I asked it to give her what it could. Three hundred years was all that could be managed."

"I am thankful for every moment. I now have a question for you."

She settled at the table and folded her hands. "What would you like to know?"

"Do you hate me for my relationship?"

Ru shook her head. "Of course not. I am a little irritated by your mourning. I had always assumed that she would live and love you as long as she could, but by the time I became a woman, you would be ready to move on. That happened a few decades ago, and I can tell you that frustration builds up very quickly when you are going into heat once a year."

He dropped into his chair. "You want me?"

"I have always known that you are the most suitable mate I would come across. I also knew that I needed a lot more time to get to this point in my life cycle than originally guessed. This dimension does not let me change myself, so reaching maturity at all was an act of will."

"I had no idea."

"You never asked. Now, I am going to change clothing, so as I know you are a little squeamish about these things, you can either turn your back or leave."

She got up and went to her wardrobe, pulling out a gown with flames in the pattern. It was daringly cut and left her neck and collar completely exposed.

She tossed it onto her bed and stripped off her clothing. Santa watched with interest, and he jolted in surprise when she turned toward him, her hands on her hips wearing only her collar. "Are you taking inventory?"

He blinked. "I hadn't realized you were really..."

"An adult? I was just a little forest force when you first met me. I have absorbed more magic in the last thousand years than most gods see in five thousand. My forest may be long gone, but I am still standing." She stalked up to him and poked him in the chest.

He caught her hand and pressed it flat against him. "I was going to say I hadn't realized that you were made entirely of curves. The clothing you wear hides it."

"I did that for Kres. She thought of me as an eternal teenager, and I didn't want to disabuse her of that notion. As you know, there was much we did not tell her."

He nodded. "I know. Does the collar hurt?"

"It is simply like wearing a belt. Well, wearing a belt at all times, even while bathing."

"I am sorry. You know why it was necessary."

She chuckled, turned and went to pull on her gown. "Of course. You don't trust me to stay otherwise. You chose to lock me in place rather than trust that I would keep to my promise. It is a sad state for Santa."

"You were a forest spirit, notoriously free. I did not know how long it would take to implement my plans, and I could not chance you returning to your forest before things were settled."

"What about now?"

He blinked and sat up. "You still want it off? You are known for the red glow."

Ru nodded. "Of course I would choose freedom. I would choose to walk the paths where my trees were."

"The trees are still there."

Shock ripped through her. "What?"

"The trees are still there. They are a protected forest. No one can touch a trunk or a branch. Families camp and animals are safe in the two hundred acres where your forest began."

Tears formed in her eyes. "Why didn't you tell me? Why did you say that it was gone?"

"I needed you to stay with me."

Ru brushed the folds of her dress into straight lines. "I need some time on my own now."

He left, and she nodded to herself, removing the dress she had just put on and running to the roof again. She found the contemporary portal, and she shifted into her reindeer form, running to see the place that had been hers and hers alone.

Santa felt the moment that Rudolph left him. It hurt more than anything he had ever felt before, and he deserved it.

He had kept her from her forest, kept her from a mate and, instead, flaunted his relationship in front of her. Now, she had told him that he was her best chance at a mate, and he had commented on her taste in clothing.

He was an idiot.

Even before he met her, Ru had acted in the best interests of those around her. When he had captured her, she had still moved to make the lives of those around her richer and more fulfilling.

His focus had been on ingraining himself into the rituals of humanity. She had helped him achieve his goals, but he had still never given her freedom.

It was time to rectify that detail. If it was all she wanted for Christmas, he would give her her freedom. Once they were on equal standing, he could address the letters of the other reindeer.

If she was amenable, he and Ru would become lovers, and together, they would soar forward, bringing as much comfort and joy to the world as they were able. He just had to convince her not to spit in his face first.

Ru's hooves stepped carefully through the snow; the trees whispered to her in welcome, excited by her return. She listened and heard the brook tapping under the ice.

She walked to the centre of a clearing, and she knelt, lying down in the snow while the world moved around her and her forest welcomed her home.

A familiar presence interrupted her all too soon.

Santa appeared in the centre of the clearing, and he walked over to her in silence, kneeling at her side and stroking her muzzle before he reached around her neck and unbuckled her collar.

He was freeing her.

She sat for a moment as air rushed around her neck, and then, she carefully took on her wolf form.

The first few steps were cautious, and then, she frolicked in the snow, enjoying her favourite form for the first time in a thousand years or more.

Santa knelt in the snow with the collar in his hands. He watched her with a smile on his lips and a gleam in his eyes.

She walked up to him and growled happily, rolling to her back and wiggling in the snow.

He laughed and stroked her fur. "You look happy."

She shifted to her human form and grinned. "I am happy. Thank you."

She threw her arms around his neck and kissed him. His mouth was firm under hers and soon began to kiss her back.

When he wrapped his hands around her and she felt the collar, she paused and pulled back. "Are you going to put that collar back on me?"

"No. I will never sneak it onto you again. If you want to wear the ruby, we will come up with something else."

She grinned. "Good. In that case, would you care to return home? The magic you expended to get here is making you look a little tired."

He sighed in relief. "Yes, please, Ru. I had forgotten how exhausting it was travelling on my own."

She stood, stretched, rubbed her neck and shifted into her reindeer form. Santa was on her back in a moment, and they returned home in the bright light of day.

When they arrived back at the workshop, she waited for him to spring the collar on her, but it never came. She shifted into her human form and smiled at him, her neck free of the collar.

"If you still want to have dinner with me, I will join you in an hour or so." Santa smiled.

Ru was standing in full view of a dozen elves, but they were all staring at the collar in Santa's hands. She chuckled and inclined her head. "Roast chicken dinner it is."

He smiled and she left, walking naked across the landing zone before she shifted into her wolf form and ran up the steps to her tower. It felt so good to be whole.

Ru finished assembling the meal just as Santa came through

Nice and Naughty

her door. This was his realm; he could enter and exit anywhere. He just couldn't manipulate things. The rules of magic were funny.

"I brought a bottle of wine."

She chuckled. "Just like the old days."

"Yes, when you were four hundred and looked twelve."

She snickered. "Yes, I never had the heart to correct any of the elves either. As far as they knew, I was an enchanted human."

He sat and poured the wine.

She served the chicken dinner, and they sat as they had in the old days.

When they finished with the meal, they were sitting back and he cleared his throat. "I have something for you."

She perked up. "Yes?"

"The dwarves put this together last minute, but I think that it will satisfy a conundrum." He reached into his tunic and pulled out a small pouch. He handed it to her.

She opened the drawstrings and dumped the pouch contents into her hand. The ruby from the collar gleamed in her palm.

"The chain fits over your head, and it will shift with you. You can take the ruby off or put it on. It is your choice completely."

She smiled at the compromise. "Well, the humans do expect a red glowing reindeer at the front of the team, thanks to that song."

"They do. It also keeps us from showing up on radar and other tracking mechanisms." He smiled.

She placed it over her head, and it glowed brightly as if happy to be back with her.

It settled between her breasts, and she sighed in contentment. "I was feeling a little naked."

"So, you like it?"

"In this format? Yes. Thank you." She trailed her fingers over the stone.

"It looks content only when it is with you." Santa smiled. "Just like me."

She looked at him in surprise. "You were content with Kresida."

"I was in love, but I knew she was mortal. We were happy, but I was never content. I could never relax because each moment with her was going to be one I could never recapture."

Ru walked to him and sat in his lap. "I am sorry for the worry."

"Don't be. There was joy, there was laughter, but it was different. You are my equal in a way that is not possible with someone else."

Ru blushed. "I am powerful, but I wouldn't say equal."

"Your power is different from mine, but it is no less strong. The reindeer have taken on the status of demigods. You have your own immortality beyond this realm. I would say that makes us even."

Ru wrinkled her nose. "You make it sound so romantic. The humans are fickle. In a matter of decades, we could be forgotten."

"And at that point, you will be free to live here and spend your time visiting your forest." He cleared his throat. "Or you would be free to travel with me."

"Travel?"

"In the old times, I would travel as an old man and assess the villages and villagers that I came across. Those who offered me hospitality, though they had little, were rewarded. I don't think it is a bad idea." He wrapped a hand around her waist.

The firm curve of his hand sent a number of reactions through her body. Ru smiled and placed her hand on his chest. His heart was thudding under her touch.

She leaned up to kiss him, and he met her halfway. Their subject matter may not have been romantic, but she was no longer trapped at his side. She could choose him and that was the headiest aphrodisiac ever.

He moved his hands over her body, and she twisted against him. When his erection was thick against her thigh through the leather of his leggings, she pulled her head away.

"You aren't just humouring me because of the girls' letters?"

Santa grinned. "No, they have just reminded me of a few things that I was in danger of forgetting."

He stood and carried her to her bed, placing her on the covers and arranging her limbs. "I love that you wear your horns at all times here. It suits you."

She chuckled and waited for him to strip his clothing off. "And wearing your normal seeming suits you, but I am used to your old, fat, human seeming. I wouldn't want to wake up to it, but even that has a certain charm."

He paused while pulling off his boots. "You know that I only wear that because I let the humans control the glamour."

His hair was sliding around his pointed ears, the scarred gleam of his chest was visible through the strands, and the muscles of his stomach were bunched as he balanced on one foot.

She reached out with her leg and pushed him over.

He shouted and thudded as he hit the ground.

Ru giggled madly and turned to her side to watch him struggle to pry his boots off from his sitting position.

"Why did you do that?"

She shrugged. "I owed you. When we are even, I will let you know." She grinned. "Plus, it was funny and I am what I am."

He yanked off his second boot with a pop, and he got to his feet. "You haven't been this mischievous in a while."

When he was naked, she welcomed him into her embrace. "Says the man missing eight reindeer the week before Christmas."

"Oh, shut up."

He kissed her giggles quiet, and they rolled together on the snowflake-printed quilt, alternately wrestling and caressing each other until she was astride him and easing him into her.

Santa grinned. "Is this your Christmas wish?"

She laughed. "Christmas I will be sleeping, but it is my Boxing Day desire."

Ru eased onto him and closed her eyes at the sensation of heat and fullness. She may not feel the cold, but this was a kind of heat she wanted to get used to.

His beautiful blue eyes closed as she started to move on him. The fall of his hair surrounded his head like a halo of silken snowflakes.

His body was bronze and marked with battles of centuries past. Every inch of him was beloved to her. The man who had sought her out and freed her before she had to do something drastic.

She rode him slowly, loving the feel of him sliding inside her, and he seemed to enjoy it so much that he rolled with her, thrust into her again and set his own rhythm.

He grabbed her arms and pinned them above her head, weaving his fingers with hers as he lowered his chest onto hers. The full contact was wonderful, the pressure against her breasts made her skin come alive and the ruby around her neck glowed and pulsed as they rocked, thrust and retreated together.

The light outside shifted from daylight into darkness while they rocked together, no rush on their time. Pleasure rose and fell, swelled and ebbed, and still, they moved as one.

When she couldn't hold back anymore, she shoved and twisted until she was on top once again. She furiously circled her hips while holding his hands above his head. Her breath came in sharp gasps, and she finally moaned, throwing her head back so that her hair cascaded down her back.

The light under her skin swelled, and as Santa gripped her hips and thrust upward with a growl of his own, she felt the energy inside her complete.

Pleasure pulsed through her limbs, but power glowed around them before coalescing and flying through the closed window.

Ru slowly collapsed on Santa's chest and smiled. "So, what was that?"

He chuckled and stroked her hair. "I think we just made a new earth spirit."

She rested against him, calm and content. A new spirit. Yeah, that summed up their union. There was going to be a new spirit this Christmas, and it was going to start with them and expand out to her eight reindeer and their mates.

Perfect. Rudolph was perfect. The heat from her body enveloping his cock had taken all of his concentration to work with, and it wasn't until she was astride him again with those glowing breasts and gleaming body his for the taking that his control cracked.

Her stamina was incredible. He had felt small, rhythmic pulses around him throughout their coupling, but it wasn't until she had worked for her own orgasm that she really let go.

For so many years, he had thought of her as the child he had first seen in the forest. Their time apart had done nothing to change his opinion, but now that she had proved that the years had, indeed, passed for her as well as for him, he was delighted by the transformation.

When he had first sought a forest spirit to imprison, he could not have imagined this result.

Santa lay back with Ru in his arms and closed his eyes. He hoped she was right about the reindeer being willing to return under the right circumstances. Otherwise, he was screwed.

Santa had shifted them so that they were under the covers. He smiled and pressed a kiss to her temple. "Hello, Ru."

She grinned. "Hello, Santa. We will need to change the archive. The girls will need some privacy."

He blinked. "Do we have time?"

She shrugged and tapped her fingers on his chest. "I have started the archive on the changes. It is going to be a snowflake pattern. I think it will be quite nice."

"You are making changes to my workshop without telling me?"

"I am making changes to the team's quarters. They are my concern, and now, their mates fall under my responsibilities. Even though they are from the nice-and-naughty list."

He brought his hand down lightly on her hip. "It is the naughty-or-nice list, as I have been telling you for centuries."

She smirked. "Whatever."

"So, you expect the elves from the list to stay here at the workshop? They were only available because I called for them."

"No, I expect them to live wherever they lived before this. I just expect them to take their reindeer with them."

"You want to let them leave again?" He raised his brows in surprise.

"I want to encourage them to leave again. They were born human; they need humans to be around them so that their hearts don't grow cold and lost in duty."

"Are you in danger of that?"

She smiled as he stroked her cheek. "No. But I am not human. I wear this body for communication and now for intimacy. I still prefer my animal forms."

He sighed. "I will have to work at keeping you in this shape. I am guessing you will need enticement."

She grinned. "It sounds like an excellent idea to me."

Sadly, Santa had had to spend the next day on logistics, so Ru spent her time expanding the archive with points and chambers on each side of the eight-sided building. The girls could come and go in any form they wished, with complete privacy. Or, they could gather in the central common space and trade stories.

This would always be their base of operations, but it was not their only option, not anymore. That was the purpose of her efforts on their behalf. She wanted to get them excited about the world. It wasn't as easy as she thought, but she was pretty sure that it had been managed.

Lying in Santa's arms that night, she felt the moment that Dasher took flight. The others launched moments later from wherever they had been during their sabbatical.

Her team was headed home.

Ru smiled and tucked herself against her ancient elf and held tight. Tomorrow was going to be one helluva party.

Ru got up and dressed, wearing a loose cloak and nothing else. She gathered eight other cloaks from the archive and went to stand in the central landing area before Santa was even awake.

From different points in the sky, light appeared, and the reindeer ran through sky toward her.

They were all there, and each one had a panicked and exhausted elf on her back.

The ladies landed on four hooves, and the moment their partners dismounted, Ru stepped forward. She handed a cloak to each one of them.

The girls grinned and covered up. When Ru had finished her rounds, she was swamped with hugs.

After the hugs came the questions, and Ru answered what she could while their amused partners introduced themselves. Several of the men were long-term placements, and the locals did not know them.

The men caught up, and Ru looked at Dancer. "Yes, things did get resolved here. There has been alteration in the status quo, and I think that the changes will be to your liking."

Dancer grinned, and they all gathered in a group, walking to the archive, and she heard them exclaiming as they saw the changes that had been made in their absence.

"Everybody now has a separate wing, each designed so that you can have privacy when you want it. The common areas are the same, and there is a snack ready for you."

The girls laughed, and their bemused men followed. The conversation pit was filled with presents covered with gleaming wrapping.

Cupid smiled. "We brought along our own gifts."

"Do we want to get dressed first?" Vixen called out.

The rest of the girls laughed, and they all gathered in the huge conversational pit and each unwrapped a segment of the new, circular couch large enough for two. The bemused elves followed, and their reindeer pulled them into the gathering.

Ru closed her eyes and called Santa. She settled in the pit with the other ladies, and when he arrived, she pulled him down next to her.

Once those gathered were used to the idea, conversation began to flow.

The adventures of the reindeer were amazing and far more than Ru could have imagined. She sat holding Santa's hand, and she opened the presents that the girls brought her. She got chocolate, jewellery, some very nice lingerie that Santa took possession of, but it was having her family back where she could see and touch them that mattered to her.

When they had finished their party, the girls headed to their rooms with their mates in tow. Ru was left sitting with Santa and smiling happily. "You picked really well."

"You called it with Donder. I would never have picked him for her, but you nailed it." He nuzzled her ear.

She turned and straddled him on the couch, her cloak covering both of them. "I think we need a bit of privacy."

He grinned. "You are not the only one who can make changes to this place."

He stood, taking her with him, bundled up her presents and walked toward a shadowed corner of the room.

"What is that? It wasn't there earlier."

"It was installed. You now have a chamber above the hub of the snowflake. You were always central, after all."

The door was familiar, and when he opened it and headed up the winding staircase, she knew that they were in her tower.

"Back to my place?"

He wrinkled his nose. "Well, sort of."

When they arrived at the floor that normally housed her bedroom, it was twice the normal size and contained an extra wardrobe. "You moved in with me?"

He grinned. "It seemed sensible as I am going to be spending every possible moment in your bed for quite some time."

"Don't tire yourself out; tomorrow is Christmas Eve." She chuckled.

"And you will be at the head of the team, as you always are." He nuzzled her ear.

She chuckled. "Don't get any ideas. I have to run around the world tomorrow, hauling your ass as I go."

"I thought I would just hold you until it was time to go."

Ru sighed regretfully. "Well, that is sensible."

He set her on the edge of the bed and peeled off her cloak. Kneeling between her thighs, he pressed his lips to her, sending heat through her folds before he used his tongue.

To hell with sensible, this was more fun.

The next morning, the reindeer were rumpled, but all lined up in front of the sleigh. When Santa hopped into the sleigh, they shifted into their beast forms and the harness elves lashed them in place under the watchful eyes of the reindeers' mates.

Santa settled in with the bags of gifts, and he flicked the reins, Rudolph started the team, and they lifted off to do their annual work.

Gifts, hope, charity and love were heavy things to deliver. Ru hoped, as she always did, that they were up to the challenge. The world was depending on them.

Epilogue

Ru led her exhausted team across the sky. Santa didn't even try to control her trajectory. She was taking them home whether he wanted to go there or not.

She landed in the central landing site, and the elves rushed to release them from their harnesses.

One by one, they shifted back to human and staggered toward the archive. The girls were picked up by their mates and carried inside for rest.

Ru staggered upright and headed for Santa. He was just as worn out as she was.

He left the sleigh and put his arm around her shoulders. "You should have something to wear."

She chuckled. "Why now? That would be a first for all of us, and it isn't necessary. The elves aren't even looking."

"And that trip around the world has made you blind. They are definitely looking."

She grinned. "They can take it up with me then. I am always willing to discuss things with rational beings."

"You would chew them up and spit them out."

Ru snorted. "You are delirious. You need to lie down."

"Only if you are with me." He nuzzled her head, careful to avoid her horns.

When they got to their chambers, there was no funny business. She helped him remove his suit, and they crawled into bed. With a smile, she pried the new snowflake made of Christmas magic out of her horns, and she put it on the bedpost. She would deal with it in the morning or tomorrow. Whichever one came first.

Santa wrapped his arms around her and pulled her close, tucking his chin on her shoulder while he covered her back.

She murmured, "Should I tell them how they became reindeer?"

"When you feel the time is right. They are content now. Let them enjoy their lives until they ask."

"If they never ask?"

"Then tell them when you are ready." He squeezed her with the arm that wrapped her waist.

"You really are all-knowing."

"It is all-seeing, and I can see that you are nervous about telling them. They will understand. You saved them."

"I turned them into the same kind of bond servants that I was."

He sighed. "But they knew how to feel love. They knew how to give love, they had family and they understood what it meant to be human, just for a little while. They had a life that would never have existed without you."

"And I would never have been in this situation without you. So, I will blame you." She giggled.

He nipped her shoulder. "A little Christmas tradition has been born, and it is only our first one together. You can blame me, and I can take it."

She wove her fingers through his on her belly. "I will compensate you somehow."

"I will put it in my letter to Rudolph next year. Now, get to sleep, little wolf. I have plans for the next year together, and I thought you would like to vacation somewhere warm."

She chuckled drowsily. "I don't think I have ever spent time in somewhere warm. Warm might be a nice change."

"Whatever my little wolf wishes. Think about it and get back to me after I have whisked you away. You might enjoy getting out after all this time."

She was too tired to answer, but it was comforting to know that he was making plans for the first time in centuries. Santa would take a break and Rudolph might get a tan.

Stranger things had happened, right?

Author's Note

So, all the reindeer have their partners, Santa is taking a holiday with Rudolph, and the world has been filled with hope, love, charity and a few gifts here and there.

My personal experience with Christmas is that it can be anything, but it is usually what you make of it. I have had horrible holidays, ones that make me cry, fill me with depression and rage. But, I have also had moments where I laughed so hard I almost peed myself, and others where I was strong enough to reach out to others.

Now, I pick the holiday that I want to have and make that my focus. It doesn't always work, but I have a plan.

So, thanks from me, Merry Christmas, Happy Holidays, hugs and kisses,

Viola Grace

About the Author

Viola Grace (aka Zenina Masters) is a Canadian sci-fi/paranormal romance writer with ambitions to keep writing for the rest of her life. She specializes in short stories because the thrill of discovery, of all those firsts, is what keeps her writing.

An artist who enjoys a story that catches you up, whirls you around and sets you down with a smile on your face is all she endeavours to be. She prefers to leave the drama to those who are better suited to it, she always goes for the cheap laugh.

Made in the USA
San Bernardino, CA
04 March 2016